OUTLAW

NEMESIS OF ROME

ADAM LOFTHOUSE

B

Boldwood

First published in Great Britain in 2025 by Boldwood Books Ltd.

Cover Design by Colin Thomas

Cover Images: Colin Thomas

A CIP catalogue record for this book is available from the British Library.

Paperback ISBN 978-1-83678-512-5

Large Print ISBN 978-1-83678-511-8

Hardback ISBN 978-1-83678-510-1

Ebook ISBN 978-1-83678-513-2

Kindle ISBN 978-1-83678-514-9

Audio CD ISBN 978-1-83678-505-7

MP3 CD ISBN 978-1-83678-506-4

Digital audio download ISBN 978-1-83678-509-5

This book is printed on certified sustainable paper. Boldwood Books is dedicated to putting sustainability at the heart of our business. For more information please visit https://www.boldwoodbooks.com/about-us/sustainability/

Boldwood Books Ltd, 23 Bowerdean Street, London, SW6 3TN

www.boldwoodbooks.com

To Steve Denton, David Baird and Paul Bennett.
The first three people from out there in the real world to
tell me the words I'd written were any good.
Thanks gents. This one's for you.

1

A man told me once that defeat can do you good, in the long run. You learn from your mistakes, become wiser for them. He said a little humility can be the makings of a man, that he will lead his warriors better in the future, be more understanding to their needs.

I have to admit I thought it a load of bollocks at the time. Just the drunken ramblings of a once-great man who had led his warband to ruin. He sat in the corner of the feasting hall, the shadows clinging to him like a wet cloak. I had thought him nothing then. A coward, a *nithing*.

I thought of his words as I sat in the shadows of a hall myself, as if the darkness would protect me from the memories of my own great defeat. They didn't. His words didn't ring any truer either. I felt no humility, no sudden worldly understanding of what it was to lead men in war. I felt no sympathy for those who were weaker than me, no sudden urge to reach out to the world and put right some wrongs.

I just felt sick. Embarrassed. Shamed. It had been six years since my great defeat. Six years of skulking in the shadows, hiding from the sun, disconnecting from the world.

I had been a great man once. Alaric, Lord of the Ravensworn. Five hundred men had ridden at my back, and our enemies quivered when we did. I was a lord of war, a battle turner, ring giver, chief killer. An oath breaker. That's what men used to call me, what they whispered as I walked by. I was feared by chief and peasant alike, and I revelled in my status. Sure, I'd work for the highest bidder. And sure, maybe a couple of times, I'd begun a war on one side and ended it on the other. But so what? I had men to feed, a reputation to garner. I never gave a shit what people thought. Anyone got in my way, I made them a corpse.

That was until my past eventually caught up with me. I'd gotten in too deep, made some dodgy deals, found myself stuck between the anvil that was my enemies in Germania and the hammer that was Rome. They'd crushed me like an egg. Five hundred men I had led into battle one glorious summer's day. You wouldn't think it to see me now.

I'd built the hall I languished in. Not myself, of course. I was a man of wealth and status back then. But I'd watched as my men sweated and laboured as beam by beam the great feasting hall began to take shape. It was the place I had brought my wife once we had made our vows, the place I planted the seed of our first child in her womb. I thought it most likely it would be the place that I'd die.

It was mid-morning, late spring, and the birds were singing and the trees were blooming. My wife was outside with the children. I could hear them whooping and splashing in the shallows of the river, enjoying the return of the warm sun. I was on my second jug of ale, already settled down to brood the rest of the day away, when there was a clamour of voices outside, the thrum of hoofbeats through the timbers, a clink of metal drifting on the air.

I sighed, briefly considering if it was worth getting up for, then quickly decided it wasn't. I was just re-filling my cup when one of my men burst into the hall, daylight offending my one remaining eye. 'There are men here, Lord,' said Batur, a young warrior who had sought me out and offered his service the year before. He was an eager enough lad, a thin wisp of a youth in dire need of bulking up if he was going to survive the warrior's path, but he wasn't the brightest spark, to say the least.

'No shit,' I spat, feeling a small sense of joy at the hurt look in the young man's eyes.

'What should we do, Lord?' he asked. He had a narrow face, Batur, raven hair that fell in curls to his shoulders, dark eyes and pale skin. His beard was sparse and fluffy, more like the left offs from a woollen tunic then a man's beard. My wife kept telling him it would thicken, though she always had been an optimist.

I sighed again. 'Ask my wife to bring the children inside. Then get my sword and shield, one for yourself too. Are the other two still out?'

I had two other men who still called me Lord. Sedric and Kai. They had left two dawns ago with our only four horses and two carts, off to the nearest tribe for provisions. I had been expecting them back that morning at the latest.

'No sign of them yet, Lord.'

'Then if these riders come to make war, we shall have to kill them ourselves. Now get to it.'

I could smell his fear as he left. It's one thing to

practise with sword and shield, to harness your muscles and quicken your reflexes. It is another entirely
to use those skills to take a man's life.

Standing slowly, swaying with the effects of the
ale, I walked through my empty hall, ignoring the
smell of the soiled hay on the floor, to the sleeping
chamber I shared with my wife at the rear. Inside was
a chest, a chest I had not bothered to open in a long
time. But open it I did, and I stood watching as the
dust from the lid floated into the air and caught the
light of the sun filtering through from the open window. Inside, wrapped in the faded red of a raven
banner – an unwelcome reminder of happier times –
was my mail and helmet.

I hadn't looked on it in months, years maybe. So it
was to my surprise that both were polished and in
good condition. I smiled to myself, wondering how a
man as ungrateful as me managed to have a wife so
continuously thoughtful. I could hear her and the
children making their way through the hall as I
begun the laborious process of getting it on.

'There are men, Alaric!' Saxa squealed as she
scurried into our sleeping chamber, my two boys,
Ludwig and Eric, in her wake.

'How many?' I asked, struggling to get my head
through the hole in my mail shirt.

'Six, Father!' Ludwig said, his voice an excited squeak. Everything's an adventure when you're seven. 'Will you fight them?'

'Not if I can help it.' I'd managed to get my head and arms into the mail; getting it over my stomach, though, was proving harder than I'd care to admit. It had been many a year since I'd bothered to wear the thing, and I'd drunk myself through countless barrels of ale in that time. 'Damn thing,' I muttered to myself as I tried to wriggle it over my bulging belly.

Saxa moved forwards and yanked hard on the end of the mail. I almost collapsed as my body took its full weight. At least I finally had the thing on. 'Sure it never used to weigh this much.'

'You're not getting any younger, my dear.' Saxa leaned in and kissed me softly on the cheek. 'Or slimmer, for that matter.'

'Thanks for the morale booster,' I said, reaching back into the chest and snatching up my helmet. It was unremarkable, as far as helmets go. Just plain iron, not too dissimilar to the ones used in Rome's cursed legions. But it had served me well in the past.

'Are you forgetting something, Lord Alaric?' Saxa asked as I made my way out of the door.

I doubled back, kissed both my boys on the head, kissed Saxa on the lips and told them to shut the door when I was gone. 'Not that, welcome as it was,' Saxa said again as I made to leave. 'This.'

She reached into the chest and unfurled the red banner, holding it out for us all to see. 'The Ravensworn!' Ludwig screamed, jumping up and down in excitement. 'You never go to war without your banner, Father!'

'Been a long time since I've been to war, boy,' I muttered, but I reached out and grabbed it all the same. 'Need a spear to fix it to.' In a flash, Eric was out the door. He came stumbling back with a spear twice his size. He was five that summer and still barely spoke a word. Short and podgy where Ludwig was tall and thin, he had a fearful face, large round eyes that seemed to quiver every time I met them. He would mumble sweet nothings with Saxa when she put him to bed each night, but I found it hard to get more than four or five words from the boy when the sun was up. 'My thanks,' I said as I ruffled his hair. He reddened with pride and embarrassment. I fixed the banner to the spear and walked out without looking back.

The sunlight outside offended my bloodshot eyes – or eye, I should say. I'd lost the left one same time I'd lost my army, though I have brooded over that enough for now. The world was a plethora of colour, the greens of the leaves, the blue of the sky reflecting on the water. I blinked three times as my eye adjusted, fidgeted in my ill-fitting mail. 'Lord.' Batur handed me my shield. It had the same black raven on the same red background that adjourned my banner. It had stood for something once; men had bled and died for that symbol, had bragged to friends and family that they were privileged enough to ride and fight under it. Alas, that was a long time ago.

'Have they said anything?' I motioned to our guests, who sat astride their mounts fifty or so paces away.

'They asked for you, Lord. I said you would be out when you were ready.' I pretended not to notice the quivering in Batur's shield and took two paces' forwards, trying to muster up the bravado I had once been famed for.

'Morning, friends. How may I be of service?' I called, hoping I was swaggering in my mail, looking a great deal more comfortable than I felt.

'We are here to see Lord Alaric. I have already told your lad there. If your lord is not here than please tell us where we can find him. We are on urgent business.'

Well, that was rude. I know I hadn't exactly been keeping up appearances for the last few years, but to not be recognised entirely seemed to bring me to a whole new low. 'What business do you have with Lord Alaric? He is not expecting anyone.'

The man who had spoken before growled in frustration. In one fluid motion, he freed his sword and kicked his mount into action. He covered the small patch of land between us in moments. 'I am here to see Lord Alaric. I have ridden many weeks to get here, through hail, wind and rain, and I did not do that to be denied at the end of my journey by some pompous guard deemed unfit enough to travel on campaign with his lord! Now, where is he? Has he travelled south to fight against Rome once more? Did he winter with his friend, King Balomar, in the lands of the Marcomanni?'

I got an immediate whiff of horse sweat and leather. Then the man's foul breath, his sickly yellow teeth so close to my good eye that given a few more moments I could have worked out what he'd had for breakfast. 'Hmmm.' I made a show of thinking, scrunching up my eye and fingering my lips. 'What was the question again?'

Truth was, I was playing for time. The man had asked if I was fighting Rome or wintering with Balomar, a king in his own right down south. Neither of which I had done in a long time. Whoever he was, whoever had sent him, they seemed to have no up-to-date knowledge of my fall from grace. I was enjoying being the great lord again, if only for a moment.

'Wotan's beard, man! Did you lose half your brain when you lost that eye! You there!' he called to Batur, who still stood trembling behind his shield. 'Where is your lord?'

Batur said nothing, just poked out a wobbly finger from behind his shield and pointed at me. I followed the finger, fixing my face in a frown as I looked myself up and down. 'Ahh, yes, I *am* Alaric Hengistson, once Lord of the Ravensworn, the greatest warband to ever roam these lands. My apologies, I didn't realise it was me you were looking for. Been a while since armed strangers rode across half the country to find me.'

To my satisfaction, he was speechless. His mouth worked for a while, but it seemed he couldn't quite get a tune from his tongue. 'Now then,' I continued, not even trying to hide my mirth, 'are you here to kill me or hire me?'

2

My visitor called himself Eadger and told me he was a loyal servant of one Chief Wilhelm of the Cimbri, the tribe that controlled the lands in northern Jylland. Eadger seemed like a decent man, tall and broad, chestnut hair that curled to his shoulders. His dark eyes bore into me as I spoke, as if he were seeking my soul. Good luck to him finding that.

'And how many men can your lord call upon?'

We sat on logs at the river's edge, the sun reaching its highest point above us. Batur was pouring ale into cups, Saxa distributing bread and cheese, for we had nothing else to offer. My boys were back to playing in the river, fighting with sticks, the water splashing up to their knees. Eadger's men laughed at their play, sitting a few paces away from him and me, giving us the pretence of privacy as we spoke.

'Three hundred, give or take. Most are farmers, though I am sure they will stand resolute when called on to defend their homes. Fifty are proper warriors; my lord had them training the rest even when we left to ride south, and that was twenty days ago.'

'So,' I said through a mouthful of bread. 'Your chief has committed himself to a war in which he is hopelessly outnumbered. Instead of finding a peaceful resolution, he intends to fight until the bitter end, despite having only fifty warriors and no allies to call to his aide.'

'Yes, but—'

I held up a hand to silence the intrusion. 'And your enemy numbers somewhere between four and five hundred, all warriors, armed and armoured. You are fighting a battle by sea and land, yet only your enemy has ships and the seacraft to sail them. Oh, and you are desperately low on supplies, since your enemy raised all your lord's barns and then burned his crops as they grew on his lands. Have I missed anything out?'

Eadger blubbered for a moment or two before regaining his composure. 'We need *help*.' He all but squealed the last word. 'My lord has no friends amongst our neighbours the Anglii. In fact, my lord is concerned they are in league with our attackers.'

'Would make some sense. These foreigners wage war on you and then the Anglii are on hand to pick up the pieces and take your lands. Who rules the Anglii these days?'

'They were in league with the Suebi for a while, but that alliance seems to have waned over the last few years. Haribert is their chief. He is experienced, cautious, but we know he seeks more land.'

'And wiping the Cimbri off the map would give him the perfect opportunity to do just that. Tell me about these tribes your lord is at war with.'

'We have been fighting the Suiones and the Sitones for a while now. They come from across the eastern sea; Kattegat, we call it. Their ships have no sails, and the currents in the water are treacherous, but they row across the waves like it is nothing more than a lake. They say their lands are no place for growing crops, and their women and children die of hunger in the winter. So they build their ships and they raid our coast, taking what they can back across the water with them.

'Last year, we fought off a large band of the raiders, ten ships' worth, killed most of them too. But a couple of ships got away. A few days later, fifty or more turned up, men from both the Suiones and the Sitones. See, the Suiones are ruled by a king, the Sitones a queen, and you'd never believe it but—'

'They married,' I finished for him.

'Yes! Wotan curse them. So now we are at war with both tribes, and our lord has refused their offers of peace.'

'Why?'

'They want annual gifts of wheat and barley. On top of that they wanted us to offer one hundred shirts of mail, and the same number of swords and shields. We don't even have that ourselves! It is only my lord's honour guard that have iron shirts and swords. The rest of our men fight with no protection other than a shield, their only weapon a spear or a sword carved from bone.'

'Bone?' I was stunned. My father would tell me stories of Germanic warriors from the past, heroic chiefs who had fought against Rome in her early days or tribes from as far off as Gaul before that. Those men fought with bone before men had known how to forge metal into sharpened weapons. I had no knowledge there were still people who used such primitive weapons. No wonder the Cimbri were desperate for all the help they could get.

We both sat in silence for a while. Saxa was re-filling Eadger's men's cups, my boys still splashed away in the water. Eadger waited until he had finished eating to speak again. 'So, what is going on with you? If you don't mind me asking. My chief would have us all believe you are a great warlord with a host at your back. I was expecting to find an army when I finally found you. Instead...' He drifted off, his hand gesturing to the empty hall behind us.

I laughed. 'Aye, I was a great man once. Sadly, that was a long time ago now. I had five hundred men back in the day, a warband the match for any in this land. Had both my eyes, too.'

'What happened?'

I shrugged. 'Made too many enemies. Got greedy, thought I could fight the world and win. Guess the world won in the end.' I rubbed at my left eye. The eye itself was long gone; the lid had attached itself to the underside after a time, and now a thin layer of skin, a different shade of white to the rest of my face, was all that remained. Saxa had made me a patch and I'd worn that for a while, but it made me itch and I hadn't left my hall for an age, so I didn't see the point in persevering.

Eadger shook his head. 'Then I have travelled here for nothing. I thank you for your hospitality, Alaric Hengistson, but I need an army. Five hundred spears would have given my lord the strength to fight both our enemies abroad and the Anglii. My lord would have paid you a fortune in amber for your army. I guess we will have to fight on with what little manpower we have.'

He rose and made his way towards his men. They spoke in low tones for a while, Eadger reluctantly shaking his head as the other five cast resentful glances my way. I could imagine what they were thinking, after travelling all that way just to find little old me, a shadow of the hero they had been sold back home. Must have been like digging for treasure just to find a chest full of rocks. Saxa came and sat next to me, the ever-anxious Batur lingering behind us.

'What does he want?' she asked. She didn't look at me, kept her eyes fixed on our boys in the river, still splashing and laughing the day away. The purity of childhood, something to be cherished.

'They come from the Cimbri, a tribe at the northern tip of Jylland. Their chief wants me to go fight for them. Seems he's got himself into a bit of a pickle.'

'Will you go?'

I scoffed a laugh. 'They're after the Ravensworn, not me. He needs five hundred spears under the red banner to put the shits into his enemy. Few years ago,

I'd have seen it as a no brainer. Now...' I sighed and trailed off. What was there I could offer him?

'You have *something* you could offer them though? Surely?'

'A one-eyed old warrior, too fat to fit in his mail.' I cackled a laugh. 'I'm sure me and my army of three – two of which are still missing, by the way – will be enough to turn the tide in a war of hundreds.'

Saxa studied me then. Her eyes poured into mine and I sensed her weighing her next words the way a farmer weighs his grain. 'You aren't happy, Alaric,' she said after a while.

I said nothing. It was true, and she knew it, I for damn well sure did. Don't get me wrong, it's not that I didn't love my family. I did, and still do. Saxa had never been my choice of a wife and she knew that as well as I did. But we had formed a bond in the years since my great defeat in the east and raised our two boys, who I loved more than anything else in the world. And I did love her. It may not have been a union of lust and passion; we had never been one of those newlywed couples unable to keep our hands off each other. But what we had was respect, an alliance, and an understanding. But did having her and the boys and nothing else make me happy? No. I craved for the old days, the way a drunken craves the wine.

For the blood and glory, the thrill of riding to battle, of testing your mettle against your enemies and emerging victorious.

'Saxa, it's not that I don't love you and the boys—'

'I know,' she said firmly, cutting me off.

'It's just that my whole life I've wanted to be the best, to have the best. When I was Alaric of the Ravensworn, I had *respect*. I had the finest fighting force in the land, all the silver I could ever need. I had fame. I...' I stumbled, trying to find the words. 'I felt *wanted*, needed, in a way I think I've craved since childhood.'

Saxa smiled as I frowned at my own words. A sudden realisation hit me that maybe all I had done with my life so far was to prove my father he was wrong. I'd walked out on him with nothing but sixteen winters on my back. I had no coin, no prospects, not even enough warm clothing to survive the cold nights, though I had found a way. He hadn't wanted me to go, hadn't wanted me to walk the path of the sword. That had just made me more determined than ever to do it. He'd given me a blade though, the very same one that was strapped right then to my waist. I held it a moment, fingers stroking the leather-wrapped handgrip.

'He came here once, you know,' Saxa said quietly.

'Who?'

'Your father.'

'What?' I was stunned. I hadn't laid eyes on the man in twenty years or more. How had he even known where to find me?

'We hadn't been back long. You had returned defeated from the east. You were feverish, your eye socket swollen to twice the normal size, seeping blood and puss day and night. I was so busy looking after you and Ludwig, pregnant with Eric. He came just as autumn was turning to winter, stayed for three weeks.'

'Three weeks?' I spluttered, outraged I had not been told this before.

'He felled trees and chopped firewood. Used what silver we had to buy grain from the nearest settlements, cleared out the barn and saw it all properly stored. Even slaughtered a couple of cattle and salted the meat. Every evening, his work done, he would come into our sleeping chamber and sit by your side. He would tell stories of your childhood, of teaching you to swim in a lake, or drilling you with sword and spear.

'One night, he told the story of how your mother died. That was the first time I have ever seen a grown man openly weep. He must have loved her dearly.'

I snorted. 'The coward did nothing to save her when the Romans came.' Every time I lay down at night, just before sleep takes me, I still remember her screams. I wanted to tell Saxa that, but I couldn't bring myself to do it. Does that make me less of a man?

'You know how I know he loved her so much?' Saxa continued. 'Because he chose to save her son. He chose to stay when he had no reason to. He chose to stay on that farm and raise another man's child, because that is what his love would have wanted from him. Can you not see that his whole life has been devoted to your mother? Even now, he will be on that little farm, fighting with the earth to scratch a living, to make it through another winter. Every morning he will walk out of his home, look down the track to the woods and hope to see you coming home.'

I felt hot tears, stinging my one good eye. Of course I knew that the man she was referring to was not my real father. That man had been a great chief, called himself a king, even, King of the Suebi, the greatest tribe in the north. He had used my mother as a plaything, my parents' farm as nothing more than a breeding ground. Once in a while he would ride up with his warriors, take my mother and spill his seed in her. He wanted options, wanted to grow old knowing he had many sons who could succeed him when he was gone.

As it happened, it didn't work out that way. Though I had made light work of ridding the world of his successor. Revenge is a dish best served cold. I had never quite faced up to what my father had had to go through, seeing the woman he loved used like that. I had never questioned his feelings, his motivations.

'I can't remember him being here,' I said, a sudden longing to see the man.

'It was thanks to him that we survived that first winter. I would never have been able to get through it alone.'

I'd spent so much time in the last six years focusing on my own woes, I hadn't once stopped to consider Saxa's. What must it have been like for her that winter? Scared, alone, separated from her tribe and her family. She must have been terrified, and desperately lonely. Married to a man she barely knew – I had been on campaign for practically all of our marriage at that point – and raising her first child whilst carrying her second. I looked at her with newfound admiration then. She had proven to me many times in the years we had spent together how strong and resilient she was. But I think it was only then I truly appreciated the hidden depths of her strengths, the courage that soared through her veins.

'There are many forms of courage,' I said to her, leaning in and kissing her on the cheek. 'Nothing, though, comes close to that of a mother.'

I got up, brushing the grass from my cloak. 'I know what I need to do.' Saxa smiled up at me, I think seeing a bit of the Alaric of old. She was the first person to see that man in a long time.

3

'How many in each one?' Eadger asked, lugging another chest from the earth.

'Not sure, exactly. And they've been down there a good while, so it might take some cleaning to get the rust off.'

Twenty chests we had all in all. Great wooden things that had once followed me on my travels wherever I went. They'd been full of silver back then, pillaged treasures and hard-earned coin, the spoils of my many victories. One or two of them still had a bit of hidden wealth within, but the rest were what interested Eadger.

He opened the first with the flat of his blade, the wood creaking and finally opening with a snap. His five men crowded round him, and I smiled to hear their excited whispers. Eadger was the first to dip his hand inside. It came back out grasping the wooden handle of a battle axe. His men rushed in next, pulling out swords and mail, helmets and daggers. 'Reckon your lord could make good use of them?' I asked with an arched eyebrow.

'Aye.' Eadger laughed. 'Aye, I reckon he just might.'

'And do you reckon he'll still make good on his promise of amber?' Amber washed up on the northern shores of our land. We used it to trade with the Romans in Gaul and Pannonia. Turned out their women were fond of shiny things, and we were fond of food and wine. Was about the only use for the Romans in my mind.

'Aye. I'd say the offer will stand.'

'How will we get all this to the north, though?' one of his men asked. 'We'd need a dozen carts and the mules to pull them.'

Eadger's face dropped at the thought. 'Wotan's eye! You're right.' He threw the axe back into the chest in disgust.

My smile grew wider. 'A dozen carts and the mules to pull them I can't help you with. I *do* have a ship though.'

* * *

I'd stolen the ship six years or so before, back when waging war on Rome and her Germani allies was my pastime. I had taken the Ravensworn to Ulpia Noviomagus, snuck in and opened the gates in the dead of night, and my men had slaughtered the Roman auxiliaries almost to a man. Three ships had been our spoils – two Liburnians, big warships made for fighting on the open sea. The third was a small Celox, a scouting ship. Shorter and narrower than the bigger ships of war, it was better suited to the shallower depths and narrow waterways of the many rivers that cut through our land.

The two war ships had been stolen from me in the first year after my humbling defeat. The Celox, though, had been well concealed, pushed out of the water and rolled into some thick woodland, not a mile from my hall. It was covered in moss and mould, and I had no pitch to hand to get it properly seaworthy. Though I reckoned with a few days' worth of cleaning and changing the odd plank of wood we could have her ready to sail.

'Does she have a name?' Eadger asked me. It was just after dawn the following day, and already Eadger, his five men, plus myself and Batur, were stripped to the waist, using a mixture of old clothes and tools to begin the clean and repairs on the small ship.

'Can't say she has, not from me anyway.'

'You really think we can get her to float? Must be a load of folk with river craft around here. Surely we can borrow or steal one from somewhere?'

I shrugged. 'Depends how much trouble you want to get yourself in. From the sound of it, your lord has enough troubles in the north. Don't need any more following us up there.'

Truth was I was suddenly desperate to see the boat I had stolen from the Romans sail once more. I loved the sea, the thrill of the white-topped water, the sharp scent of the salt spray in my nostrils. It was a freedom like something a land lover would never experience. The sea could take you anywhere you wanted to go. All my concerns and worries would melt away when sailing, left behind on the beach. I could not wait to return; just the thought of it invigorated me, and I felt the added spring in my step as I worked.

'True enough, I suppose,' Eadger muttered. 'Her hull seems awful shallow, though. I've no doubt that will be fine on the rivers, but out at sea?'

'We'll stay close to the shore. Besides, it won't take us long to get there.'

We worked for over a week, dawn to dusk. I sweated out the years I had spent languishing in my hall, throwing myself at the work. When we were done, my body ached from head to toe. I was more exhausted than I could ever remember being. But I felt *alive* once more. The sense of having achieved something seemed to lighten my soul, and Saxa even remarked it was the healthiest she had seen me look in an age.

'You've got your spark back,' she said to me on the night before we were due to sail. We had just made love, the second time that night, yet more evidence of my renewed enthusiasm for life, and we lay content on our straw pallet, letting the cool night air dry the sweat from our bodies.

'Aye, I feel you might be right. I have you to thank for that, my love,' I said and kissed her brow. 'You were right, I did need this. I need something to focus my mind on.'

'I know you did. I wish it wasn't war you wanted to focus on, but you are a warrior, and war is what you do.'

'Will you sail with us tomorrow? I can drop you upriver, near your father's people. It won't be safe for you and the boys to stay here on your own.'

I had been debating with myself if it was worth

leaving Sedric and Kai with Saxa and the boys to
keep them safe. But they were young, and far too
fond of the ale. They had returned three days late
from their shopping spree. They stank like the rear
end of a brothel and had spent all the coin I had
given them for provisions for the journey on ale and
women. They had at least come back with the supplies I'd asked for, supplies that were now already
loaded onto the ship to keep us fed for our upcoming
journey.

'Yes, if it makes you happy, my love, we will.
Though I think we would be perfectly safe here for
the summer. It's not like anyone travels this way.'

That was true enough, I agreed, but I insisted they
come with me anyway. I had picked that sight to build
my hall for one specific reason: no one ever travelled
that way. We were on the conflux where the rivers
Elbe and Saale met. I had first discovered the sight
many years ago and had used the shell of an old
Roman watchtower to make camp for the
Ravensworn when we weren't out on campaign. It
had become our spot, our little hideout, where we
could rest and recoup after a hard summer's fighting.
It had seemed the natural choice to build a hall once
I'd saved up the coin, and I hadn't regretted that
choice a day.

Our journey the next day would be made all the easier for our location, for the River Elbe flowed right to the tip of Germania, leaking into the sea, where we would then have a short sail up the western coast of Jylland.

'I know. But the thought of something happening to you and the boys whilst I am gone... It would be better if you were with your people.'

'*Our* people, you mean. You forget you are Chauci too.'

I smiled. 'My father was. Well, the man who raised me. But I turned my back on them the day I walked away from him. You know that.'

'A man should have a tribe. Our children should have a tribe, should know where they come from.'

'And they will. They will spend the summer with their grandparents, who I'm sure will fill them in on the proud history of the mighty Chauci.'

Saxa snorted. 'We won't be far from your father's farm; maybe we could spend some time with him?'

I paused at that, raising myself slightly as my brain worked. I had blocked all thoughts of that man from my mind as I worked on the ship, but at his mention they all came flooding back. 'Yes,' I said after a time. 'Yes, maybe you could. He would like that.'

'And so would I.' Saxa purred, pulling me back

onto the bed. We kissed, long and deep, and once more gave in to our bodies' desires.

It was near on midday by the time we were finally ready to set sail. I had tasked Sedric with setting free the remaining animals we had in our barn that we couldn't bring with us. Two aging horses, one pig and a mule. 'Just set them on their way through the trees, they'll know where to go to find food,' I'd said. Sedric had moaned about wolves and even bears. I had just laughed away his concerns. 'It is the natural order of things, young Sedric. They'll survive or they won't. But we can't take them onboard and we don't have the time to waste dropping them off to someone else. Set them free and be done with it.'

We also had ten hens in the barn; those I had caged and put aboard. Fresh eggs would be welcome, and if the grain got spoiled in the hold, we could always eat them. It took all nine of us to heave the Celox into the water, rolling the ship on freshly felled logs until it wobbled into the lazy current. By the gods it was a sight. I thought it a ship fit for the Hanged One himself, though of course I would say that. We waded out into the shallows of the river together and one by one clambered onboard, getting Saxa and the boys out of the water first.

It filled me with pride to see the excitement in my

sons' eyes as they raced around the deck, barrelling from prow to stern, taking everything in. Their whole lives they had only known their father as a lonely old drunk, spending the daylight hours hiding from the light, longing for the comfort of darkness once more. Now they would see the *real* me, and I hoped in the short time they would spend on the ship we would make a few lasting memories. 'Batur, would you raise the sail?' I called, silently hoping he wouldn't make a hash of it. We had practised some of the basics the afternoon before, the ship still safely on land. Eadger's men had picked it up well enough, and I thought they would respond well to being out on the open sea. Sedric and Kai had struggled through, the two youths muttering and giggling to themselves as I tried to patiently explain the workings of a ship. My patience had soon worn thin though, the flat of my sword across their backs its replacement. They had listened then.

Batur, though, had struggled with everything. He was a wisp of a youth; just one look at his arms and you'd wonder if he could even lift the sword strapped to his waist. I had a secret concern that he would not be able to withstand the wind once we exited the river and things began to get lively. He'd made some effort in his appearance ready for the big day though, and his poor excuse of a beard was gone. The red pimples on his cheeks where his skin had revolted against the blade of the razor just gave another reason for the others to poke fun at him. He took it all in his good-natured way, and dutifully pulled on the rope to lift the sail when asked. Kai took pity on him after a while, and two of them together managed to get it raised and tied off.

'What do you think?' Sedric asked me when the job was done.

I hadn't been looking at the sail, was too busy watching my boys as they raced from the steering oar to the prow, a beaming smile fixed to my face. Looking up, my smile grew wider as I saw the crudely painted raven on the off-white fabric. 'It's perfect,' I said, and I was surprised to find I meant it.

A few years before, I'd have been outraged to have been presented with such shabby artwork. But times had changed; I was no longer the great warlord, no longer a young man. Maybe I had changed, as the old man had told me long ago in that hall I would. Maybe as the grey streaked through my hair and beard, I was growing to appreciate the simpler things in life.

I looked once more to Ludwig and Eric racing back and knew it to be true. 'The boys helped,' Saxa said, sneaking up beside me. 'We've no way to get it dyed red, but we thought it was a nice gesture.'

'It's perfect.' I kissed her, hugging her tight. Our boys reached us and I knelt down and scooped them both up, breathing in their scent, suddenly aware I had two or three days left to do it and then I might never get another chance. 'Right then, let's get this voyage underway, shall we?'

4

It took us seven days to reach the sea. Three days to the drop off point for Saxa and the boys. It had been hard, saying goodbye to them, much harder than I could ever have imagined. My vision blurred from tears for many an hour once we pushed off from the bank and resumed our journey, my one good eye fixed on the three waving figures until they were out of sight. None of the men had spoken to me for the rest of the day. I think they all understood I needed some space, and I had been grateful for it. Although I think they also lacked the energy to muster a word between them.

The raven-painted sail was all well and good out on the open sea; on the river, though, it was worse than useless. The Celox had space on each side for twenty rowers; we were just ten men. Since I was the only sailor among us, I had spent my time at the steering oar, keeping us well to the centre of the narrow river, avoiding the reed beds and occasionally running to the prow to check for rocks when I felt the ship grating on the riverbed. That left the other nine men to row. Eadger and his men had fared pretty well. They were warriors, used to marching and riding long hours in mail. They were fit and strong, packed muscle covering their torsos. My three men, however, were not built for such endeavours.

Batur was a wisp of a boy, all skin and bone. He had been raised in a poor farming village to the west, his people not belonging to any particular tribe. Food had been a luxury for him growing up; if he'd got two meals a day, he would have considered it a feast. But to give the lad credit, he didn't once moan about what he was being asked to do. He sat on the bench, sunrise after sunrise, and pulled the oar with everything he had. I purposely made sure he was overloaded with milk and as many oats he could fill his belly with. After just seven days there was a subtle change in his body, the first hint of muscle showing beneath his baggy tunic.

Sedric was a bear of a man, a head taller than me,

and the coming winter would be his twentieth in this world. He was all puppy fat though with a rounded belly the vigour of youth should have shaken off. He shaved his head almost daily, revealing a pox mark of white scars on his scalp that he claimed had got there from incessant scratching with a blade at the lice that had plagued him for years. It was common enough amongst our people; we had never been acclaimed for our cleanliness. We had no great bath houses like the Romans, no big cities with barbers lining the pavement, offering a trim for a few bronze coins. He moaned and sweated the days away at the oar, bemoaning his blistered hands and aching back. His head had reddened from the sun, and by the fifth day he had taken to wearing a dampened cloth tied around his scalp to try and keep the skin from peeling.

Kai was the one I had the highest hopes for. He was shorter than the other two, but well built, with thick legs and rounded shoulders. He had the physique of a warrior, the desire to be the best and bravest, but still lacked the skill. It had been three years since he had appeared at my hall, saying he wanted to train under one of Germania's greatest warriors. To this day I have no idea how he knew where to find me; half the tribes had assumed I was dead. But he had found me, and I had accepted his service, although I had little enough to offer. He pulled the oar as if it presented him with a personal challenge, seeing it as a foe he needed to overcome. I pretended not to notice his winces and groans as I ordered them to stop as the sun waned in the west each evening, though his stoop when he rose from the bench was hard to miss.

They all cheered as the sea came into view, the nine men rising from their benches in glee, the sail raised, a northerly gust driving us out into the open water. It was mid-morning, warm and dry, the sky a pale blue bowl overhead. We heard nothing but birds squawking and the rush of the waves as they bounded towards the shore. Once we had cleared the last of the land to either side, I stripped off my tunic and dived from the stern, feeling more alive than I had in an age. Surfacing, I wiped the hair from my face and looked up at the ship, laughing at the shocked expressions of the men I had left onboard.

I had a memory of the last time I had done this. Sailing these very waters with three ships loaded with five hundred fighting men. They had cheered my name until they were hoarse, and I had known I was doing the will of the gods. I was lost in that memory, and for a moment I expected to see Ruric as I looked up into the ship. Ruric had been my second in command since the Ravensworn had first been formed, and never had there been a braver soul, a finer fighter. I had marvelled time and time again as he continued to defy age, hefting his giant battle axe and carving a path through any shield wall that stood in his way. *Gods below, boy, would you get back onboard before Rán takes you!* he would have called, his bearded face set in a scowl as men cheered all around him.

My face dropped when I could not see him aboard the Celox. Nor was Ketill there to throw me down a rope and pull me aboard, shove me on the back and insist I drink a barrel of ale with him. I felt my old melancholy return, the tug to retreat back to the darkness of my hall. So many souls lost to the Heroes Hall. One day I will see them again.

I swam for an hour, maybe two, my arms, legs, chest screaming at the exertion. I was old, my body run to fat. That is no condition in which to go to war. Battles are not often decided by heroes, or the most fearsome warriors. In my experience, they are won or lost by discipline and fitness. The Romans knew this, and that was why they always won. I had always insisted that any man fighting for me should be able to ride or march a full day in mail, then have breath enough to spar for an hour at the end. In the condition I was currently in, I would not have survived as a warrior of the Ravensworn. So I carried on swimming.

'Never seen a man swim like that,' Eadger said to me as he hauled me over the rail.

'You ever tried?' I shivered in the breeze, my legs at once accustomed to the easy motion of the ship as it rocked on the waves.

'No, can't say I intend to, either.'

'Maybe that is why your people are losing your fight. If you wish to fight raiders from the sea, you should be comfortable in the water.'

'I'll settle for us winning the battles on land.' He laughed as he threw me an old tunic to dry myself with. 'How long until we reach home?'

I paused in my drying to consider the question. 'Seven days? Depends on the wind. If it blows to the north like this the whole time, we'll be there in no time. If it changes then we may have to row some more, or even beach the ship and wait for it to change. The sea is unpredictable, and flows with Rán's will.'

It had been a long time since I had given the gods any attention. As far as I was concerned, they had abandoned me at my time of need, and I had no further need of their services. Before, I had been a follower of Loki and considered myself a disciple of the Sly One. Every battle I turned through deception, every new direction a tribe took because of my meddling, I prided myself that he was watching, steering the oar that propelled me to glory. But then my men had been defeated and my enemies had conspired behind my back, united to bring me down. Loki had abandoned me that day, and the Hanged One had not even seen fit to bring me to his hall. So I was still here, still stuck on this world, whilst my friends drunk their fill on the benches, feasting until the End Time. I could not shake myself from the unfairness of it all.

'Anyone waiting for you back at home?' I asked Eadger to distract me from my thoughts.

A shadow passed over his face, and he frowned as he spoke. 'No, no one waiting for me.' And I saw then the face of a man with a troubled past, demons lurking in the back of his mind. It was a feeling I could relate to. 'But I am keen to get home all the same. Much counts on it.'

'Then pray for a northerly wind.' Of course, we didn't get one.

It was afternoon the following day when things took a turn for the worse. I swam again in the morning, spent an hour sparring with Kai as I dried off, showing the lad different thrusts he could make with his sword in battle. Battles are different to fighting one on one – you have less room to manoeuvre, two or three men within striking distance. To survive, you have to be quick and alert. It pleased me that Eadger's men were paying as much attention as my own were. We would need as many stout hands behind shields as we could get when we reached our destination.

It was Batur of all people who first noticed the change in the wind. The ship rocked to a different beat as the wind blew the sail from north to south, as if Rán herself had decided we had travelled as far north as we were allowed. The air stung as it whipped salt into my eyes; I could feel it clinging to my lips and beard. It was another clear day, a pale sun high in the sky, but something was changing, I could feel it.

'Whose lands are those?' I said as I pointed off to the east. We were sailing up the western coast of Jylland, the land flat and featureless to our right.

'That'll be the Anglii,' Eadger said with a shrug. 'All the lands to the south of Jylland are. We won't reach our own people until we pass the great river that splits the land in two. As to who holds power over this particular stretch, I couldn't really tell you. Haribert is their chief, but his hall is a long day's ride from the western shore. The Anglii are few in people and spread over a vast land. Could be we could camp there a day or two and see no one.'

'Or could be we are ambushed in the night,' I finished for him, licking the salt from my lips.

'Aye. What concerns you, Alaric? It is just wind, far as I can tell.' He raised his hands above him, circling them in the air.

'It's not the wind that bothers me, my friend, but what it will bring south with it.' I ran to the mast and climbed, up and up until I stood on the netting to the side of the sail. Squinting as I looked into the wind, I scanned the northern horizon, sending up the first prayer I'd muttered in an age to any god that would listen. *Let the skies be clear.*

I stayed there for an age, eyes fixed on the distance, before my worst fears were realised. To the northeast, over the flat lands of Jylland, there was a black smudge in the sky. I watched long enough to determine its trajectory, before scampering back down to the deck. 'We need to make land, now.'

'What is it, Chief?' Sedric asked me through a mouthful of oats.

'Storm clouds to the northeast. The wind is bringing them this way.'

'So what do we do?' Eadger asked, nervous eyes fixed on the horizon.

I hung over the side rail of the ship, eyes scanning the western coastline of Jylland. I was looking for a cove, a small beach, anything we could aim our prow at and row towards for all we were worth. My eyes roamed back to the sky; the black smudge was already getting bigger.

'There!' I pointed to a semi-circular beach with a small grass-topped knoll behind it. 'Get to your benches, we aim for the beach.' There was no grumbling from the men this time, the nine of them running for their oars and pulling for all their might. I made for the steering oar and felt the rising aggression in the water as I turned the ship landward – the storm was going to strike with a fury.

Back in the day, when I had foolishly considered myself one of the greatest warlords in the land, I had worshipped Loki, the Trickster. It was to him my prayers went then. I prayed for the guile to steer the ship to safety, the luck to make it onto dry land before the storm hit. I hoped the gods had forgiven me for whatever transgression had caused them to desert me so. When I die, I would go to the Hanged One's Hall, feast with my fellow warriors and await the End Times. I would not leave this world in a watery grave.

The spray became blinding as we rowed east, the tide retreating from the shore, as if Rán herself forbade us to make it to the safety of land. And what Rán wishes, she usually gets. The men rowed like gods of old, straining on their oars, Eadger bellowing out the strokes. Sweat and salt water poured down them as I spat and cursed in the stern, willing the small Celox to find its way to land. There was a loud boom of thunder overhead and a crack of lightning had me seeing stars. The wind roared all around us, waves assaulted the ship's hull as we sliced a path east, the ship lurching up and down with so much force I had to hold on to the steering oar so tight I thought my knuckles would burst, my feet being lifted from the deck entirely.

'We're not going to make it!' one of Eadger's men bellowed over the howling wind, his voice shrill with fear.

'Shut your mouth!' I roared back at him. 'Shut your mouth and row!'

The sky was dark now, black clouds rolling through the heavens. Thunder cackled above us as if the gods were laughing at our small ship, battling the might of the great storm alone. I cursed the gods as we rode the waves, water cascading over the rails every time the sea sent us crashing down. Batur lost his seat as we rose up one wave. He slid down the deck as the ship crested the wave and began to descend, screaming in terror, before smashing into the ram at the prow. He lay in a heap at the front of the ship, unmoving, I could see the blood matted in his hair from the stern. I willed the lad to get up, to grab hold of something, *anything*, to stop himself sliding overboard, but he didn't move.

Lightning cracked again, twice, vanishing in an instant and plunging the world into darkness. I was momentarily blinded, nose full of salt, ears battered by the wind. I tried to call Batur's name, but only a choke came out. The lightning returned for an instant and my water-logged eye saw two things. The first was the grassy knoll atop the small beach, not fifty yards ahead of us. The second was the empty patch of deck Batur had been sprawled on moments before.

It was too much for me take in and in a moment of madness, I let go of the steering oar and made to move forwards, hands outstretched in a feeble attempt to maintain my balance. I managed two lurching steps before losing my balance, falling backwards. I seemed to stay suspended in the air for an age before colliding head-first with the deck. I just had time to mouth Batur's name before the world went black and I could think no more.

5

It was dark when I awoke. Not the raging dark of a harrowing storm, but the comforting blanket of night. I heard the rustle of the sea embracing the shore somewhere off to my right, the chill breeze blowing gently onto my face. An owl hooted in the distance, sea birds squawked; the world seemed calm.

I remembered the raging storm, the terror, the certainty we were all about to meet our doom. I gingerly stretched out a hand and it clutched wet sand. I let it run through my fingers. We had made land then, and that was enough for now.

'Batur,' I muttered, then I urgently tried to rise as I remembered the slumped form of the lad at the prow before recalling he had disappeared.

'He's awake!' someone shouted, and I heard foot-steps rush to my side.

'Don't move, Alaric,' a hushed voice said, warm breath on my face. 'I don't think you've broken any-thing, but you took one hell of a bang to the head.'

Took me a moment to recognise Eadger's voice. He spoke to me in the tone Saxa used when she tucked our boys in at night: quiet, calm, comforting. 'What happened to Batur?' I croaked. I was becoming more aware of the thumping pain in my head, the aches and pains spreading from my arms and legs to my rattling chest.

'He fell, Alaric. The sea has taken him.'

'Wretched gods,' I cursed, and I tried to move to make myself more comfortable. I lifted my left leg and stretched it. At once it came alive with the tin-gling burn of pins and needles, the blood rushing freely to my foot and back once more. I cursed again. 'And the ship?'

'Somehow made it onto the beach, seems to be in one piece. We'll know more come the morning. Do you want some water?'

'Had enough of that for a lifetime,' I muttered, the tingling in my leg subsiding. I turned, lying on my left side, and listened to the wind and the waves. Eadger said nothing else, and I guess I must have passed back into oblivion. When I woke again, the sun was high in a cloudless sky.

I blinked rapidly, sunlight offending my one remaining eye. My skin felt like leather as I worked the muscles on my face. I felt it crack even as I grimaced at the discomfort. I rose gingerly; my head still hurt like hell, but the aches across the rest of my body had lessened. Slowly, my eye became accustomed to the light and I took a moment to take in our surroundings. We were on the same semi-circular beach I had spotted from the ship the day before. The ground was sand mixed with shingle. Behind me was the grassy knoll, ten, maybe fifteen foot high – practically a mountain on this notoriously flat terrain.

Our small Celox did indeed appear to be in one piece, sitting proudly on the beach. Her sail was down, the oars hanging out of their holes, dragging on the sand. I hoped it was a sign that the gods had not completely deserted me. Perhaps this had been a test of my wavering courage, Loki looking down to see if the gnarled old warrior he had once bestowed with his favour was still worth his attention. I afforded myself a small smile that I had passed the test. There can't have been many sailors who could have steered their ships to shore in such conditions. Alaric, though, had prevailed.

Sedric and Kai were aboard the Celox, Sedric with his customary rag around his bald head. They seemed to be checking on the livestock and supplies. I thought then of the sacks of grain we had stored in the hull, the water that had engulfed the deck the day before. Surely there was no way that had survived?

'We've lost a lot of food, but should still have enough to see us home,' Eadger said with a smile as he approached, as if reading my mind. He held out a water skin and I snatched it with relish, draining every last drop in huge gulps. 'Gods, man, remember you need air, too!' he joked as I raised the skin high.

'What about the armour, weapons?'

'They'll survive. Some will need a good clean when we reach the north, but they should still do the job just fine.' That was a relief, at least. 'Worse news with the livestock though. The hens are dead; your lads are skinning them as we speak, so at least we'll have some meat for a night or two, though I will miss the eggs.'

'And your men?'

'Bumps and bruises only. You took the worst of it; the rest of us were holding on to our oars for dear life.'

I thought of Batur then, the poor lad thrown down the deck, the sickening thud of him hitting the ram. My face must have darkened as Eadger once more seemed to read my thoughts. 'I am sorry, that was insensitive of me. Had Batur been with you long?'

'Couple of years, maybe a bit more. He was the first man to come and offer me his services after the Romans had left me for dead. I know he wasn't the sharpest tool in the shed, but he was steadfast and loyal. I shall miss him.'

I'd always had a soft spot for young misfits, I think because I had once been one myself. It was Ruric who had taken me under his wing when I was young, shown me what it was to be both a warrior and a leader. I had always tried to do the same for other strays I had come upon on the road. I'd had a scout once, a lad named Birgir, whom I had thought the world of. My face darkened once more, for Birgir had not been the bright young lad I'd thought he was, and he had betrayed me in the end.

Life is one big lesson; I remember my mother telling me that once.

'We scoured the hull for holes this morning. She appears to be intact. There's a lot of water down there to be drained out, and we didn't know whether to risk removing one of the beams to drain it, or whether to just form a line of men and buckets and do it the hard way. What do you think?'

I clicked my tongue as I tried to kick my knackered brain into gear. Removing one of the planks at the bottom of the hull was all well and good, but we had no pitch to seal it back up with, and it could end up costing us more than a little time if we got it wrong. 'We don't have the equipment to get it sealed back on,' I said after some thought.

'Buckets then?' Eadger asked with a sigh.

I nodded. 'Buckets.'

The weather stayed mercifully cool and dry, the wind easing the sweat from our bodies. We were bone tired, traumatised from what we had gone through the previous day, and I had doubts as to whether the men would be ready to get back onto the water once the ship had been drained. I said as much to Kai as we passed buckets up the line from the hold.

'Don't see we have much choice, Lord.' He shrugged. 'Can't carry all this gear north, and no point us turning up without it.'

I asked him to share that theory with the others. He and Sedric were starting to bond more with Eadger's men. I didn't know whether it was the shared experience of the storm or losing Batur, but the two groups of men had kept a respectful distance from each other until then. There had been no malice, no tension bubbling under the surface, but a visible reluctance from both parties to get to know each other.

I thought I could understand it. Sedric and Kai would be wary of the six battle-seasoned warriors, and they in turn probably didn't think much of the two young fools who were to be considered immature at best. But that morning, the air was alive with chatter, cheap jokes exchanged and experiences shared. I smiled to see it. If we were to go to war together then we would need to have common ground to share, the beginnings of a bond formed. Friendship gave men another reason to fight harder. They would want to boast of their courage and prowess after battle, want to be seen to excel in the slaughter in front of their brothers. Eadger could see it too, and we exchanged encouraging looks as the men began to sing together.

Breaking for a meal as the sun began to set, I walked to the top of the knoll at the back of the beach, breathing in the cool evening air and preparing myself for another day at sea. It encouraged me that I managed to scamper up the grassy bank without getting out of breath, and I rubbed a hand around my waistline, wondering if it was indeed a bit slimmer than it had been the day Eadger and his men had arrived at my hall. I felt stronger, fitter, despite the wounds of the day before. It was a nasty cut, the one on the back of my head, but it would heal as all cuts do, and I hoped it would be some time yet before I would need to don a helm and have the base of it rubbing away at the open wound.

The Trickster must have laughed at my innocent mind. Atop the knoll, I could see inland for miles. The ground was as flat as a summer calm sea, and didn't I wish I'd been sailing on one of those. There was nothing remarkable to look upon; a few trees to the south and an endless expanse of grassland covering the rest. It was from the north that they came, twelve men, armed and mounted. They rose at an easy canter across the plain, and at once I ducked behind a thorny bush, though if I'd managed to see them with one waterlogged eye, they sure as hell had seen me.

They were half a Roman mile off, no distance really, and I could see the glimmer of their mail in the waning sun, the outline of round shields and spears. I chewed my lip a moment, trying to determine how far north up the coastline we had travelled. Eadger had said the Anglii were no friends of his people, but was it possible we had passed their lands and reached the Cimbri? I decided it was unlikely.

I shuffled back down the knoll, not willing to raise

my voice to alert the men, for surely it would carry to the approaching riders. 'Weapons, now!' I hissed as I reached our campfires, stirring tired limbs into action.

'What is it, Lord?' Kai asked as he reached for his sword belt, wrapping the leather around his waist.

'Twelve riders, armed, coming from the north,' I said as I reached my own blade, ripping it from the sheath and scooping up my shield.

'Quick, lads, mail,' Eadger ordered the five Cimbri warriors.

'No time, weapons and shields, they'll be here any moment.' And sure enough, the first sounds of drumming hoofbeats could be heard over the lapping of the waves. I cursed myself for not having the foresight to keep a man on watch on the knoll. That's what the Alaric of old would have done, the warlord of the Ravensworn. He'd have had men out in every direction, scouring the land for potential foes, especially in land he knew nothing of.

Alas, I was not the Alaric of old. I had not even made the men wear armour whilst ashore. Silhouettes appeared atop the knoll, the dull gleam of helmets in the orange glow of dusk. 'Form a line,' I said quietly, ensuring I was in the centre, Kai to my left and Eadger to my right. I won't lie, it felt good to be standing in a line of warriors once more, my raven-painted shield in one hand, the sword my father had given me in the other. However, I did quickly notice a problem I had never been presented with before.

A warrior fights with his shield held forwards in his left hand and his sword in his right. He stands with his left leg to the front, right leg braced behind. This means a warrior's head naturally points slightly to the right, which is fine if you still have both your eyes. I was missing my left, a sea-soaked leather patch that now desperately needed replacing strapped around my head. Unless I craned my neck to turn to the left, I couldn't see a fucking thing.

'Good evening,' a cheery voice called from the knoll. 'You are camping on my land, and I have come to collect the tax due to me for the privilege.'

The rider that had spoken eased his mount down the bank. It was a steep drop, if not particularly long, and the horse took its time descending. When he reached the bottom, I could make out more of his face, and I saw a young man with soft skin, bright eyes and the smug look of someone used to getting their own way. I guess I used to look like that.

'Tell you what I'll do, pup. If you turn that mount of yours around, I'll let you leave with your life, and we'll call that payment enough.' Eadger and his men laughed at the cheap joke. Kai and Sedric to my left were silent though, and I could make out the slight quiver of Kai's shield. No one forgets their first dance in the wall of death, and the two young men were sensing their debuts approaching.

'Big words from a man a bit long in the tooth. And who might you be, greybeard? You got a name large enough to match your bravado?' He was putting on a show for his mates, the arrogant young'un, and I smiled at his self-assurance. It was time to see if the old men still spoke of the great Alaric around their fires at night.

'Look at my shield, boy. Really look. What do you see?'

Black on red, a raven flying through a torrent of blood. Back in the day, those shields had been as feared as the men who'd stood behind them. To see those shields facing you on a field of battle was to see your own death. The pup looked. I realised then the sun was bleeding out behind us, and the pup had to squint to make out the details. Squint he did, and I smiled to see the realisation dawn across his hairless face. 'Yes, you see it now, boy, don't you? I am Alaric Hengistson, Lord of the Ravensworn. Men sing songs of me, all across this land. Oath breaker. Battle turner. Chief killer. Take a good look at me, boy, then ask me about your fucking taxes again.'

It was like I could see his cock shrivelling into his groin. He was suddenly uncertain, his horse twitching, throwing its head from left to right, sensing its rider's fear. 'I have nothing to fear from you,' he called, a shrill high-pitched squeal. I knew I had him then.

'Then tell us your name, oh mighty lord. Give us the name of the great warrior that will send us squealing to the Heroes Hall.'

'I... I am Sigimund Haribertson, and my father rules these lands.'

'Quite the mouthful,' Eadger muttered, and all of us shook our shields as we laughed.

'Fancy yourself as quite the little lordling, do you then, Sigimund?' I spluttered through my mirth. I saw him and his men for what they were then. The son of a great lord, out touring his father's lands with his friends, imposing themselves on the peasants and making right tits of themselves in the process. It was possible his father had told him to do it, get himself used to the burden of rule and all that. Though I'd have wagered this lot had just been harassing pretty farm girls and helping themselves to as much ale as they could drink. And by ill chance they had spied a beached ship, manned by just nine men, and thought they'd found some easy pickings.

Life is full of lessons; the trick is living long enough to learn from them.

'Well then, *my lord*' – I gave a mocking half bow – 'we are on *your* lands, as you so rightly pointed out, and I have to say I have absolutely no fucking inclination to pay you any tax. So what are you going to do about it?'

My blood was up, my heart racing in a way it hadn't for years. Skin prickling the back of my neck, throat dry, bladder full. Gods, I'd missed that feeling. Sigimund had given it the big'un in front of his mates, and now he couldn't back down without losing face. He knew it, I knew it. He had to attack us, and I could see him coming to terms with that. He didn't want to; in truth, I think his nerve had already gone, slunk away with the evening tide. But he was the son of a great lord, and sons of great lords have to prove themselves worthy of succession. Ridding the world of Alaric of the Ravensworn would do that and more for his reputation. So he did the only thing he could.

6

They came at us on foot, leaving their horses tethered to the bushes atop the knoll. A questionable choice, for a mounted man will always be the favourite when up against a foot soldier. But the ground was littered with rocks and other debris, the mix of sand and shingle unfavourable to a galloping horse. So they locked their shields together and approached.

'Steady now, lads,' I said to Sedric and Kai to my left, their colour fading with the light of the sun. Kai seemed to be shivering, and I wanted nothing more than to put down my shield and give the lad a quick hug, spend a moment or two whispering encouragements in his ear. Kai wanted to be a warrior though, and to be a warrior one has to be able to summon their courage alone, to quash down their fear and hold their ground. He would learn that today, or he would die.

Their line was the same width as ours, but the four men in the centre each had a man behind them. I could see the axes in the hands of the four men in the front and knew already their plan. The axes would snake out and hook on the top of our shields. Once the shields were yanked down, the men behind them would use their spears to attack our unprotected torsos. It was an old tactic I had used with the Ravensworn many times before.

'If you're facing an axe, keep your shield high. They will try and hook over the top of them and pull them down, and the men in their second rank will use those spears to gut you like a fish.' I spoke quietly, though the approaching party were still thirty paces off. 'Men on the flanks push hard and try to claim your kill quick. Seems to me they will look to split us into two groups, encircle us and finish us that way.

'Look at their faces, lads. They are not men, they are boys. There's no man over there who has done this before, no proven warrior. It's twelve lads off on a grand tour of their friend's father's lands. They did not come expecting this. Hold your nerve, stay calm, and we'll be fine.'

'Let's charge 'em,' Eadger said to my right. 'They won't be expecting that.'

I considered it a moment. It was usually beneficial to be the attacker rather than the defender, unless you had time to prepare the ground before the battle. I thought of the battle I'd fought against a cavalry wing of Batavi years before. We had been the defenders then, but we'd had time to choose where to stand and dig pits and hide them. I realised that the men were looking to me then, and I was too busy smiling at the memory. Good times. 'Fine by me. Wait until they are ten paces away, then we go.'

Sigimund and his men approached us with the pace of a reluctant snail. They were silent, beardless faces licking dry lips, shields being adjusted in sweaty palms. They were nervous, not a one among them with the character to encourage the others. My smile widened; they were nothing but sheep for the wolves.

Once they came within ten paces of our wall, I raised my sword and bellowed 'Ravensworn!' at the top of my lungs, then burst forwards, shield held high so my enemy saw nothing but the top of my helm and my one good eye. I covered the ground in less time it took the shit-scared boys to register what was happening, and had claimed my first kill before they could react. I just had time to see a pair of quivering eyes behind a shaking shield before I thrust straight and true with my sword, the tip punching through the coward's mouth and bursting out the other side. The lad died without a sound.

Stepping over his body, I hacked at a shield to my right and lunged at the one to my left. Space around me, enough to dodge the tip of a probing spear, feel the rush of air on my cheek as it passed my face. Sedric pushed up on my left flank, and I heard the clank of metal on metal as his sword met his opponent's axe in a blaze of sparks. Eadger and his boys caught up with us, and the momentum of their weight on Sigimund's line of shields swung the battle, with our enemy coming to an abrupt halt and having to take two steps back.

'Ravensworn!' I bellowed once more, just for the hell of it. Just to feel the *power* of it once more. Sedric battered his man with his shield, and with a squeal the man fell back, slipping on the shingle and crashing to the ground. Sedric leaped at him, hacking down with his sword and carving a bloody mess from his face. 'I think he's dead, Sedric!' I called as I once more dodged a blow from the spear. My opponent was young, too young, his mail hanging off him like it was his father's. It probably was. I snarled, hefted my shield and charged him. The youth screamed in terror, dropped his spear and turned to run. I stabbed him through the back.

Eadger and his men had made small work of the rest of them, and with a laugh dancing in my throat, in my head I turned to see Sedric and Kai, already celebrating a fine victory. Kai, though, was struggling. He was locked with a youth both taller and broader than he, the bigger man using his strength to push Kai back. The youth roared in Kai's face, seemingly unaware his friends were already dead or dying, and laughed as he kicked Kai's shield, knocking him flat on his arse. Sedric was still transfixed on the man he had killed. Sweat rolled down his face so fast it seemed to be racing gravity. He was looking from his sword to the bloodied pulp that was once the face of a man, the mushy brains on the sand once full of hopes and dreams.

'Wake up, Sedric!' I called, already hopping bodies to get to Kai, but I was never going to reach him in time. Kai had his shield raised high over his head, and his opponent stood over him, sword gripped in both hands. He lifted the blade above his head and sent it crashing down, splintering the shield and driving through into Kai's face. 'Sedric!' I screamed again. Raising my own blade high, I skipped over the corpse at Sedric's feet and buried my sword in Kai's attacker's back.

Silence then. The quiet after the storm of shields, as each man still standing gave thanks to the gods that they'd survived. Panting, I heaved my sword from a dead back, twisting the blade so it slid free from the bone and mail without too much fuss. I made for Kai, who was silent as a summer breeze on the shingle. Pulling away the ruined shield from his face, I saw his eyes were open and moving, a ruined mouth trying to spit out words through broken teeth. 'Calm now, lad,' I said softly, stroking his blood-drenched hair. 'Calm now.' I turned and shouted to Sedric, still standing wordlessly over the corpse he had made, and told the man to fetch me water.

'Seems there's still life in the old dog yet!' Eadger called over to me, an ear-splitting grin on his sweaty red face. He had Sigimund by the arm. The youth was disarmed, blood spilling from a cut on his forehead, his nose broken and leaking crimson. 'What you reckon we should do with this sack of shit?'

'Bound his hands and feet, leave him with his men for now,' I said, not really caring what happened to the bastard. Sedric came back with the water and I tipped some gently over Kai's face. His hands twitched with the pain. Sedric had to hold his friend's shoulders to stop him writhing away. He groaned, Kai, groaned in agony and despair, unable to form the noise into words. 'Breathe. Breathe, Kai. In and out, slow as you can. You got to fight this, lad. You got to be strong, you hear me?'

The wound was awful. Kai must have turned his head as the sword smashed through his shield, and in doing so may have just saved his life. The blade seemed to have cut through his left cheek, burst through his mouth and out the other side. His teeth, the ones not on the shingle anyway, were bloodied stumps. There was blood everywhere, and I was trying to get a grasp on whether his tongue had been severed, but red was red, and I couldn't really make anything out. I tipped more water into his mouth and he choked on it. 'We need to sit him up, Eadger, help me.'

Eadger passed Sigimund on to one of his men and knelt at Kai's right shoulder, me on the left. Sedric, still coming to terms with the brutality of battle, held the skin of water as Eadger and I raised Kai to a sitting position. 'Aaogh,' he moaned, tears running rivulets down his face, disappearing into the open wounds on his face.

'What do you think?' I said to Eadger.

The man scrunched his face in thought, eyeing

the wounds with professional curiosity. He ran a hand through his chestnut hair, sweat soaked and flattened to his head by his helmet. He rubbed at the five-day old stubble on his chin, the yellow of his teeth showing as he grimaced. 'Need to stitch the wounds on his cheeks, stem the bleeding. Once that's done, we'll have a better chance of seeing the damage in his mouth.'

'Any of your boys a steady hand with a needle?' I'd always been more of a maker of wounds than a stitcher of them, though every warband usually hand a man or two handy with a needle and thread. Surgeons were rare our side of the Rhine. Our warriors didn't have the luxury of pop-up hospitals like the Romans had, manned at all times by skilled men. You had half a chance of surviving a wound with people like that to stitch you back up at battle's end.

'Rolf, over here,' Eadger called to one of his men. A stolid-looking man, greying hair and matching beard, round shouldered and thick in the waist. He could have been any of a thousand warriors from Germania. We bred men for one thing only: war.

Rolf set to his task, cleaning his hands with the skin of water before applying the thread to the needle. Eadger, Sedric and I held Kai down as Rolf got to work, stopping every now and again to wipe away the blood with a clean tunic. It didn't take long to get it done, but by the gods it felt an age.

We slept fitfully that night, the sky a purple backdrop, the odd glint of a star. Kai moaned his way through the darkness. We'd force fed him enough wine to knock out a village, but still it seemed to not take the pain away. Sigimund lay with his legs tied to a log, hands bound behind his back. He was awake when I eventually gave up on grabbing a couple of hours shut eye, wide eyes staring at me as I rose from the vague comfort of an itchy blanket and wandered down to the shoreline.

I stood there a while, the cold breeze on my face, listening to the rush of the waves, the occasional hoot of an owl. I'd been couped up in my hall so long I'd forgotten how much I loved the simple things in life. It was peaceful, standing there, and I thought of my wife and boys, tucked up warm and safe back south – at least, I hoped they were. Saxa's father would have seen her well, and the boys would be causing mischief around his hall. I smiled at the thought.

There was a crunch of boots on shingle behind me, and I turned to see Sedric, gingerly making his way towards me. 'Can't sleep?'

He shook his head. 'Killed your first man today, eh?' He nodded. 'Like to tell you it gets easier, but it doesn't.' I offered him a sad smile, reached out a hand and touched his shoulder. 'You did well, Sedric.'

'No, I didn't.' Sedric spoke with a shaky voice, a quiver I'd not heard in the usually brash young man before. 'Should've saved him,' he whispered.

I shook my head. 'Don't think that way, brother. If you think that every time a man next to you in the line dies then you will go mad with grief. It was a battle, lad, and in battle, men take wounds. That's just the way it is.'

'Will he be okay?'

I shrugged. 'I don't know. He won't die, if that's what you mean, but I'm not sure he will make a full recovery. I've seen men hurt before, Sedric, and I remember all too well the first time I saw a man killed. Stayed with me for a long time.'

Sedric scoffed. 'You are a warrior born, Lord. You must have killed a dozen men by the time you were my age.'

'When I was your age, I found myself down in the south, in Goridorgis, capital of the Marcomanni. They dig pits there, deeper than a man is tall. And in them, two men fight to the death. One man climbs out victorious, the other is buried where he dies. That's where I first saw a man die. Lying there in the mud, guts splattered on the ground in front of him.

Help me, he'd mouthed as I'd just stood there, dumb-struck, like you were today.

'I went back the next day, saw the same thing happen again. Then one day, for some reason I cannot explain, I decided to jump in myself. Never looked back.'

My mind took me back to the darkness of the pit, the only light coming from the flash of my opponent's blade. I could have died a hundred deaths down there in the mud and sludge. But *he* always had my back, the Trickster, guiding my every move.

'When I was a child, my mother was raped and murdered, not ten feet from where I lay, though thankfully it was dark and I did not see it happen. We become products of our past, more so with the passing of each winter. I am what I am because of what I suffered that night, a boy of fifteen, listening to the screams of his world going to shit. You haven't suffered the way I have, Sedric, not truly known an-guish. I don't say this to demean you, lad, for I have come to value your service. But to give you some un-derstanding of why I am as I am.'

Sedric was quiet a while, and for that I was grate-ful. My mother's screams filled my ears, the farm-house flames warmed my skin. My father's voice, soft in my ear, telling me to close my eyes, to stay still and not struggle. I felt the old hate towards him burn within me then. But if that was me, and my sons, would I have done anything different?

Parenthood puts everything into perspective.

'I couldn't stop looking at him,' Sedric said, his breath misting the air. 'Couldn't believe I'd done that. He was a person, you know? He probably had family, parents waiting for him to come home.'

I turned to Sedric, put a hand on each of his shoulders. 'If you hadn't have killed him, do you think he would have killed you?'

Sedric didn't reply, couldn't look me in the eye. He nodded, eyes downcast. 'Then you did the right thing. No point dwelling on it, lad, though I know it's hard.'

I used to have dreams. Dreams full of all the men I have slain. They would stand on the far bank of a river, and I would be sailing towards them. 'Come to us, brother,' they would call, their faces full of forgiveness, their hands outstretched, waiting to pull me ashore. Years they haunted me, the smiling faces of the dead, though I dare not tell Sedric that. 'Go get some sleep, Sedric. It will be another long day at the oar tomorrow, and you'll need your strength.'

He nodded once more, still mute, and trudged off into the darkness. I stood there a while longer, my one eye facing the sleeping sea. I don't know how long I was there, but I stayed until my mind was empty, the shadows of my past retreating to the darkest corners of my consciousness. When I turned back to the beach, the sky on the horizon was an orange haze; the sun had sent its outriders out, spreading the word that dawn was forthcoming. I walked slowly back to the sleeping huddle of men. Sigimund was still awake, and once more his eyes were fixed to mine. The smugness of the previous day had gone, the anger and defiance too. There, in the half light of pre-dawn, I saw him for what he was. A scared youth, realising, perhaps for the first time, that he had made a grave error.

I sighed, weariness creeping up on me like daylight attacking the night. 'Let's get you up,' I said, kneeling at Sigimund's feet and freeing him from the log.

7

'Are you sure it was wise to let him go?' Eadger asked as we sailed away from the beach.

I sighed, weary to my old bones. 'What good would killing him have done?' I could see him if I squinted, a lone rider, silhouetted against the rising sun.

'He will go back to his people. His father will want blood.'

'I'm sure he will. But the lad knows nothing of where we are going, doesn't even know who we are, apart from the fact that I am Alaric. We sail out to sea far enough that he can't see which way we're travelling, then we swing the ship north and carry on our journey.'

We were a sullen group that morning, and if a stranger happened upon us, they would be forgiven for thinking we had been defeated in battle the previous day, not victorious. But Kai would not cease with his moaning, and Eadger and his men were uncomfortable with my decision to let Sigimund live. 'If you wanted the lad dead you should have slain him in battle,' I had said to them, before helping Sigimund onto his horse. For myself, my thoughts were with poor young Batur, an eager young man who had wanted nothing more than to be a famous warrior. In truth, I was resentful to Eadger and his men. Wasn't their fault, of course. They hadn't summoned a storm from the east, they hadn't encouraged those youths to attack us. But right then, on that bright, sunny morning, I cursed the day Eadger had rode up to my hall, asking for the great Lord Alaric, commander of the Ravensworn.

We had butchered one of the dead youth's horses, and the meat was hanging beneath us below deck. We would not starve on our journey and would arrive ready to fight. Still, though, we were sullen.

I kept the men at their oars, hoping exhaustion would wash their woes away. I swam for a while after we turned the ship north, and just as I was clambering back aboard, there was a roar of water off to the left, and a giant whale broke free from the surface, water streaming into the air from its blowhole. It was a sight to bring a smile to even the most downcast man, and when a school of dolphins swam alongside the ship a short time later, it seemed all bad humour from the day before had evaporated like morning dew, for a time at least.

The weather held over the following days, a pale blue sky stretching away above, a light northerly breeze on our backs. We ate the horsemeat with relish, each of us dreading the day it would run out and we'd have to go back to sodden oats. It was the fifth day of sailing, though, when Sedric came to me with disturbing news.

'You're certain?' I said through a mouthful of meat.

'Aye, Lord. It was all there this morning when I went to check on Kai. Saw the lock had been removed, just assumed you or Eadger had been in there. But it was open just now. I went over to inspect and saw it empty.'

It was mid-afternoon. I'd just been for a swim and was enjoying a late lunch. The sea was calm, the wind mild but strong enough to fill our sail. I'd been having happy thoughts as I chewed, thinking of the fun Saxa and the boys would be having, the slaughter

I was going to reap when we reached the tip of Jylland. Three chews later though, my mood had soured. 'Show me.'

Eadger and his men were lounging on their benches, bellies full of horsemeat, enjoying the sun on their faces. I said nothing as I walked past them. Sedric muttered something about going to check on Kai, who was recovering below deck, out of the sun. We went down the ladder and made our way through the gloom, thin strips of light leaking in from the gaps in the planks above us. It was a cramped space, the Celox being a shallow ship, and I had to stoop my head as we made our way towards the prow.

Kai's condition was improving. His tongue had suffered only mild damage, and he was awake more than asleep. Sedric fed him a watery bowl of oats three times a day, and I was confident he would recover sufficiently enough, even if he would be sucking oats from a spoon for the rest of his days. It wasn't Kai, though, that I had come to see.

We'd stored the food supplies at the stern of the ship. There was slightly more room, better light from the hatch above, making it easier for us to access on a daily basis. The chests full of weapons and armour we had stored in the prow, firstly to keep the weight distributed across the hull, secondly because we would have little need to access them whilst at sea. I had fitted poorly made locks to each chest before we departed, and the only key to them was around my neck on a length of string. It wasn't because I didn't necessarily trust Eadger and his men – the gear was for their people, after all. My first thought had been it provided security to the contents of the chests if they were thrown about in heavy weather. None of us wanted to climb down and find armour rusting in pools of water across the floor.

Sedric led me past the first two chests, stopping at the third. 'Here, Lord,' he motioned. I squinted in the semi-gloom, cursing myself for not thinking of bringing a torch. We had a few, but they were all above deck, and I didn't want to arouse suspicion by sending Sedric up to fetch one. The lock had been smashed clean off the chest. A casual inspection was all it took to find a large rock on the ground between the third and fourth chests. I picked it up, testing its weight. 'That would have knocked it clean off easy enough,' I muttered, tossing it to Sedric. 'So you saw the lock was off this morning, but the gear was still inside?'

'Aye, Lord,' Sedric said, nodding.

'And after lunch you came back down to check on Kai and you saw the gear gone?'

'The lid was open, Lord. The lid wasn't open this morning, but the lock had been smashed off.'

'How do you know it had been smashed off? I could have removed it this morning when I came to see Kai?'

Sedric blubbered, momentarily a fish out of water.

'I'm not accusing you, lad!' I raised my hands, professing my innocence. 'I know it wouldn't have been you, and it damn well weren't young Kai, so that means it was one of our friends up above. Someone up there ain't too keen to see these weapons and armour reach the north. Now, if I'm to bring that accusation to Eadger, we need to make sure your story is as well pitched together as this ship, understand?'

It's no small thing to accuse a man of treachery, especially when that man is one of a small group on a ship out at sea. There's nowhere to run when you're sailing the Whale Road, nowhere to hide. 'So from the beginning, Sedric, I need you to tell me exactly what you saw.'

* * *

'No, Alaric, I don't know why any of my men would have done this.'

I'd brought Eadger below deck, on the pretence Sedric and I needed an extra pair of hands to help with Kai. I confronted him with the empty chest and for a while the man said nothing, running a hand through his hair, rubbing his newly shaven chin. 'How do we know it was one of my men anyway?'

I rolled my eyes. 'Well, for one it wasn't me. Kai's weak as a babe and has been passing in and out of consciousness, and Sedric was the one who reported it to me in the first place, so it's hardly likely to be him, is it? I need you to think, Eadger. Were there any of your men who weren't too thrilled about the mission you were given?'

'What, recruiting you?' I nodded. He sighed and shook his head, eyes frowning as he thought. 'None that voiced it if they were. They're my men, Alaric. *My* men. I know them all, trust them all. Long time we've fought together, and you know as well as I that battle forms a brotherhood not lightly broken.'

I agreed, though I had been on the wrong side of a betrayal six years ago, and it had cost me everything I had. 'None of the men have been acting suspiciously in the last day or two? Noticed anyone slipping below deck when they had no reason to be?'

Eadger vigorously shook his head. 'No, Alaric, nothing.' Eadger chewed his lip. 'Can you tell me everything you saw this morning?' he said to Sedric, who looked to me before nodding. Sedric spoke a while, re-telling the same tale he had told me. I was comforted that it didn't vary at all. That's how you find a liar – ask them the same question over and over, see how many different answers you get given. Sedric, though, was no liar. I knew it, and I could tell Eadger did too.

'So, what do we do?' he asked me once Sedric had finished.

'I think we keep this to ourselves for now, keep a look out for anything suspicious. We'll also have to take turns coming to check on Kai more regularly; the more often there's someone down here, the less chance of anything else going missing.'

'So where exactly *has* it gone?' Eadger frowned as he looked around the cramped space. There was nothing to suggest where our culprit may have disposed of the weapons and mail, just wooden planks all around us, the chests squeezed in tightly together.

'I don't know. But I can't see how someone would have managed to get it all above deck without one of us noticing.'

'Could have happened whilst we slept?' Eadger ventured.

'No, it was all here this morning, I've told you that,' Sedric piped up.

'Of course.' Eadger nodded, slapping a hand on Sedric's shoulder. 'I'm sorry, I just can't fathom why one of my lads would do this.' He walked off, hanging his head, rubbing his face in despair.

'You go up,' I said to Sedric. 'I'll sit with Kai a while.' Truth was I didn't trust myself to not start a row if I went back on deck. I was angry, ashamed even, that I had let another traitor into my life. Thought I'd left all that behind me out there in the east. That and my left eye.

I sat down next to Kai, holding his hand in my own, just so he knew he wasn't alone. He stirred at my touch, eyes opening, grimacing through the pain. 'Re... ear...' the lad stuttered. The effort of speaking made him convulse with pain; his whole body shuddered and I had to put hands on his shoulders to steady him.

'Hush now, lad. Just stay calm. You're going to be all right. Just takes time is all.'

He shook his head. 'Re... ear, wa... ere...' he slurred, eyes willing me to understand.

'Okay. Okay now. Do you want some wine?' Kai nodded. I looked around for a flask but couldn't find one. 'Hang on, lad,' I said as I ran up on deck. 'Need a skin of wine for the sick note!' I called, putting on a cheer I did not feel.

'Take mine,' a voice called. It was the man they called Red Beard, for reasons that should be obvious. He was a jovial man, pushing fifty if he was a day. If he'd have tried to sign up for the Ravensworn back in the day I would have told him to lose some weight before he even thought of riding with us. Eadger, though, said he was the finest swordsman he had at his disposal. To reach his age and still be casting a shadow suggested there was some truth in that. 'How's the lad doing?' he asked as he handed over the wine, face full of concern.

'Better every day, thank you, friend.' I clapped him on the shoulder and went back down below. Kai had fallen back asleep, and rather than disturb him, I sat and sipped the wine, enjoying the solitude. I pondered what Kai might have been trying to tell me. Had he seen someone below deck? Surely he would have heard the lock smash off the chest?

My thoughts were disturbed by the groan of wood, footsteps thumping down the ladder. Eadger appeared, an eagerness about him. 'Just had a thought,' he blurted out, 'your lad, Kai.'

'He can't write,' I finished for him.

'Bollocks!'

'Bollocks indeed. I was just thinking the same thing. He was trying to tell me something a moment ago, couldn't make out a word of it.'

'He will get better,' was all Eadger said, before returning up the ladder.

It was two days later we had another incident. Dawn was a finger's width on the horizon, a small streak of blood against an iron-grey sky. The wind was still blowing us north, but I had fallen asleep the previous night fretting over another storm. Eadger woke me, shaking me gently on the shoulder. 'Come,' he whispered.

I had been sleeping at the stern, close to the ladder. Eadger, Sedric and I had been taking turns to keep watch below deck throughout the night, and Sedric should have been down there now. I followed Eadger down the ladder, blinking the sleep from my eye. Kai was asleep on the floor, and Sedric lay next to him. 'Gods,' I muttered, thinking he had fallen asleep on his watch. Rome would have you killed for that.

'It's not what you think. Look.' Eadger pointed to the back of Sedric's head. I grabbed a torch that hung next to Kai, brought the flame down to see better. There was a lump on the back of Sedric's head, a bruise purpling on the flesh.

'I have checked his skull, nothing broken. He'll have a sore head when he wakes though.'

'He'll have more than that,' I growled, feeling the fury in me rise. How could he have been so stupid? 'Another chest gone?'

'Aye. You need to see.' I followed Eadger to the prow of the ship, noticing water pooling on the deck where it hadn't been before. Another chest with the lock smashed off, another chest empty. I did not curse and lose my temper, but instead pushed down the furies fighting to consume me. I exhaled slowly, keeping my composure. Using the torch, I scanned the deck of the ship, looking at the dry planks in between the slurring pools of dark water.

'What you looking for?' Eadger asked.

'Footprints.' Sure enough, in between two small puddles, I saw one. It was pointing away from the chests, further into the gloom at the very front of the ship. I followed it, finding another, then another. There was something distinctive in their pattern, but my tired mind could not discern what. They stopped at the very point of the ship, and I passed the torch to Eadger as I began running my hands across the wooden beams that formed the wall in front of me.

'What you looking for now?'

'Whoever smashed that lock and emptied the

chest, they emptied it somewhere. No way a man carried all those weapons and mail up the ladder without any of us noticing. So stands to reason they've found a way of throwing them into the sea from down here. Or...' I smacked a plank, hearing nothing but the hollow thud of flesh on wood. I smashed another one, hearing nothing but the same.

'Curse you to the Hanged One himself. Men say you've got the Trickster in you, now I see why. What *are* you looking for?'

I knocked the next one, again getting no reply other than the same hollow thud. But the next one came with a distinct metallic chink. 'This, my friend, is what I've been looking for.' I motioned for Eadger to help, and together we heaved out the wooden plank, laying it gently to the ground. Inside was a hollow space, not wide enough to fit a man, but plenty wide enough to hide two chests worth of mail and swords. 'Seems our traitor doesn't just want to stop us delivering this to your lord in the north, but perhaps wants to see it to the hands of his enemies?' I left the thought lurking in the silence.

'Wotan's fucking eye,' Eadger muttered, lowering the torch to see the stash of weapons and armour better. 'We have to act, now.'

And we did.

8

'One of you, one of you doesn't want our mission to be a success. One of you would see your people fall, die at the hands of a foreign invader. Maybe one of you is in their pay, or maybe it's just where your loyalty lies. I don't know, I don't much care either. But I care about my reputation, I care about getting back home and seeing my wife and boys again. One of you is trying to stop that happening, and when I find out who it is, I'm going to kill them.'

The sun was fully up now, a burning fireball that matched my mood. My blade was bared, I wore no armour, but I was as ready for a fight as I'd ever been in my life. Five men stood in a line in front of me. Five warriors. Five killers. One traitor. Red Beard was on the left, looking sullen and ashamed. He'd gasped when I revealed what had happened – the empty chests, the wound to Sedric. He seemed a good man, Red Beard, kind and honest. But I had to remind myself the man was a killer, and killers don't get to reach old age without a knack for survival.

Rolf was next, the man who'd stitched Kai up after he'd taken his wounds. Again, he seemed a decent enough man. Quiet, studious, had the kind of face that easily vanished in a crowded place. A background man, a supporting cast member, and likely happy to be that. Gunnar was different. Tall and broad, he'd become famous aboard the Celox for the amount he could eat. By all the gods, that man was never full. He'd eat a hearty breakfast and not an hour later be complaining of an empty belly. He was loud whatever mood he was in, boisterous and full of wit. I liked his gap-toothed smile; it seemed to raise my mood whatever sort of day I was having. He wasn't offering me one right then, though.

The last two were brothers. Rudi and Mellow. Rudi was Rudi because that's the name his parents had given him. Mellow was Mellow because he had a well-earned reputation for being a miserable bastard. You know, the type of character that could fall in a barrel full of tits and come out sucking his thumb. I'd seen corpses with more personality.

I marched up and down that little line, Eadger sitting on an oar bench behind me. The Celox was rolling the waves, the gentle breeze filling the sail still edging us north. Sedric was still below with Kai. He'd woken briefly, thrown up down his front, then passed back out. It was a small comfort that there was no break in the back of his skull, but it still irked me that one of these men would so brazenly attack a man they knew was sworn to me. It was another reminder of how far I had fallen, how low my reputation had sunk. There had been a time where being my man meant you were almost untouchable, such would be the fear of my retribution. Seemed those days were long gone.

'So, any of you have something you want to confess? Now would be the time.' I continued my pacing, hand gripped tight to the sword at my waist, cold iron in the glint of my eye.

'I will not believe that any of my friends would do such a thing.' Redbeard shook his head at the thought. 'We are honest men, fighting men. Our mission, to find you, to save our people from the invaders, it is too important to all of us.'

'Then how do you explain what has happened?' I shot back at him.

'I cannot.' Redbeard shrugged. 'I just will not believe that one of my friends is desperate to see us fail.'

'Can't say it's the sort of work I have the stomach for,' Gunnar said as he scratched his head.

'Good to know there's one thing you don't have the stomach for.' I also doubted he had the intelligence for it, but I kept that to myself.

'Well, it sure ain't anything to do with me or my brother.' Rudi motioned to Mellow as he spoke. The former said nothing, just pulled a knife from his belt and started picking at his fingernails.

'Nothing to say for yourself?' I challenged Mellow, stepping forwards and lowering the knife down by his side. Mellow sighed, shrugged, then took a step back and began picking his nails again. He muttered something under his breath, too low for me to catch.

'What was that?'

'I said I didn't realise a man so revered for his opposition to Rome could behave so much like a Roman officer.'

That got a few laughs from Gunnar and Rudi, and for a moment I considered gutting the little shit there and then. He had long dark hair as straight as an arrow, and it covered his pale face as he looked down to study the nails he was picking. 'Learnt a lot from Rome over the years, I'll have you know. You know why they're so hard to beat in battle? No? Discipline and training. Nothing more, no great secret, no great tactical innovation that none of us could think of. They train their men to within an inch of their lives, and then their officers maintain an iron grip on them. No bad thing to respect your enemy, to learn from them. My Ravensworn were more than a match for any tribe this side of the Rhine or Danube for those two reasons alone. Discipline is something I think you could do with a little more of.'

Mellow didn't even look up, just shrugged his shoulders once more, let out a little sigh, the way a sulking child does after being given the same lecture from their parents for the hundredth time. Well, this little shit wasn't my son, and I was pissed. I had two good lads below decks carrying wounds, wounds they'd only received because they'd agreed to join me in this little venture up north, all to save Mellow's skinny arse. Not to mention poor Batur, lost to a watery grave.

I levelled my sword. Two quick steps and I was on him, handgrip of the blade in my right hand, the tip of the sword in my left. I laid it bare across his throat and pushed him back towards the rail.

'What you doing, you crazy old bastard!' Rudi screamed. I watched what little colour there was on Mellow's cheeks fade as he was forced back, unable to turn his head to look behind him for fear of catching his neck on my blade. He couldn't have been much older than Sedric or Kai, but I swear to the Hanged One right then he was reduced to nothing better than a snivelling child.

'Discipline,' I hissed in Mellow's face. 'Discipline saves lives, keeps men in line, keeps warriors equal and on the same side. No discipline, then you give the opportunity for some little cunt to exploit you, and I've been around for too many winters to let something so trivial as a lack of discipline ruin my reputation.'

We had reached the rail, the water sloshing beneath us. Mellow wore no armour, which bore well for him where he was going. 'Ever learnt to swim, boy?' He shook his head, the fear in his eyes giving his face more life than I'd seen throughout the whole voyage so far. 'Well, now's a good as time as any, hey?'

I threw him overboard. The little shit didn't even have the character to scream as he tumbled towards the waves, hitting them with a wet slap before disappearing beneath.

'No! Mellow! What have you done? I'll fucking kill

you!' Rudi hadn't even bared his blade when my own was pointing at his chin.

'Three questions. First, did you do it?'

'What?'

'The chests and Sedric. Was it you?'

'Fuck! No!'

'Was it him?' I asked Rudi. I gestured with my head to the empty sea beneath us.

'No! You have to fucking save him—'

'Do you know who it was?' I cut him off.

'No! I swear, I don't know. Fuck! Please save him.'

I waited a moment more, studying Rudi's face. He was quivering, frantic hands rubbing dishevelled hair. His eyes were wide, moist, tears running down his face. I saw his fear, his panic, but I saw no lie. I'd always trusted my sense of character. Even though it had let me down before, I'd had far more hits than misses. I nodded. 'Had to be sure,' I said before launching myself over the rail and diving beneath the white-topped waves.

9

It took us a further ten days to reach our destination. To say they were tense would be an understatement, but we had no further incidents. Mellow recovered from his first swimming lesson, though he complained of an aching chest for a few days. It had taken the work of moments to find him flapping beneath the sea's surface, and to be honest he and Rudi should have been more grateful the ship had been travelling as slowly as it was. A fact neither brother could quite grasp. The ignorance of youth.

Sedric had made a full recovery, though there was still a shining bruise on the back of his bald pate. Kai had been making further progress, though still he could not rise from his cot. He was awake more, though, and the swelling on his face had subsided. His speech was still atrocious, and I feared his days of chatting up pretty girls in the halls across Germania were long gone. But he would survive.

It was under a deep blue sky that we rounded the tip of Jylland, the point where two seas met. The Skagerrak to the west, whose green waters had carried us north, and the Kattegat to the east, the darker waters a stark contrast to the ones beneath us as we turned to meet it. The land was flat, featureless, much like the rest of Jylland, though a deep white beach shone brightly in the golden sun; almost looked inviting.

Would have looked a whole lot more inviting if it wasn't for the hundreds of armed men fighting on it.

'We have to land!' Eadger called over the rushing of the wind. The breeze had been almost non-existent in the last day. The rest of the lads and I had been hard at work on the oars. My shoulders ached, the small of my back was a ball of agony, and I'm not too proud to admit the thought of donning mail and leaping ashore to join that melee didn't feel me with glee.

The wind was easterly, the current beneath us a turmoil. The two seas crashed together, white-topped waves spilling over the rails and onto the deck.

Landing was easy in theory, though I worried about the practicality of it. 'We clear the headland first, make landfall on the eastern shore!' I roared back.

'Those are my people dying down there! We need to land now!'

What good would nine of us do? Well, eight; we couldn't really count Kai. But I understood his urgency, sympathised with his emotions. 'Lower the sail and get everyone on their oars, this is going to be rough!'

The sail was lowered in the time it took me to reach the steering oar. I yanked it hard to the right, the small Celox reeling and tipping as her timbers strained against the current. We tilted left, water flooding our feet, the wind ripping in one ear and bursting out the other. 'On my word, row!' I bellowed, unsure whether any of them could actually hear me. The Celox righted itself as we straightened off. I eased my grip on the steering oar for no more than a moment, hoping to ease the growing cramp in my hands. No sooner had I done this, the ship lurched once more, carried by the ferocity of the sea, and we were facing back west before I knew it. 'By the fucking Hanged,' I snarled, this time wrenching the oar to the left and sending Mellow and Rudi crashing to the deck as the ship tipped in the water once more.

'What are you doing?' Eadger called to me, both his hands with a white-knuckled grip on the side rail.

'Trying to keep us afloat! I told you this was going to be rough!' We were once more facing the right direction, the wind a howling screech in my face. I couldn't open my eye fully for it, could barely squint to see which way we were facing. Rudi and Mellow were once more at their benches, though Mellow's oar had slipped overboard when he'd fallen. Gunnar was ordering him to grab one of the spares strapped down on the deck, but the miserable youth could barely take a step towards them.

Gunnar was up in an instant, his every movement bristling with the urgent need for violence. He threw Mellow his oar, cursed the lank-haired youth as he fumbled the catch and the oar struck him in the face. He ripped open the strapping and freed a new oar, then staggered back to his bench. 'Wait for my command!' I called, trying to open my eye enough to get a feel for the current. We were facing south, maybe fifty yards from the safety of the beach – if you can call a beach full of armed men safety. Fifty yards might as well have been fifty Roman miles though, if Rán had had her way with us.

There was a rhythm to the current, a distinct beat at the heart of the raging monster. I closed my eye and allowed myself to feel it, swayed with the waves as they rocked up and down. Sailing was all about timing, choosing your moments, much like a battle. I had to make sure I chose mine right.

The sea pitched down, the water retreating, gathering itself for the next charge. That was my moment. 'Row!' I screamed, holding the oar steady as Eadger began bellowing the strokes and oars dipped and rose in the water. The sea came back, a bubbling cauldron of death, Rán eager to drag us down and see us to a watery grave. The ship rose with the current, water exploded over the rail to my left, and I clung on for dear life as we rose higher and higher, the oars still cutting through the water. 'Keep going!' I called, almost certain none of the men could hear me. Still, wouldn't want anyone saying I hadn't done my bit.

We crested the biggest of the waves and as we came crashing down, I felt the hull scrape on the seabed and knew we were nearly home. 'One more push, lads!' I called before being thrown from my feet at the impact of the ship levelling back out. I landed flat on my back, wind driven from me, sword hilt digging in my hip. 'Fuck you, Rán,' I muttered as I staggered back upright. Rán was said to have had nine children, named for each of the waves. I'd never bothered to remember their names before, and I sure as fuck wasn't going to now.

We lurched over the last few feet, the ship protesting as it was dragged along the seabed. We came to a shuddering halt on the beach. Sedric was thrown from his bench, and Red Beard was struggling to put down a rebellion from his breakfast. Rolf had managed to snap his oar but stay on his bench, and Rudi and Mellow were huddled together, looking like two drowned rats caught in a downpour. Gunnar and Eadger seemed to have survived unscathed, the latter already on his feet, ordering his men into their mail. Gunnar had magicked a hunk of bread from somewhere and was busy cramming the whole thing into his mouth. 'Sedric, get below and check on Kai,' I said as I took my shield from its leather cover. 'Then get back up here and be ready to fight.'

I shrugged my mail over my lank hair, fastened my helmet and grabbed my shield, pausing for a second to take in the black raven on the red background. It was faded, scarred from the last battle we had fought on a beach, but still it helped to remind me of who I was, of who I used to be.

Eadger was the first onto land, leaping over the rail at the prow and landing with a splash in the shallows. He roared, shaking sword and shield in the air, as if challenging the gods themselves. Gunnar followed him, bread supposedly swallowed. He had no shield, just a great single-headed axe grasped in both hands. Just for a moment, he reminded me of Ketill, the former chief of the Harii, and perhaps my closest friend. He had died, as had his men, for my folly, for my arrogance, my hubris. I felt a sudden need to protect Gunnar then, to ensure he came to no harm. So many had crossed to the Heroes Hall on my behalf, I didn't think I could bare to let another make the journey alone.

My breath was coming in ragged gasps, blood pounding in my ears. My hands shook so violently my shield clanged to the deck, and before I knew what was happening, I had sunk to my knees, hands on my chest, trying and failing to catch my breath. I saw Ruric, my old second in command, my teacher, my rock, looking at me with wet eyes, raging at the lives we had lost fighting the Fourteenth Legion down by the Danube. 'Their deaths are on you, Alaric!' he boomed at me, an accusive finger waved at my face. I reached out and tried to grasp that finger, tried to speak, to beg forgiveness, to tell him I had changed. I was no longer the arrogant prick who ordered men to their deaths without a second thought. That man had died in the east; I was merely his shadow, lingering in the land of the living. 'I'm sorry, my brother,' I whispered through shallow breaths. My vision blurred, and I collapsed in a heap, arms and legs tingling, fingers numb.

* * *

'Lord? Lord, can you hear me?' Hands on my shoulders, someone was shaking me, stirring me back to life. 'Lord? What happened?'

'Ruric,' I mumbled.

'We have to get you up, Lord.' He grasped my hands and lifted, and reluctantly I allowed myself to be pulled to my feet. My hearing was clouded, as if my ears were full of wool. I wobbled, legs aching as the blood returned. I breathed deep, counted to ten then slowly let it out. Bit by bit, my sight returned, my one remaining eye burning with the effort. Another deep breath and I could hear the rushing of the waves behind me, the cacophony of battle to my front. 'Are you okay?'

Sedric had me gripped by my shoulders, his head as close to mine as a lover. 'I don't know what happened,' I stuttered. 'I've never experienced anything like that before.'

'The others are all off the ship, Lord. Kai is comfortable, going to stay below.'

'Then it is time to go,' I said with authority I did not feel. My hand was still unsteady as I scooped up my fallen shield. Sedric was looking at me uncertainly, but I moved off down the ship before he could say anything more, desperate to put the whole incident behind me. I reached the prow, clambered up and leaped down, losing my footing on the wet sand as I landed and fell on my face. The waves came and covered me, and for a moment I allowed myself to be lost in the peace of their embrace. But Rán ordered them back just as quickly as she had sent them in, and I was thrust back into the land of the living, the white noise of battle ringing in my ears. 'Which side are we fighting on?' Sedric called to me. I hadn't even noticed him land, but there he was with sword and shield, helmet fastened tight over his bald head.

For the second time in as many minutes, I clambered unsteadily to my feet and took in the scene before me.

The beach was whitewashed sand, the odd sprout of green as it gave way to the land beyond. We were at the point of the peninsula, the beach curving round to our left and right. Ahead of us, atop a small knoll in an otherwise flat landscape, was a wood-built fort, the walls standing high and proud, light smoke seeping up to the clear blue sky from within. In front of the fort, hundreds of men were making slaughter. There seemed to be no order to the battle, no neat lines of shield walls facing one another. There was just chaos, carnage, and I grinned at the sight, feeling the life return to my limbs.

'I reckon we just kill anyone that tries to kill us. Can you make out Eadger and the others anywhere?'

'I see what you see.' Sedric shrugged, wiping a nervous hand across his face. It was my time to comfort him then, remembering he had only fought in one battle, and that was very much small fry compared to this.

'You've two eyes, lad. I'd wager they're both sharper than my one. You keep them open today, you hear? And stay close to me. We make for the walls, stick together, and I'm sure things will look clearer from there.'

So we hefted our weapons and made our way into the bloodbath.

10

'Watch your right!' Sedric called, and I turned just in time to block a sword with my own. I pushed the blade back hard, wrenched it wide, my attacker thrown off balance with the ferocity of my defence. Whilst he staggered back, arms outstretched, I hacked at his neck and felt warm blood spurt up my face. 'Good call!'

Two more steps and I was defending again, this time blocking a spear with my shield. The point dug into the wooden board, then clanged off the bronzed boss. Snarling, I punched out with the shield, missing my target but making the spearman leap back to avoid the blow. He backed onto the toes of a swordsman behind him, who spat and pushed him in the back, and he all but fell on my sword. 'Behind you!' I called to Sedric as I ripped my blade free.

A red axe on a blue sky, tearing down from the heavens to end a life. Sedric had the wit to sidestep the blow, strike the axeman in the face with his shield and follow it up with a neat lunge to the chest. 'That's how you do it, lad!'

Chaos all around us, a manic grin beneath my greying beard. I could *feel* the Trickster at my shoulder. This was his making, his bread and butter. I knew then that he would see me through, that he had not abandoned me. Gods, but it felt good to be alive again.

There was grass beneath my feet, the sand behind me. Looking up, over the top of the shields and the helmets and the banners, I saw the wooden walls of the fort, a half circle of men fighting a desperate defence in front of the gate. 'Think that's Gunnar!' I pointed with my sword.

'How can you make him out?' Sedric called over the din of the battle.

'Pretty sure he's got a hunk of cheese in his hand! Come on, let's go!'

We fought and killed as we moved, working as a tandem. Sedric caught blows with his shield and I returned them with interest. We got into a pattern, shouting in each other's ears to be heard over the constant clash of iron. We had no idea who we were killing, whether they were Eadger's people or their enemy. Anyone tried to kill us, we killed them. In situations such as the one we found ourselves in, it's always best to keep things simple.

'You made it!' Eadger greeted me with a savage thump to my back, smiling a manic grin made to look worse by his blood-stained teeth. 'Welcome to Tastris!'

We joined our shields with theirs, standing in the centre of the crescent that protected the gate. Gunnar was there, minus the hunk of cheese. Still, he had no shield, no helmet, the blade of his great axe dripping with gore. Rolf stood at his shoulder, panting heavily into his beard, almost leaning on his shield. Truly, war was a young man's game. Rudi and Mellow fought side by side, the latter sporting a nasty cut on his left cheek. I was going to war with these half dozen men once more, except this time I knew one of them was a traitor to our cause, and I still had no clue as to which.

'So are these the Suiones, or the Sitones?'

Eadger shrugged. 'Both, I expect. As I told you before, they are one people now.'

'Where are their ships?'

'They landed on the eastern coast this morning. If we'd have sailed around the northern edge of the beach, we'd have probably seen them.'

I regretted that for a moment. An assault on their ships would have almost certainly given them pause in their attack, and maybe given Eadger's people a chance to fight on the front foot.

'These walls are pretty high. Why aren't your people fighting from behind them?'

'We have no arrows, no siege craft, no way of fighting from behind them. Plus the gate is fucked. A strong gust of wind would blow it open. Best to fight out here.'

'Where is Wilhelm, your chief?'

'Ahh.' Eadger hawked and spat blood. 'Not exactly the warrior type, our chief. He prefers to coordinate our defence from inside the fort.'

'So he's a fucking coward?'

'Pretty much! Look lively, they're coming again!'

There had been a small break in the fighting, a collective pause as warriors took a moment to gasp in air and regroup with their comrades. More and more men were retreating to the safety of the half circle. Shields bristled as our line thickened. 'Men of the Cimbri!' a high-pitched voice called out. 'One more push, give us one more push and victory will be ours!'

I looked around, frowning in puzzlement. Was that the voice of a boy I could hear, rallying the warriors of the tribe? And then I saw the source. Cladded in armour made from bone, rattling as the figure made their way into the centre of the semi-circle. Iron sword bared and pointing up at the sky, long blonde locks curling around a smooth, soft-skinned face. Deep, dark eyes that took in every detail around them. Eyes that locked onto mine.

'Is that...?'

'Ahh, yes. She is our champion, commander of the chief's warriors.'

'She?' I stood dumbfounded. It was not unheard of for women to fight amongst the men in war. There were certain tribes on the eastern steppe who thought nothing of it at all. Boys and girls alike were taught the ways of sword and spear from an early age. But to see a woman as a war leader, a champion of a chief of Jylland's biggest tribe?

'Yes, was going to tell you, just never found the right moment. Her name is Hilde, in case you were wondering.'

But I had no time to wonder any more. The enemy were charging at us, their own shields raised high. 'Close your shields and brace!' Hilde bellowed, and at once the men around me complied.

'So, your chief is a coward and your warriors, what few you have, are commanded by a woman. You don't have enough iron for weapons so your men are forced to arm and armour themselves with bone.'

'Aye! Once again, Lord Alaric, we're very grateful you came!'

'Once this is over, you and I are going to have a very stern conversation.'

'Gotta live through this first! Get that shield up, old man.'

And then they were on us. The smack on my shield was like being kicked by a donkey, and I felt my boots sliding back across the grass as I was forced to relent to the intense pressure. Men screamed and cursed, spat and roared, a deafening cacophony of metal on wood assaulting my ears. I hunched down behind my shield, Eadger to my left, Sedric to my right. From the corner of my eye, I saw an axe head hook over Sedric's shield and he stumbled forwards as the axe was wrenched back. I struck out, as hard and fast as my ageing muscles could manage, reaching under Sedric's shield with my sword and jabbing away until I felt the blade bite into flesh.

'Keep that shield up!' I said to him, leaning into my own and slashing over the top, cutting nothing but air. Eadger was yelling Gunnar's name. Looking to my left, I gasped in horror as I saw the big man cutting a bloody swathe through the enemy ranks. He had no shield and no helmet, but the great axe twirled in a brilliant arc, blood dripping from the blade. In five heartbeats or less, he had cut himself a path, and it was an opportunity Eadger did not want to miss.

He leaped into the gap, sword darting out to his right to cut into an exposed neck. Mellow followed, snaking left, ducking low, blade swiping the ankles from one man, piercing the calf of another. Rudi followed his brother, shield held dutifully high, seemingly content to do nothing but stop the blows rain down on his brother's head. Rolf side-stepped right and hooked his shield onto mine. 'Do we follow them?' he asked. His skin was a waxy grey, sweat pouring down him like rain off a roof. He was an old man, still brave and strong, but no one can live the life of a warrior forever. A fact I was beginning to come to terms with.

'You hold here,' I called as I slipped out in Rudi's wake, using the protection of his shield to advance unnoticed, my sword striking a spearman's neck, snatching a life.

'Die, you fuckers!' Gunnar was snarling, axe still scything a path through the throng. Men were giving him space, fearful of that axe, and Eadger took full advantage, advancing past Gunnar and throwing himself at an enemy shield. The man behind it buckled and fell, dead before his arse hit the grass, a gaping hole from Eadger's sword in his chest. For the first time, I saw the men we were facing wore no armour. Some did indeed wield nothing but spears with heads cast from bone. I smiled, the old wolf-like grin that had spread so much fear back in the day. It was time to get to work.

I pounded past Rudi and Mellow. I was astride Gunnar when I blocked a spear with my shield, turned with the blow so the tip was deflected past my body, then ducked under the shaft and rammed my sword home into an unarmoured torso. Easy. I freed the blade, more blood spattering my face. I hacked down on a bald head, slammed my shield into a toothless face. Three more steps, enemies to both sides, I blocked a blow on my shield to my left whilst taking a life to my right, then let a spearman prod me with his bone-headed blade, laughed as it tickled my mail, then punched a hole in his shoulder. I could feel the tide of the battle changing, the enemy retreating to my front, my friends coming up on my rear.

Red Beard's beard had never looked redder as he

prowled like a hunter stalking a wild boar. His shield was in tatters, barely anything left around the boss, but still he gripped it, sword held high in his other hand. Our eyes met for a moment and we shared a grin as one the warriors of the Cimbri moved forwards, our energy renewed, scenting victory. The combined armies of the Suiones and the Sitones could smell defeat, and they showed us their backs as they streamed down the beach, off to the east and their ships. 'Don't let them get away!' Hilde's high-pitched voice rang out, somewhere behind me. 'Follow the men! Hunt them down!' As if we needed any encouragement.

I was off down the beach with the rest, boots pounding on the sand. I whooped with the others, laughed with Sedric as we gave chase. I could feel the press of the Cimbri all around me, and for a moment I allowed my worries of the broken chests, Batur's death and Kai's wounds to fade away. Got to enjoy the small things, after all. But it was at that moment, when my glee had reached its zenith, I felt a sharp burning in my lower back, and before I knew what was happening, my knees gave way and I crashed to the sand with all the grace of a beached whale.

I coughed, the lancing pain in my back a ball of fire. Spitting sand, I reached around and felt something sticking out of me. A knife. I breathed deep, welcoming the pain, trying not to panic. I'm no expert on the human body, but I know enough to know that the lower half of your torso contains some of your more important organs, and having a knife pierce them does no good for your life expectancy. Scrunching my one good eye closed, I wrenched the blade free, burying my head in the sand once more to hide the squeal of pain. I lay there a while and just breathed, in and out, felt the warm blood trickling down my back, tasting iron in my mouth. *So this is how my story ends.*

I didn't die immediately, which was a smaller comfort than you might think. But when the tears had cleared from my eye enough for me to be able to see, I brought the knife in front of my face and saw it for the first time. It was a simple blade, leaf tipped, well forged, a small, wooden handle. I knew it was well forged because I'd seen a hundred others just like it, two hundred, even. I'd seen them all in a chest that I'd locked below deck on the Celox that had brought us here.

My good humour of just moments before had well and truly evaporated. Not only had some bastard tried to kill me, but it became inexplicitly clear that the turd that had tried to do so was also the same turd that had been trying to destabilise our entire mission. A rage filled me, a burning desire for vengeance. I pictured all their faces: Red Beard, Gunnar, Rolf, Mellow and Rudi, Eadger too. One of them had done this, one of them had taken advantage of the press to slip a knife into my back, without even the courage to face me.

I wasn't going to die; I knew it then. If nothing else, I was simply too fucking angry. Snarling, I pushed myself to my feet, determined to go and confront all six of the whoresons there and then. But just as I regained my footing and went to take a step, my vision blurred once more, my legs went to jelly, and I passed out of consciousness before my body came slapping back down to the ground. Guess there'll always be time for vengeance later.

11

I returned to the world of the living in a pitch-black room that stunk heavily of herbs and sweat. A lantern burned in a corner, the flittering light painful to look upon. I frowned as my senses returned, an instinctive hand reaching around to the small of my back, the burning anger returning.

'Careful there, old man,' a hushed voice said to me. 'Hell of a wound you took. Best you take it slow.'

I hissed as the pain kicked in, a slow burn at first, then an explosion of fire, spreading from my back to the tips of my toes, pounding in my ears. 'Where am I?'

'Inside the fortress of Tastris. I'm told you fought bravely in the battle outside the walls. In fact, I am told that without your timely intervention, it would be the enemy inside these walls this day, and not us.'

'Water,' I croaked, my face scrunched up against the pain. With soft skin on the back of my head, I lurched forwards in the darkness, feeling queasy. 'How long since the battle?'

'Two days.'

I drank deeply, the water ice cold, soothing my raw throat. 'My wound?'

'You will survive. It has been cleaned and stitched; the blade missed all your important parts.' That was a relief.

'Who are you?'

'My name is Isvilt, wife of Wilhelm, our chief.'

I took notice of the pitch of her voice for the first time, the smoothness of her hand, the curve of her cheek in the lamplight. I could not think of a single chief in all Germania who would happily let their wife see to a wounded man alone. A chief's wife was forbidden fruit, out of the reach of mere mortals. Not that they tasted any better; I'd bedded a couple in my time. I remembered Eadger saying to me that Wilhelm had been behind the walls during the battle, the grim resignation on his face as he confirmed his leader was a coward.

'I thank you for your care,' was all I said, too tired

to question her further. I lay back, my head on a straw pillow, and thought I caught the scent of something floral as I did.

'Rest now,' the hushed voice said once more, and I fell back into a deep sleep.

* * *

It was light when I awoke once more, this time immediately alert to where I was. Thin strands of light slipped through the slits in the wooden walls and roof, crisscrossing the small room in which I had been left. I sat up slowly, feeling the stitches in my back protest. The wound still hurt, hurt a lot, but the pain felt more manageable than it had when I had awoken before – whenever that was.

I took a moment to take in the room. There wasn't much. The pallet I lay on was raised on two wooden crates, the straw cot dumped on top. There was a small round side table, a jug of water and one cup resting on top. The lamp had burned out, still smoking in the corner, mixing with the shards of light, giving the room a smoky haze. An empty bucket sat in the other corner; my bladder twinged as I locked my eye on it.

Unsteadily, I got to my feet, alarmed to find my

legs bare. I had been stripped down to my tunic. I staggered over to the bucket and pissed out half the sea, slightly disappointed there was no one there to witness it. I was just shaking off when the door opened, and Sedric's bald head peered around the frame. 'Lord! You're awake!'

'Not only that, come and see the size of—'

'Well, damn me to the Heroes Hall, I thought you were a dead man for sure!' Eadger barrelled his way past Sedric, engulfing me in a bear hug before I'd even had time to take my hand off my prick. I stepped back with a smile, wondering if I should point out the small damp patch I'd left on the front of his trousers, but decided to keep my mirth to myself.

'Surprised you didn't have a wager on it.'

'I did! I owe Red Beard a skin of wine, a price I'm happy to pay. How you feeling?'

'Wound hurts like hell, but I'll live. What news from outside? Is Kai okay?' This was directed to Sedric.

'Aye, the lad's doing fine, got himself a cushty little room in the chief's hall. We unloaded the weapons and armour from the ship and have already started distributing it amongst the men. You're a hero, Alaric! Your name is toasted by Wilhelm each night around his fire.'

'So, we won the day in the end?' A feral-looking dog had slithered into the room, all scraggily fur and bone. It sniffed my leg before turning its attention to the bucket, burying its nose inside and drinking noisily.

'Yes, we won. More of the bastards got away than we wanted, but I reckon they'll be reeling from that beating for a good while yet. Is that dog drinking your piss?'

'Seems to be. Was a mighty fine piss, to be fair.'

The dog stopped drinking and looked up, as if sensing my amusement. It had an eye missing, the left one, same as me. With a wince, I lowered myself to a crouch and held out a hand, the dog approaching slowly, cautiously, before allowing me to give it a scratch around its ears. 'Good dog,' I whispered, rubbing its belly, feeling nothing but ribs where there should have been meat. 'I take it food is sparse?'

'How do you know that?'

'No one has fed this dog in a good while.' I wiped dirt from the corner of the dog's remaining eye, and it growled in anger. 'Whoa there, little thing, I'm not going to hurt you.' The dog backed away, head tilting as it considered me with that one eye. 'Are you going to be my friend?' It scampered back, tail wagging, once more letting me stroke it. 'Good dog.'

The dog let me stroke it a while longer, before moving off to the crates that held my pallet up, sniffing them, then cocking its leg without a care in the world. 'A boy then. I shall call you Loki.'

'Surely Wotan would be more appropriate?' Eadger said, holding a hand over his left eye. 'You know.'

I laughed, stitches burning. 'I have always been a student of the Trickster. Loki will do just fine. Plus, it seems I am in need of friends in this place.'

I told Eadger and Sedric how I'd got my wound. Sedric boiled with anger, and Eadger shook his head in sorrow. 'I still cannot believe one of my men would do all this.'

I rubbed at the wound on my back, wondering how the stitches would fare when I was forced into mail once more. 'Well, we know it was one of them on the ship. And when we gave chase down the beach, they were all around me. Plus, it was one of the knives from the chest that I pulled out of my body.'

'How can you be sure?'

'Because I recognised the design, Eadger! I know you find it hard to accept, but one of your men is a traitor, and if we don't find out who, they may yet be the death of us all.' I sighed, cursing myself. Eadger had been nothing but steadfast since we had met, even if he had been a touch reticent on the details concerning his chief and his tribe. He had become a friend, and I needed to keep my friends onside. 'I'm sorry, Eadger. But as you might be able to understand, I'm feeling a little rough around the edges. Where is Kai? I would like to see him.'

We left the small hut they had kept me in, and I had to squint in the sun's light as we made our way down a mud track. To our left was the wall we had fought outside two days before. I had time to study it now and did not like what I saw. There were gaps between the wooden planks that ran vertically along the wall, gaps big enough to get hands and feet through. I thought that even in my weakened state I could climb up in moments. There was a fighting platform of sorts on top, but it looked rickety, mould showing on the underside of the timber. Maybe our best chance was to let the enemy clamber up the wall and fall through the platform once they had reached the top. A wry smile touched my face at the thought.

To my right was the main compound of the fortress. 'Fortress' was a flattering term really; fort would have been generous. 'Outpost' is what the Romans would have called it. There was a hall, its front door adjacent to the northern gate, a patch of mud in front which could have served as some sort of assembly area. To the left of the hall was what appeared to be a granary. I was pleased to see wooden stilts on the bottom, raising it off the ground. The Cimbri may not be able to fight, but they could at least keep their grain away from rodents. On the opposite side of the assembly area was a collection of small huts, similar to the one I had been kept in. They had just strips of fabric for doors, and as we walked past, I saw children running in and out, laughing and playing with wooden swords. They were dressed in rags, their feet bare, skin filthy. I wondered at the desperation of their parents, thinking this poor excuse for a fortress was their children's best hope of survival.

I can't say I've lived a good life. When I die, there won't be people grieving in their hundreds, spilling stories of my valour and big heart. But when I saw those children playing, it just reminded me of my boys. I thought of them there, stuck in that desperate place, skin the colour of old mud, ribs showing on their flanks. I may not have been the man I once was, may not have commanded vast armies or determined the fate of the people around me, but right then I was grateful for what I did have: a good home, food aplenty, sturdy shelter to see my family safe through the long winter months. There is so much I had taken for granted, especially in the years since I had lost my friends, my army and my eye. I vowed to myself that when I returned home – *if* I returned home – I would not do so again.

Entering Wilhelm's hall brought around the feeling of walking through a defeated army after battle. Men sat slumped in small groups, faces streaked with blood, talking quietly amongst themselves. No one looked up when we entered. There were no guards on the door, no visible sign of discipline. This, as I have said before and will repeat many times, is why a German army has never sustained victory over Rome. We have won the odd battle, the Tuetonburg forest some years before being the standout example. But we have never *sustained* a victory, never built on it and gone on to achieve something more. We do not have the cohesion, the discipline, the chain of command and the respect for those we call our allies. We would sooner be squabbling amongst ourselves than uniting under one leader and taking the fight to Rome.

There are those of us who hold this hope, that one day it may be achieved, but it is a fleeting one at best. My old friend Balomar of the Marcomanni, his tribe bordering Roman lands, is a man who holds such an ambition. But every time he reaches out to the chiefs around him, he is met with scorn and challenged on what right he has to be the one to lead a united German army. His right is he is the only one of them with the vision, the strength of will to see it through. Though I fear his dream will be destined to fail. I looked around that hall, at the slumped, tired forms that littered the floorboards, and I saw just why such a dream would never bare fruition.

These men had just won a great battle, fought off the enemy from their gates, succeeding in keeping their women and children safe. From the look of them, you'd have thought they'd lost it all.

My eye was drawn to the far end of the hall. There was a raised dais, a little rectangular table, where the chief would dine with guests of honour. A small man sat there, eating a bowl of thin soup with a wooden spoon. He had mouse-like features, a thin face with a long nose and high cheek bones that stuck out like boulders either side of his sunken eyes. His beard was a whisp of whiskers on hollow cheeks; his head sat hunched over thin shoulders, a tattered robe hanging like a main sail around his threadbare torso. 'This is your chief?' I muttered to Eadger.

'Aye. Wilhelm Erikson. You must remember his father?'

I did indeed. Erik had been a fearsome man, a born warrior, and men had flocked to fight under his banner. I'd had the honour once. On a grim and bitter winter's day, my newly formed Ravensworn had fought with the Cimbri against his southern neighbours and carried the day after a long and bloody fight. It seemed his son had not inherited his personality. Erik had dominated any room he entered, and it wasn't only down to his physique; he had a winning smile and a certain charm, a knack for finding the right words at the right time. First impressions of Wilhelm were underwhelming at best. 'I remember Erik well enough. On first impressions, I'd say the apple hasn't exactly fallen close to the tree, if you get my meaning.'

Eadger winced, then reluctantly nodded his head. 'He's still my chief, Alaric. And he'll pay you handsomely for your work here.'

'Oh aye, I don't doubt. Not sure what I'll be doing with all that amber though, once I'm a corpse on top of your rickety walls.' I stood and watched the so-called chief slurp his soup for a moment more, deciding if I had the energy to go and introduce myself to him. No doubt we would exchange a few moments of awkward conversation, he would declare himself favoured by the gods for having a warrior such as me come to his rescue, and I would feign delight and honour at being asked to come. Both of us would smile at the other until our backs were turned, then our smiles would drop into frowns. No, I didn't have the energy. 'Where's Kai?'

Eadger led me down a small passage, along the right-hand side of the dais. I was struck by the same repugnant stink that lurks in the depths of any hall, no matter how great or small. The stink of cattle, of old hay and piss and shit. A smell one might find in even my own hall, if I had any cattle, that was. I paused as we walked past a door on our left, then backtracked two steps and breathed in deep. For the first time, I remembered Isvilt, Wilhelm's wife, coming to treat me as I woke feverish in the night. I got the same scent now, and knew I was standing outside her chamber.

'Not that door, Alaric. No one goes in there. Come.' Eadger led us on a few more feet, stopping at a door on our right. My mind was still further down the passage, my nostrils filled with the flowery scent. I tried to picture Isvilt's face, but couldn't. It had been too dark when I had first met her. I forced myself to think of Saxa and our boys, reminding myself of what I had. 'What's the matter, Alaric? Is it your wound?'

'Isvilt came to see me last night, I think.'

'Liked what you saw, eh?' Eadger smirked and arched an eyebrow. 'Don't expect too many late-night visits from her, my friend. I've a feeling you're not her type.'

I was almost offended by that, having seen the state of her husband a moment or so before. But I was prevented from questioning Eadger further as he opened the door and entered. I followed into a gloomy but spacious chamber, with a cot in one corner, a table and two stools in the other. Kai was sitting up on his cot, sipping water clumsily from a cup, the liquid leaving a trail on his tunic as it spilt from his wounded mouth. He smiled as we entered – at least I'm assuming it was a smile – and rose to wrap his arms around me, his grip reassuringly tight.

'It does me good to see you up and about, young Kai,' I beamed in genuine affection. He and Sedric had become as kin to me, seemingly without me even realising. Losing Batur, the useless oaf that he undoubtedly had been, had only strengthened my bond with the other two. The three young men had sought me out and offered their service at a time when I had nothing to give. Might have been because they had nowhere else to go, might have been they were running from a past they'd sooner leave behind. It didn't matter to me. When I was at my lowest ebb, those three had stood behind me. I would be eternally grateful for that.

Kai tried to speak, but nothing but groans came from his mouth. 'Slow it down,' I said to him, placing calming hands on his shoulders. 'Try and speak slowly.'

'You... urr?' he managed eventually.

'Am I hurt?' He nodded. 'No, lad, I'm fine. Just a scratch is all. How are you? Are you eating?'

He held a palm out vertically, tilted it from side to side.

'A little,' Sedric piped up to help him out. 'Seems all our hosts have to offer us is a thin gruel and mouldy bread. The bread has proven too much for him, but the gruel goes down just fine.'

'How is your pain?'

'Aaaaa,' Kai groaned once more. He seemed to be struggling to move his tongue at all, and couldn't purse his lips together.

'Bad?'

'Yeeee.'

'Okay, lad. Look, it won't last forever. You just need rest. But I need you to try to tell me something. On the ship, when you were wounded and down below, a man came down. He emptied some of our chests, and even caught Sedric a nasty blow around the head. Did you see anything? Anyone? If I brought all the men that were on the ship with us into here, would you be able to point him out?'

On the peripheral of my vision, I saw Eadger and Sedric share a knowing glance. I kept my eyes on Kai though. He knew something, that much was obvious. Suddenly, he would not meet my eye, shifted from foot to foot as he studied his boots. 'You can tell me, Kai. I am your lord, and you swore to serve me. If you know something, now would be the time to speak up.'

A poor choice of words perhaps, but he got my gist. Kai shook his head, still staring at the floorboards. There was a quiver to his face, a twitch in the wounds on his cheeks. He knew something, all right; he was too scared to say.

'Tell you what, why don't we let you rest, and I'll come back later. Maybe we can talk some more then?'

He nodded, and we hugged once more and then Sedric, Eadger and I left him to his isolation. I worried for him as we made our way back down the passage and into the hall. Too much time alone isn't good for anyone; I was proof of that. Took all this to finally wake me from my reverie and kick some life back into my wearisome mind. Kai should have been around people, around his friends. I vowed to return on my own later in the day.

Nothing had changed in the hall. The same men still sat quietly in their little groups, hunched and disinterested, and once more I wondered how I was supposed to turn the tide in this war with men such as these. Wilhelm had vanished from his spot on the dais, though the man seemed to lack such presence I doubt if I'd have noticed him crawling over my boots.

I sighed. 'Right, let's go and have a proper look at the walls, shall we? Then I'd like to tour the beach and surrounding land, see if there is anything worth taking note of.'

Loki the dog was laying in the mud when we left the hall, tail wagging as his one eye saw us approaching. He fell in line with the three of us as we exited the north gate, off to explore how in all the Hells I was supposed to keep us all alive.

12

Somehow, the fortress was even less impressive from the outside than it was from within. We turned east from the north gate, walking the perimeter slowly, taking in the landscape around us. It was a bright and warm day, a clear blue sky unburdened by the weight of cloud. I felt the difference in the temperature, my tunic sticking to my damp back as I sweated in the sun. Summer would bloom soon, and the fighting season would be well underway. 'Was that the first raid of the year?' I asked, kicking at the dried blood that stained the sand.

'Second, apparently. First one was a week or so before we arrived, though Hilde says that time they only came with half their strength.'

I nodded. 'First one to test the water, second to go for the kill.'

'Aye, except we turned up.'

I scanned the beach with my one eye, a feature-less landscape that rolled away into the sea. The water seemed calm from back here, but looking at the lapping waves, I remembered the torrent caused by the two bodies of water meeting, how close we had come to capsizing our vessel as we tried to make land. My boat itself was where we had left it, hull down on the beach, the tattered white sail with the crudely painted raven flapping in the light breeze. I smiled at the sight.

Walking around the broken walls, peering through the gaping holes and shaking the mouldy timbers, I wondered how this tribe had held out for so long, with nothing but this and weapons of bone for protection. A flicker of doubt crossed my mind. There was something I hadn't been told, something Eadger was keeping from me.

We were halfway down the eastern wall when I first saw it. 'What is that, over there?' I pointed to a ramshackle collection of burned-out wood and de-bris, seemingly the only other thing of note in that flat land of sand and grass.

'It is the town of Tastris, or at least it was. That is

where most of our people were born and raised. That was where we first tasted our enemies' weapons.'

'Do people still live there?'

'There is nothing there now, nothing but the ghosts of our past.'

'So the people inside these walls, those are all that remain?'

Eadger nodded, running a hand down one of the wonky planks. 'This is all that is left of our people. I told you, did I not, that our need was dire. I would not have been sent to seek you out if it were not.'

I walked down the beach, aware that Eadger, Sedric and Loki the dog were following. Birds squawked overhead; the waves sighed as they crept inland. It was peaceful, if you didn't look at the brown blood plastering the sand. The town of Tastris must have been a sizeable place once upon a time. I could make out where there had been streets, where houses had lined the sides, could picture the place bustling with life. I reckoned there could have been a couple of thousand people at least living there, and once more wondered how this tribe could have fallen so low. Surely there were a thousand or so men of fighting age at one point. Where were they? What happened to them?

Eadger was frowning heavily as he trudged next

to me, and I wondered what horrors he was reliving, and how many dark and lonely nights he had been reliving them for. He stopped in front of a wooden wreck that I guessed must have once been a house, his lips murmuring a silent prayer. I remembered asking him on our journey north if he had a family awaiting his return and the darkness that had clouded his face. He'd said he hadn't, but was that because he'd never had one? Or could it be that they were already lost to him?

'Tell me,' I said to him, putting a hand on his shoulder.

'I... I have never spoken of it.' His voice shook with his pain, his arms hugging his torso as he sought to keep his emotions in check.

'Nothing worse than speaking the words that hurt you the most. I kept mine inside me for years, locked away as I drank my way through the days in the darkest corner of my hall. All that pain you feel, that anguish, it eats you up from the inside, consumes you, without you ever knowing. Let it out.'

Loki nuzzled into Eadger's legs, his one eye staring up at him imploringly, almost like he under-stood. Sedric had walked a few paces away, close enough to listen in, far enough away to stay out of the conversation.

'I was a carpenter, back then,' Eadger began. 'Back before those bastards from across the sea decided they liked the look of our land. I built a good portion of the houses down this street. They weren't much to look at, granted, but they were hale and strong, kept the rain out and the cold at bay during the winter. People were grateful for my work, and I made a good living. I was up at the fort when the first ships were spotted. There were children playing on the beach, women in the shallows washing clothes. I remember it was hot. I was up on the wall, western side, sweating away as I repaired some moulding timber. I was taking a swig from my water skin when I heard the first screams.

'My wife, Ida, was at the beach. She'd made me a new tunic and thought she'd give it a wash before giving it to me. She was good with a needle and thread, always making or repairing something for someone. There weren't many better than her. So she took our daughter Unnr with her. Down to the beach in the sunshine they went. Unnr, she was seven... just seven years old. Tall and slim, raven-haired like her mother. She was always getting into scrapes around town; felt like not a day went by I didn't have to wipe blood off her elbows or knees. One time, she climbed atop a pile of timber a few of the lads and I had been using for the fortress walls. Should have seen the state of her when she fell off.' Eadger scoffed a small laugh, tears streaming down his face, mottling in his beard.

'Gods, she had spirit, that girl. Her favourite toy was a wooden whale I'd carved for her when she was still a babe. I'd seen one, out at sea, when Ida was pregnant. Been helping a friend on his fishing boat. Couldn't believe my eyes when it burst from the water, damn well nearly capsized the boat! Unnr would take that whale everywhere with her. That was the first thing I found... you know... when I made it to the beach.

'We heard the screams, up on the walls, but couldn't see anything from the western side. I sent a lad I had working with me down to investigate. Time went by, the screams got louder, and the lad never came back. Then the alarm went up from the chief's hall, horns blowing, his guards clambering out the gate, swords glinting in the sun. I tell you now, Alaric, I've never known fear like it. Felt like my heart had stopped, my blood gone to ice. Not for me, at least I'd like to think not, but for them. My girls.' He was sobbing now, sucking in air through his mouth, unable to keep his breathing under control. I felt tears welling in my one remaining eye, my hand trembling on his shoulder.

'I ran, hammer in hand, ran like I'd never run before. Rounding the walls, all I could see was chaos. Soldiers slaughtering our women and children, innocent people, good people, butchered for no reason. No reason at all.'

Looking down onto the beach, I could picture the slaughter, the tang of blood on the air. I'd seen massacres before, heard the screams of the innocent, smelt the stink of the corpses. I said nothing; I had no words. There were no words.

'I killed my first man that day. I was screaming, bellowing, calling Ida and Unnr, though of course they did not answer. A man came at me, sword held high. I batted it aside with my hammer, then drove it down onto his head, again and again until his brains were mush beneath my feet. Then I found another man, another enemy, and I did the same to him. It was only when the last of the cowards had fled back to their ships that I found the whale. It was half buried in the sand, coated in brown blood. I knew it then, though I would not let myself believe. But I found them soon after, further down the beach.

'Ida lay on top of our daughter, arms wrapped around her, protecting her even in death. My wife had been stabbed through the back, the sword going clean through, far enough that the same blow also took the life of my daughter. I had to prise them apart, untangle the cold fingers that had once been so warm, just so I could hold my baby girl one last time.'

Eadger collapsed. Loki squealed as he jumped aside, but he was licking Eadger's tears before I could even lower myself. Sedric was there then, crying like a babe, his mouth blubbering like a fish out of water as his grief-addled mind sought for the right words.

I spoke through gritted teeth, the stitches burning in my back. 'And this is why you fight. This is why you came south to find me. These people took from you everything you loved in this world, and for that you want your vengeance.'

Eadger nodded, unable to speak. Gently, I pushed Loki away so the poor man had space to breathe before speaking again. 'I've done a lot of horrible things in my life, Eadger. Some for revenge, some just for the hell of it. I'm not a good man, never have been. I've killed people who didn't deserve to die, took money from people who didn't deserve to win. But I got mine in the end. Lost my eye, my army, and all my friends.' I paused as I tried to think where I was going with this. 'I took my revenge on the people responsible for that, the cowards who conspired to see the deed done. And I have to tell you, Eadger, it didn't make me feel any better. Vengeance does not always equate to justice, though we often think they walk the same path.'

Eadger sobbed, the years of pent-up emotion pouring out of him. I knew too well what it was like to keep your feelings bottled up, locked away in the depths of your mind. There they lurked, taunting you, haunting your dreams. It was no way to live.

'What else am I supposed to do?' Eadger spoke after a time. 'What else can I do? Every spring, the bastards come back, and every spring I relive that day. I can't walk that beach without thinking of them, re-membering the anguish, the pain, the suffering. Should have been me that died. Should have been me they slaughtered. Ida and Unnr hadn't done any-thing to anyone. They were good people, the best people. And now they're gone and I'm left here alone, left with nothing but bitterness and regret. But I tell you now, Alaric Hengistson, I will see them beaten, slaughtered like dogs, just like my wife and child were.'

I nodded. It was another feeling I knew well. Vic-tory over these invaders would not bring his family back, but he knew that as well as I, and it seemed un-necessary to point it out. 'I will fight at your side, Eadger, until we are either toasting a glorious victory or I am killed fighting next to you. This I swear.'

'Aye, me too,' Sedric added.

'But I cannot do that if this traitor we have stalking us kills me first. I need you watching my back, both of you. Kai knows something, I could sense it; he wouldn't meet my eye. Whoever this whoreson is, he has Kai scared half to death. We need to try to get him to talk – well, murmur anyway. I need you, Eadger. Your people are relying on you.'

With a nod, Eadger rose back to his feet, wiping tears from bloodshot eyes. 'I know, I know. And I am most grateful you have come; I know you had no particular reason to.'

'Not apart from the two carts of amber your lord has promised me,' I said with a wink. 'Where is that, anyway?'

'He has it, that and more. It's with the livestock in the back of his hall. Don't worry, my friend – you help us to victory, Wilhelm will see you paid. Coward he may be, but he pays his dues.'

We walked back along to the fortress, a sombre group, all lost in our thoughts. To the south of the fortress, set back from the beach in the flat lands of swaying grass, there was a huge mound of earth clawing its way up to the sky, an odd thing in an otherwise featureless landscape. Eadger kept looking that way, and I looked at Eadger looking at it, but did not feel the need to ask. It was clear to me that it was a burial pit, and after the conversation we had just had, my guess was it was the final resting place of his wife and daughter. I thought it strange for a people whose custom was to burn their dead to make such a thing. But then I thought of the countless hundreds who must have lost their lives fighting for this most northernly peninsula, and then didn't find it so strange at all. There's only so much timber you can cut down to burn, after all.

My wound was a ball of fire as we made our way back through the gates, and I found myself relishing the thought of spending the rest of the day in that life-sucking hall, drinking sour ale and slurping thin gruel.

However, the Trickster, it seemed, had other plans for me.

13

'That's the man, Father!' the youth said, pointing and spitting his accusation my way. 'That is the man who called himself Alaric Hengistson, leader of the Ravensworn!'

We had just set foot in the hall. Eadger's eyes had dried and a weariness cloaked me. I hadn't noticed the tension in the hall as we entered, being more concerned with finding a seat and taking some of the strain off my back. But I could feel it now, a taut silence, an accusation lying thick in the air.

There were twelve men in total, standing on the raised dais at the rear of the hall. Twelve armed warriors, all with helmets and mail, their war spears glinting in the fire's glow. It took my tired mind a moment or two to make out the face of the pale youth whose trembling finger thrust out accusingly towards me. But I soon livened up as I recognised who he was.

'Sigimund Haribertson,' I muttered. 'Well, fuck me.'

The youth strutted from the dais, filled with the courage of having his father's warriors at his back. His broken nose was swollen, dark rings surrounding two black eyes. 'This is the man that slaughtered my friends, that was trespassing on *your* land! All I did was ask him to pay the proper taxes, taxes that you are owed by the laws you uphold. This man refused, then he and his men slaughtered my friends in an unprovoked attack! I demand justice!'

I smiled; Gods help me but I smiled. I smiled at the foolishness of it, of the youth's brazen lie and the irony that in sparing Sigimund that night on the western coast, I may have doomed myself. They say one good deed can't hide a lifetime of bad, but I didn't think my one good deed would be the thing that ended me.

'So, you are Alaric.' A deep voice reverberated from the dais. A bear of a man stepped down onto the rushes. He had long sandy-brown hair with a beard to match. Deep set eyes either side of a wide, flat nose. He met my smile with one of his own and I saw two incomplete rows of cracked and crooked teeth. He was a head taller than me, which most men weren't, and a damn sight thicker. He looked every inch the brawler; could have been a fighter in the pits down in Goridorgis, killing for King Balomar's gold. I've a feeling he would have made a fortune.

'And you must be Haribert, Chief of the Anglii,' I said, the sardonic smile still fixed to my face. 'Must say, I've met most of the war chiefs in this land we call our own. It is surprising our paths have never crossed.'

'I seem to remember you fighting against my father once. Alas, I was too young to hold a spear that day. That being said, we nearly ended up crossing swords ourselves a few years ago.'

'That so?' I was oddly calm, melancholic. I felt as though I'd used up my emotions for the day, just hearing Eadger speak at the foot of his ruined house. I wanted some adrenalin to kick in, even if just to dull the pain of the wound in my back. But it remained allusive.

'I was asked to join the fight against you, by Dagr, chief of your own tribe. Alas, I was unable to bring my warriors south at the time, though from what I gather he and his pup Warin did for you in the end.'

'I did for that cunt too, in my own time.'

Haribert laughed, a booming, belly-shaking cacophony that seemed to shake the rafters of the hall. 'Aye, that you did. Came back from the dead, that's what I heard. Slipped into the little weasel's bedchamber and run him through. His whore too. I reckon you must be one of the only men I've heard of who's killed his wife's brother.'

'Then clearly you do not get out of your hall as much as you should. You never know, big man, you might even shift some weight. How many men *does* it take to get you in that mail every morning?'

Again, he roared with laughter. 'Aye, not quite as trim as I used to be. But then, what's the point in getting old if you can't enjoy life's little treats? Is it true, what my lad said?' He hooked a thumb to Sigimund, who was staring daggers at me from the dais.

'True enough, though we didn't slaughter those boys in cold blood. They came at us, shields touching. Didn't quite find the easy win they were hoping for.'

'I'd wager they didn't.' He turned and looked back at his son, a calculating expression fixed to his face. 'Not sure if I should bend him over my knee or pour him a cup of ale. Fancy that, my son meeting Alaric of the Ravensworn in the heat of battle and living to tell the tale.' He roared with laughter once more, and my gaze turned to his armed retinue on the dais. They didn't laugh, and I wondered how many of the seasoned warriors had sons out riding with Sigimund that red day, sons who never returned home.

'I let your son live, Chief Haribert. We were caught in a storm and beached our ship for the night, somewhere down the western coast. I had no notion of where we were or whose land it was. We saw no one, bothered no one, until your son and his retinue approached us as dusk gathered. I had no quarrel with him, though he attacked me anyway. And I want no quarrel with you. I am here to help fight off the invaders, not start a war with the Anglii.'

Silence in the hall. A bird squawked outside, and Loki sat up at the sound, sniffing the air. Eadger moved forwards slowly so he stood beside me, and on a table to my right I could see Gunnar, Red Beard and Rolf on their feet, weapons to hand. Rudi and Mellow sat with their heads down, clearly wanting no part in what was to come. I took note of that.

'You speak well, Alaric, Lord of the Ravensworn. And I am wary of a man with a reputation so formidable as yours. But I lost some young lads to you, lads who were the sons of men I rely on. I cannot allow that to go unchallenged. I'm sure you understand.'

I nodded, because I understood it well. Haribert could not allow the deaths of the sons of some of his most prominent warriors to go unavenged. For if he did, how could he expect those men to stay loyal to him? Leadership was precarious at the best of times, a constant juggling act. I had never ruled a tribe, but I had kept in line five hundred blood-hungry warriors for a time. It isn't easy, and if you do not have good people around you, it's impossible. Therefore, if those good people have a grievance with someone, then you have a grievance with that person too. 'So, what do you propose we do about this?'

'You will pay a blood price, a price set by me, mind. And there'll be no haggling.'

I nodded once more, relieved that this was going to cost me no more than silver. Haribert was just about to name his price when one of his warriors called out to him, asking his chief to come back and confer. Looking at the man, I saw a fury in his eyes such as I have never seen before. He was short and squat, a shaven head with slits for eyes. His nose was long and sharp, a beardless face around a thin-lipped mouth. His eyes burned into me, and I had time to take note of a scar above his right eye and a white-knuckled grip on the shaft of his war spear. 'Here we go,' I muttered.

'Lord, what is happening?' Sedric whispered to me as Haribert stalked back to the dais.

I sighed. 'I'd wager that man there lost a son to one of our swords when Sigimund attacked us on the beach. He is going to argue with his chief that silver is not enough, that I must pay for this with blood. It is a common enough custom.'

'But why would a chief listen to a mere warrior?'

'You know nothing of the world, do you, young Sedric? Haribert relies on his warriors, just as Wilhelm relies on Eadger and his men, and Hilde for that matter. If a chief loses the faith of his closest warriors, how long do you think he can sleep soundly at night without fearing a knife in the dark? Many people think a chief to be the most powerful position in a tribe, but often, often the real power lies with those who whisper in their ear. Do me a favour, boy, go get my mail and sword. I've a feeling you're going to be making a circle outside before the day bleeds out.'

And so it was. Haribert walked back to me, eyes downcast. He came closer this time, put a paw-like hand on my shoulder. 'My man back there, his name is Ludwig. He has served me over twenty years and is a most valued warrior of my tribe.'

'And his son died fighting against me with your son,' I finished for him.

'Aye. Ludwig says a blood price is not enough, says that blood should be paid for with blood. Turns out the rest of my men agree with him.'

'I know how it goes, Haribert, Chief of the Anglii. I will fight your man; we will make a circle outside the hall. We have a few hours till sunset, plenty of time to see this finished.' Haribert nodded and went to back away, but I caught his arm before he could. 'But once I have killed your man, then it *is* finished.'

He smiled. 'I admire your confidence, Alaric. But yes, once the fight is done, the victor can consider the matter closed. Good luck, Alaric Hengistson, you're going to need it.'

* * *

The sun was a red orb hanging low in a purple sky when Ludwig and I faced each other in the circle of shields. The wound in my back still burned, the stitches itching on the rough fabric of my tunic. I had eaten, rested for a short while, and felt as well as I could.

At my back stood Sedric, Eadger and his five men. All had volunteered to hold a shield for me – well, I'm not sure Mellow and Rudi had *volunteered* as such, but they were there nonetheless. Ludwig was crowing like a jester, the men around us a group of small children whom he had come to entertain. He regaled them with tales of how he was going to kill me, of how my guts would trail in the wake of my corpse, dragged at the stomping hooves of his horse. I smiled, a small, secret smile. Tired, wounded, jaded I was. But I was Alaric, once the great lord of war, and I thought myself more than capable of putting this fool in the mud.

The sun had slipped a finger's breadth down the horizon by the time Ludwig had finally built himself up for the fight. My mail felt heavy. My shield, with the faded red paint and the black raven, hung loose in my left hand. It burned my wound when I raised it, and I was reluctant to do so before it became utterly necessary. But my sword was sharp, the grip a reassuring presence in my palm as I stood as still as stone, waiting for him to make the first move.

The rules of the circle were simple: two men fought until only one was left alive. The men around us would close up, shields facing in, penning us in a circle of death. I had faced this before, many times. From the pits of Goridorgis to the various tribal champions, I had fought on a battlefield, when one chief or other decided they were not prepared to risk their entire army on one battle. I had fought them all, won them all. Ludwig was a big man, broad and well-muscled. But I reasoned he would be slow, that he would tire quick. My only concern was that the same could be said of me.

With a clash of iron on shield, Ludwig approached and the men around us roared, their blood-lust kindled by imminent death. Ludwig swung first, high to low, and with a wince, I lifted my shield and grimaced as his blade bit into the wood. I did not respond. Taking a small step to my right, I readjusted my grip and awaited his next move.

'Come on then, great Alaric, Lord of Battle!' Ludwig spat, stepping to his right as I took another step to mine. I smiled once more, not a secret one this time, but a provocative grin, aiming to goad him on. It worked. He leaped at me, slashing left and right with his sword. I took the first one on my shield, but it sent a jarring pain all the way to my shoulder, and my wounded back spasmed in protest. His next swipe I met with my own blade, and the swords sparked as they clashed, the men around us cheering at the sight.

I stepped back, then took another to my right. I was panting, didn't really know why; I'd barely done anything. But my heart was pounding, blood thick in my ears, pent-up adrenalin building within me, awaiting the chance to burst free. I kept it in check, for now.

'Come on, you coward! You *nithing*! Come on and fight me!'

My smile came back. A wolf grin from over the rim of my shield. 'I remember your son saying something similar to me, Ludwig. Didn't work out so well for him.'

Ludwig bellowed in rage and anguish. Emotion can be a powerful weapon, but in the heat of battle I have often found that the man who lets his emotions rule him ends up the loser. I stepped to my right again, using my sword to fend off another wild slash as I did. This time I did respond, pushing Ludwig's blade to his right before snaking out with my own, the tip burying itself in his right arm. I yanked it free, the sword withdrawing with a satisfying sucking sound. Blood poured down Ludwig's arm.

He had lost his senses now, lost his reason. And more importantly, his focus. He mirrored my steps until I had turned ninety degrees, then charged at me once more. Ludwig may have lost his wits, but mine had been in check all along. As he came for me again, bounding across the circle, I lowered myself to one knee, and just as Ludwig raised his sword for a chop at my head, the dazzling light of the setting sun struck him full in the face.

Ludwig recoiled from the light, his sword arm going up to his face as he instinctively tried to rub his eyes. It was a foolish mistake, the kind of error a man of his experience should not have been making. And it cost him his life. As his hand was over his face, I leaped back to my feet. Letting my shield fall to the mud, I rammed my sword home, right through Ludwig's heart. He was dead before his body hit the ground. And once again, I had survived the circle of shields.

14

I was cleaning the blood from my sword in a trough of brown water when she approached me.

'That was a good kill,' she said, leaning against the side of Wilhelm's feasting hall.

I shrugged. 'Thanks. Nothing I've not done a hundred times before.' I wiped the wet blade on the hem of my cloak before putting it back to rest in its scabbard.

'How is your wound?'

In truth, it was agony. The strain of the combat within the circle had torn the stitches, and I could feel warm blood trickling down my back and legs. 'I'll survive,' I said with another shrug. My limbs were aching, and I had a fierce headache. I felt more fatigued than I think I'd ever done before. It had been a long day, and I wanted nothing more than to crawl into my cot and curl up until the sun was once more high in the sky.

'There will be a council tomorrow morning. Wilhelm will ask Haribert if the matter between the two of you is settled, and Haribert will agree. We had been hoping Haribert could be persuaded to fight with us, but now I think...' She left the rest unspoken.

'I am sorry, lady, if I have ruined the chance of support from your neighbours. But those lads attacked us for no reason on that beach. They brought this on themselves.'

Hilde smiled, stepped out of the shadows so I could see her better. She was, I noticed, quite beautiful. High cheek bones, thin lips and fierce eyes; I could see why men would follow her into battle. 'Wilhelm has been saying for months the great Alaric is the one to save us. We are all disappointed you chose to leave your army at home.'

I laughed, but the action made me wince and cough, my hand going to the burning wound on my back. 'What army? It has been a long time since I have considered myself a leader of men. I was all but washed up, lady, when Eadger arrived unexpected on my doorstep. I had been quite happily drinking myself into an early grave before that.'

'And yet you came.' She moved towards me, her face inches from mine. Her breath was warm against the chill breeze of the night. She smelt of sweat and leather, of roasted meat and wine.

'Let's just say I couldn't resist one last chance at glory.'

'And will you have it?'

'I do not know, lady. I am yet to appraise the state of your men, or get a proper chance to study your enemy. First impressions, though, are that your situation is more desperate than I was initially told.' I made to walk off, but her words stopped me before I'd taken three paces.

'You mean you weren't told you were going to be fighting for a vastly outnumbered army led by a woman?'

'The numbers don't bother me, lady, nor in truth does the army being led by a woman. But your people have no real defences. This fort of yours is rotten to its core.'

'Do you speak of the wooden walls or the people that live within them?'

'You know, I'm not entirely sure.' Again, I made to move away into the night, and again I was held back.

'Come with me, Lord Alaric. I will find us some wine.'

I pictured Saxa and our boys. I recognised the hunger in Hilde's eyes, looking me up and down the way a wolf does a lamb. She didn't want to share a cup of wine with me, of that I was sure. But, I am a man. 'Lead the way,' I said.

She took me through the feasting hall, past the small room in which Kai recovered, to another small chamber, lit by the glow of a small brazier in the corner. There was a bed and a round table, a jug of wine with two cups. 'You are late my love,' a voice said from the bed. I had not noticed the figure, lying still beneath the furs. But a silhouette untangled itself from the bed, and to my astonishment I saw another lady unfurl herself from them, as naked as the day she was born. Dark hair cropped tight around a narrow skull. A face that was all sharp angles, with piercing dark eyes that seemed to look straight through me. Isvilt, wife of chief Wilhelm Erikson, met my eye with some amusement as she rose and kissed Hilde on the lips.

'Is he always this quiet?' Isvilt asked Hilde, her lips brushing the blonde curls that fell around Hilde's ears.

'He was more talkative earlier. Maybe he is just

saving his energy for what is to come? I think he is going to need it.'

May the Hanged One curse me forever, but my groin swelled so much I had a sudden urge to sit down. I blushed so deep all the blood in my head – which wasn't much by that point admittedly – could have burst through the skin. It was only then I remembered Eadger telling me not to expect too many late-night visits from Isvilt. And now I understood why I wasn't her type.

'Lady Isvilt,' I said, not quite knowing where I should be looking. 'It is good to see you again.'

'I'm sure it is.' She moved away from Hilde until she was standing right in front of me. I raised my gaze when it was no longer appropriate to look down. 'How is your wound?'

'The day's events have not done it much good, if I'm being honest.'

'Take off your clothes,' she ordered, walking past me and exiting the small chamber.

'Best do as she says.' Hilde threw me a wink as she begun to undress herself.

'Are you sure...' I'd found myself in some pretty odd situations over the years; this, though, took the biscuit.

'I am afraid, Lord Alaric, that if you are looking

for a fuck you will be better off visiting the stables. Take your clothes off and sit on a stool. Isvilt will see to your wound.'

I did as I was told. I could not help but catch a glance of Hilde's body as she too undressed and lowered herself onto the bed. She was firm and strong, lithe muscles showing on her pale skin. I also saw the number of scars she bore; her arms and torso were covered in them. Far more than I had.

'You have the privilege of better armour than me, I think,' she said, seeing the direction of my gaze. 'You wear mail where we wear breastplates of bone. They stop a glancing blow easily enough. Anything with any meaning behind it, though, tends to get through. Your gift of mail will be most useful to us. How many did you bring?'

I told Hilde of the chests packed onto my ship. I spoke also of the treachery at sea, the two broken chests, and how I had come to be wounded on the beach. At some point in my retiree, Isvilt returned and began seeing to my wound, and Hilde and I spoke of war, of past battles won and lost. My respect for her grew. She was clearly more than capable of leading men into war. What she lacked was men and equipment, and I had proven to be very little help in either regard. Even with the weapons and mail we had managed to recover from the broken chests, the equipment I had brought north with me would only arm a small number of her men. 'But I have fought many wars,' I said to her. 'And won more than I've lost. I've a fresh set of eyes on this – well, an eye, at least. Come the morning, we can get a better look at your men and work out the best strategy to win this fight.'

'We have to win, Alaric.' It was Isvilt that spoke. She had stitched me back up and was reclining on the bed with Hilde.

'I will give everything I have, I assure you.'

It was at that point I became aware of footsteps on the floorboards outside, and then the door to Hilde's small chamber was opened and Chief Wilhelm entered.

He wore just an unbelted tunic that hung from him like a sail on a mast. His feet were bare, hair wild like a bird's nest. His eyes roamed from me to Hilde and Isvilt on the bed, then back to me. I had become quite comfortable being naked in front of the two ladies, especially since it was all too obvious they had no interest in me. But right then, I had the sudden urge to be somewhere else.

'What is going on in here?' His eyes squinted

through his hawk-like face, and I realised he was having trouble seeing who I was.

'Chief Wilhelm,' I said, springing to my feet. 'We haven't actually been introduced yet. I am Alaric, once chief of the Ravensworn. I am here to fight for you, Lord.'

'I know who you are, mercenary,' he spat. 'You are here for my amber; it remains to be seen whether you will fight for my people.'

'The *lord* Alaric,' Isvilt cooed, rising from the bed to put a hand on my shoulder, 'has already fought once for you, my lord, and he has the wound to prove it. I tended to Alaric's wound in the two days he was recovering, and he has come to me to have it re-stitched. It would appear his "endeavours" earlier on today did the stitches little good.'

There was silence for a moment. Wilhelm squinted at me once more, and I thought as I had earlier when I had seen him in his feasting hall, how a man such as this could come to lead a tribe in a time of war. There were many tribes in our lands that would have done away with a chief as weak as this one seemed. Although I saw a different side to him then, a ruthlessness lurking underneath. A great warrior he may never be, but a cunning man with a cold heart could have as much success in this world as a courageous man with a kind one. I reconsidered my opinion of the man and felt a little wary of him.

'So this is why you *expose* yourself in front of my wife?'

'That and no other reason, Lord.'

'I hear you killed your opponent in the circle today. I did not witness it; violence is not something that sits well with me. You have cost me a potentially valuable ally, Lord Alaric.'

I could see where this was going, and I didn't like where I ended up. 'I think if the Anglii were going to fight with you, Lord, they would have committed themselves long before now.'

'And why would you think that?' Wilhelm spoke in a quiet voice, but there was a menace in his tone.

'Well, they're the closest tribe to you. Look at where we are, the land you live on. You are isolated up here. You have the sea to your north, east and west. The only way your people can travel by land is south, and that path leads you through the lands of the Anglii. Now, you would be well in your rights to say to Chief Haribert that if your tribe are wiped out his would be next. And he would be well within his rights to agree with you.'

'But...?'

'But that hasn't happened, has it? There is something I'm not being told here, something even Eadger is unwilling to tell me. There is a reason Chief Haribert, a war chief renowned for throwing his men into battle, has not decided to fight with you. I would know that reason.'

There was a moment's silence, just a smattering of seconds, in which I noticed Wilhelm, Isvilt and Hilde all share a glance. It was all I needed to know I was right. 'Reckon I'll head off to bed, if it's all the same to you.' I threw on my tunic, slipped into my boots and gathered up the rest of my belongings in my arms. Whatever was going on here, I had no part in it.

'I will see you in the morning, Alaric,' Hilde called as I shuffled past the chief and exited the chamber. The door closed behind me; I did not linger to hear what was said. I racked my brain all the way back to my chamber, thinking on what Eadger had told me, what I had seen. There was something I had missed, *something*, I was sure of it. It made no sense why this war had been going on for so long. Sure, it was the way of the tribes to raid each other for grain and cattle, and occasionally it would spill over into all-out war. But a foreign tribe going to the effort of sailing across a sea to wage war on the same tribe time and time again? A tribe with clearly so little to offer?

Something was off.

Loki the dog was sitting outside the door to my little cabin. I ruffled his ears as I opened the door and he followed me inside. The chamber was as I had left it; no one had even bothered to relight the smoking brazier in the corner. I didn't mind; I was exhausted. I smiled to myself as I saw the giant piss still pooling in the chamber pot in the corner. Felt like an age since I'd eased myself from my cot that morning.

It had been quite a day. What I needed was some time to relax and let my wound heal. I was not to get it.

15

The first fingers of light were reaching out from the eastern horizon when I rose once more. My wound was stiff, but the pain had lessened. I emptied the chamber pot out into the mud-churned alley before filling it once more, and then struggled into my mail. Loki the dog watched me from the floorboards, tail wagging furiously the whole time, but he did not rise until I called him to me and told him it was time to leave.

Breakfast was a bowl of bland oats that had been boiled with water instead of milk. I wolfed it down, trying not to taste it. Loki found a scrap of bone amongst the rotting rushes on the hall floor and attacked it with relish. There were only ten or so other people in the hall, and they muttered together, each taking it in turns to slide me a snide look. I guessed word would have spread of the fight in the circle the previous evening, and even had they not witnessed it, they would have heard. The thought cheered me. For that day I would need to appraise the men of the tribe, to judge how they fared in battle. I did not have high expectations, but I remained hopeful. Surely it would help my cause if they had heard of my victory in the circle; surely then they would realise that I was a warrior to follow.

I felt certain that my reputation would have preceded me to the far north. Stories would have been told around fires at night, of the great Alaric and his Ravensworn. They would have spoken of how we had turned the tide of many a battle, fought the Romans on the Danube, invaded one of their forts and captured three war ships. I was famous, after all. At least, I had been.

Ignoring their lingering eyes, I finished my dour oats and exited the hall, uncertain of where to go next. Hilde had said there was to be a council that morning for Wilhelm and Haribert to decide if the matter between me and his son had been resolved. I felt no fear at the prospect of the meeting, for

Haribert had declared that once the duel in the circle was over then the matter would be closed.

Loki followed me from the hall, and I had to squint my one remaining eye against the fierce light of the sun. On the small patch of land outside the hall's doors, where I had fought Ludwig the previous evening, men were making another circle of shields. My curiosity piqued, I walked towards them, hailing Eadger when I saw him, standing with his shield raised, locked together with Red Beard's and Gunnar's.

'Lord Alaric! We were wondering where you had got to. I'd just sent young Sedric round to rouse you.'

'I was in the hall breaking my fast, though clearly too late to do it with you! What's going on here?' I gestured to the circle.

'Wilhelm and Haribert are to meet between the shields to discuss your victory last night.'

I thought it a touch dramatic, but just shrugged. Wherever they held their discussion was no business of mine. Sedric returned; he had bunked up with Kai the night before and assured me he was doing fine. 'He keeps trying to tell me something, Lord, but I can't work out what it is.'

'If only he could write,' I mused for about the hundredth time since he had been wounded. 'I will see him later. We'll get this meet out the way and then you and I will spend the day seeing if there are any fighters here worth their salt.'

'There's a couple over here, Lord,' Gunnar piped up, and I smiled and clapped he and Red Beard on the shoulder. 'Where are the brothers?' I asked.

'Still deep in their slumber as far as I know. Rolf has a rotten belly; don't think we'll be seeing him out on the beach today.' I smiled, wondering how much ale the rust-bearded warrior had consumed the night before.

Just then, there was a commotion behind me, and Wilhelm came out of the main door of his feasting hall, flanked by Hilde and Isvilt. A half-smile danced across my face at the sight of the three of them as I wondered what had gone on in Hilde's chamber after I had left the night before. Eadger saw my smile and asked what I found so amusing, so I told him about Wilhelm walking into Hilde's chamber as the three of us sat there naked.

Eadger struggled to stifle a laugh. 'Rumour is he visits every night. I heard that he likes to sit there and watch them in bed together.'

Not for the first time, I wondered at the insanity of agreeing to support this chief in his war. And not for the first time, I pondered if it was a war of his own making. Haribert came to the circle then, his son and retinue in tow. He looked every inch the warrior chief, with his coat of bear over a mail shirt and a gleaming helmet trimmed with gold atop his head.

Wilhelm entered the circle and squinted as he looked up to meet Haribert's eye. The difference between the two men was there for all to see. Wilhelm was short and slight, though today at least he wore a better-fitting tunic and a fine green cloak that billowed in the breeze. 'Good morning, Chief Haribert. I trust you and your men rested well?'

'Rested well? After seeing our comrade cut down by your man last night?'

An awkward silence ensued, into which I took the opportunity to push myself into the spotlight. 'I am my own man,' I declared in a firm voice. 'I do not belong to anyone else, nor am I oath sworn to any lord or chief. I am here of my own free will, and you know as well as I, Chief Haribert, that I had no wish to fight your man in the circle yesterday. He brought about his own doom, as did his son.'

Wilhelm winced; he was clearly already uncomfortable enough with this charade. The last thing he wanted was anyone's ego getting in the way and dragging the meeting out. Haribert had the grace to smile, even extended a hand to clasp mine. 'You fought well last night,' he said in a gruff voice.

'I did what I needed to do.' I shrugged off the reluctant praise. 'I trust you will stick to your word, Lord. You said before the contest yesterday that once the fight was done that would be the end of the matter.'

Haribert turned to look at his son, who had the sense to keep his own mouth shut and study his boots. 'Sigimund always was an impulsive boy. In truth, Lord Alaric, I can well believe that he and his stupid friends would charge down a beach to attack a group of men without stopping to think of the consequences. Youth is wasted on the young, as they say.' He held out his hand once more and I shook it, trying not to grimace as he squeezed my bones as hard as he could. 'Truly, your reputation precedes you. I shall honour my word; the bad blood between us is settled.'

I nodded, looking past Haribert to his son. Sigimund glared back at me, fury in his eyes. The father may have forgiven me, but I knew the son never would. Couldn't, more like; his youth and pride would not allow him. I grimaced. I had been a proud man once; powerful, too. I'd made an enemy there. An enemy that would one day rule a strong and powerful tribe. Choose your friends wisely, I was once told. But a wise man chooses his enemies. Perhaps I had not chosen mine well.

'Have you given any thought to the offer I made you?' Wilhelm piped up, easing me out of the conversation. This was, I knew, Wilhelm's main cause for concern today. He had hoped he would be able to persuade the Anglii to fight alongside his own people. It was a mystery still to me why they were not already. I studied Haribert as he spoke.

'I have not changed my mind, brother chief. The Anglii have no need to enter a war with strangers from across the sea. We have our own battles to fight, our southern border to keep secure. I do not know what started this bad blood between your people and the foreigners from across the sea, but it is no concern of mine. You are on your own, Wilhelm.'

Haribert turned and made to leave. He stopped though, just as he was exiting the circle and his men were hefting their shields and spears, ready to march. 'Lord Alaric, walk with me a moment, would you?'

With a shrug to Eadger and Sedric, I followed, ensuring I gave Sigimund a wide birth as I followed in his father's wake. The chief of the Anglii had horses waiting by the southern gate, and his men mounted, stowing shields and spears on the back of a cart. Haribert took me by the arm and led me away a few paces, out of earshot of his men. 'What have you been told of Wilhelm and his people?'

'The Cimbri? Nothing, Lord, other than that they are desperate for support in their ongoing war.'

'And why, do you think, are they at war with these foreigners from across the sea?'

I thought a moment, thinking on what I had been told, and what I had seen for myself. I knew something didn't quite add up, that there was some secret the Cimbri were keeping hidden. 'I was told the raiders came out of the blue one day, slaughtered innocent people on the beach, and that they have been coming back every spring since.'

'And why now? Why would these tribes suddenly take it upon themselves to raid across the water?'

'Food? Land, even? It is nothing our people do not do, Chief Haribert. You telling me you've never sent your spears south when your harvest came in thin?'

The chief chuckled, clapping me on the shoulder. 'Aye, don't we all. It is healthy, from time to time. Bleeds in the young warriors, keeps the older ones sharp. But this war that Wilhelm has got his people into, this is a war that was entirely avoidable. There is a pit, south of the fortress, just off the road my men and I are about to ride. You can't miss it. I urge you to take a look, when you can get yourself away. There are some things you should see for yourself.'

With that, he was gone. Two warriors helped him heave himself into his saddle, and he did not look back as he rode out. Sigimund did though, eyes fixing me another murderous glare. I gave him a smile and a wave, just to piss him off. He was a pup, a spoilt little brat who had been taught his first lesson in leadership. He would learn many more, if he lived long enough.

With Haribert's words swirling through my mind, I made my way back through the fort of Tastris, collecting my sword and shield from my hut and striding out of the north gate and onto the beach beyond. There, a hundred or more warriors were grouped, chatting in small groups, a variety of makeshift weapons held in their hands. There were swords of bone, spears without heads, the tips of the wooden handles sharpened into pointed stakes. Many men carried hammers, a couple bore wood axes, but depressingly few had a good sword or spear.

Swords had always been a rarity outside of Rome's borders, for they required large amounts of iron and skilled men to make them. Both of which we lacked in the tribes. Spears, though, should have been more commonplace, and it was alarming to see first-hand how few of the men actually possessed decent weapons. The next thing I noticed was how few wore armour of any description; even breastplates of bone were hard to spot. I stood there, taking it all in, wondering how the hell I was supposed to lead this rabble to war.

'Wishing you were still tucked by your fire at home?' a voice said behind me, and I turned to see Hilde strutting across the sand. She wore her bone armour, a helmet hung from a hook at her right hip, her sword on her left. She flashed me a brilliant smile. 'These men may not look like much, but they have kept the enemy at bay so far.'

I tried to think back to that desperate battle on the beach a few days before. It was all a blur. I remembered jumping from the ship, roaring and fighting with Sedric. Finding Eadger and his men as they fought in a semi-circle around the northern gate. I did not remember much else. 'You know, I had a horse named Hilde once,' I said absently, my mind still lost in the battle.

'That meant to be a compliment?' Hilde asked, a hint of a smile dancing on her lips.

I shrugged. 'Don't know, just a fact I suppose. How many warriors do this enemy of yours bring when they come to raid?'

'It varies. There must have been over two hundred men the day your ship arrived on our lands.'

'And how is it you have managed to fight them off for so long with so few men?'

'We were not always so few, Lord Alaric. There was a whole town of us once, a thriving people, who traded with our neighbours and prospered. This' – she gestured to the rotting walls of the fortress behind us – 'this is all that is left of the Cimbri. Those few of us that remain are determined to fight for its survival.'

I nodded, though still there was something unsettling me about these people and their struggle. 'Then let us see how they can fight.'

Hilde rallied the slumbering men that sweated under the high sun. There was very little enthusiasm that I could see for a people in as desperate a situation as they were. I stood before them and introduced myself, Sedric and Eadger moving to stand at my shoulders. Eadger and his men had already been spreading the word of our battle on the beach against Sigimund and his youthful companions. And most of the watching warriors would have seen me fight Ludwig in the circle, and those who hadn't would certainly have heard the story. There, on that sun-drenched beach, I could leave the bitter taste of defeat behind me. That had happened far to the south and east, another world away. On that beach I was once more the lord of war, the battle commander who had ravaged armies and downed kings. Every man standing facing me had heard the tales of Alaric and the Ravensworn. I sensed the need in them to see him, to feel the presence of leadership and be renewed and comforted by that.

'You all know who I am,' I started. I did not need to raise my voice much, for there were only a hundred men on the beach, less than a fifth of the force I once commanded. 'You have all heard the stories of the battles I have fought, the victories I have won. I have travelled here, to this remote place, to you remote people, to help you win another. And we shall win! Together, you and I will drench this beach with the blood of your enemies, we shall strike such a blow to them that they will fear to bring their ships back to your shores!' I raised an arm in salute, awaiting the cheers that would surely follow my rousing speech.

I was greeted with nothing but sullen faces and the odd squawk of the sea birds floating in the wind far above.

'Tough crowd,' I muttered to Eadger.

'You are a stranger, still, Lord. Let them warm to you, they'll come around.'

I split the men down the middle, forming them into two shield walls, facing one another. I paced down the middle of the facing lines, straightening shields and correcting postures. 'Your left leg should be in front of your right, bent at the knee, toes pointing forwards,' I said to one callow youth whose shield was shaking like a leaf in the breeze. 'Your right leg should be braced behind the left, knee bent, ready to take the weight of a charge on your shield.' I demonstrated the position, my own raven shield held out in front of me. 'When the enemy charge your shield wall, you will be forced back. That's why you need to be low. You there, bend your legs!' I pointed at one sweating bald man, who stood bolt upright with his shield held at arm's length. 'What's wrong with you, man? It's a shield, not a flaming torch! The shield is your friend, your best friend in battle. It will save your life, but only if you treat it right. Now, hold it close to your body, let it cover you. Better!'

I moved off down the line, satisfying myself that the front lines of both formations were in position. 'Now, men in the second ranks. You need to lean into the men in front of you. You men are the muscle of the wall, for when your comrades in front are charged, it is up to you to make sure they do not break. Lend them your weight, keep them upright, and maybe you and your friends will survive.'

I was teaching them how to defend, not attack. It was clear to me that none of the men on the beach were natural warriors, men who had trained with sword and spear since childhood. Those men would have been the first to die when the raiders beached their ships and reaped a bloody slaughter. Even Eadger, who was by far one of the more experienced warriors there, had admitted to me that carpentry was his real profession. Had it not been for this war that had been forced upon them, I doubt the man would have known one end of a spear from the other. Men who have had war forced upon them are not suited to charging an enemy. For that you need skill, and above all courage. These men possessed neither.

'You men,' I said to the fifty or so warriors to my right, who stood in a shield wall two deep, 'will charge these men.' I pointed to the men to my left, who were lined up in an identical formation. I used my foot to scrape a line in the sand and ordered the men to my left to stand on the line. 'Your objective here is to not be pushed back behind this line. You have to hold! And *your* objective,' I said to the men on my right, 'is to get them over that line as quick as you can.'

I moved out from between the two formations, so I stood with Hilde and Sedric with our backs to the fortress. The men in the lines seemed cheered by the prospect, and good-natured taunts were called across the sand, wagers placed, fists shaken in mock fury. I smiled, remembering the simple joy of training men for war. When the Ravensworn had numbered over one hundred men, I had decided to split them into two. Then I'd had to divide them into three units, then four, before eventually I had five units, all numbering one hundred men. Much of this work had been taken from me then, as the captains of each Hundred drilled their own warriors. My role became an overseer, almost a clerk, with the amount of admin one must maintain when commanding a force of that size. I did not have time to train each man how to fight; I was too busy worrying if we had enough grain to see us through winter, or resolving some dispute or other between two of the men – nearly always involving a woman. I missed this, the simplicity of it. 'Charge!'

The right-hand column let out a roar and scampered across the sand. They were quick, they were aggressive, they were keen. Perhaps too keen. For they lost all cohesion in their unit. Their shields, which had been held in an overlapping line, split apart so great gaps appeared as they charged. They ran with swords held overhead, with spears reaching out in front of them, and I had to remind myself that these men were not the warriors I had once commanded, but amateurs, learning how to survive.

They hit the men of the left-hand line with a staggering slap, rather than the crunching impact I had been hoping for. They had become so disjointed in their small charge that ten men hit the opposition a good three heartbeats before the rest did. And once their companions had caught up, enough of the wind had been taken out of their assault that it was easy for the defenders to keep them at bay. They, to give them credit, stood resolutely with their shields held high. The men of the second rank leaned into their comrades in front, and not an inch of ground was given to their enemy.

'Break!' I called, sensing that things could get out of hand if I didn't put a quick stop to it. 'Enough now! I want no corpses left on this beach today!' The men responded dutifully, and there were more jokes shared; even two mock-wrestling matches broke out on the sand, much to the amusement of all.

'Back to your lines!' I called once everyone had

settled down. 'This time, the left-hand line will charge the right.' I went over to the men of the left-hand formation and bade them to form a small circle around me. 'What do you think went wrong for them?' I asked, gesturing to the other group of men, who were still slapping each other on the backs and boasting of their prowess.

'They didn't keep formation when they charged.' It was Gunnar that spoke, and I smiled when I turned to greet him, and he returned it with that same gap-toothed one of his that never failed to lift my spirits. He wore just a sleeveless tunic, his muscled arms reddening in the sun. Gunnar stood a full head taller than any other man on that beach, and I thought his physical presence was something I could use to our advantage when it came to fighting for real.

'You are right, my friend. They broke apart, some ran ahead of the others and what should have been a cohesive line ended up drifting apart. They hit you in ones and twos, and I don't think I saw a single one of you give them a step of this beach. For that, I salute you.' I paused to allow them all a moment to congratulate each other. 'But now the tables are turned, and it is you that are attacking them. So, what shall you do?'

'We stick together, keep our shields locked, walk

across the beach. We don't charge until we are five or ten paces from them. That way, when we strike their shield wall, we strike it with our full force.' It was Red Beard that spoke. He was an older man, with some experience in warcraft, which he had shown me on another beach on our journey north.

'Exactly! I've never understood why men will waste so much energy running over a hundred paces to meet an enemy shield wall when all you have to do is run five. Once you are in mail, once you are helmed and weighed down by spear, sword and shield, you will find your energy dissipates like morning dew on a warm spring morning. More often than not, the winners of a battle are not the side with the better warriors, many times not even the side with the most warriors. But the side who are freshest, fittest. The side who has full canteens of water at their waste, that have eaten a hearty breakfast in the morning, got some decent rest the night before. You do not need to run all the way. Conserve your energy, feel it building inside of you. When there are five paces left, Gunnar – who will stand in the centre of your wall – will order the charge. Remember, keep your shields locked together, and hit them as one!'

I moved away, allowing them some time to or-ganise themselves. I ordered the defending formation to stand on the line the others had previously, running my foot back across the sand to make sure it was clear to all. I gave them their own pep talk, reminding those in the second rank to lend their weight to their brothers in front. Eadger was with them; Rudi, Mellow and Rolf too – a late arrival looking a tad pale. Hilde stalked me like a shadow, listening to all I said, and I hoped, taking it all in. 'Ready, and charge!'

The line moved off at a walk, their shields locked tightly together. The men in the defending formation took this as a sign of weakness and harangued their opponents with mocking jibes, calling them women and cowards. I could see Gunnar grinning from the centre of their line, his hulking frame hunched behind his shield. 'Watch Gunnar,' I said to Hilde.

'Why?'

'Because, dear Hilde, if you can break a shield wall in two, you win the battle. Every time.'

'I know this. What is the relevance of Gunnar?'

'Look at the size of the man. He must weigh twice what I do. He will force his way through the man in the centre of their shield wall.' I pointed to the defending wall of shields, an unbroken line of wood and iron. 'And then they will be split in two. They will give ground the instant that happens, and in that instant they shall lose.'

We watched on. The attacking formation continued their slow march across the sand, even pausing once on Gunnar's order to realign their shields. Then once more they were off, and at just seven or so paces from their enemy, Gunnar ordered the charge.

They battered into their opponents with all the force of a winter storm. Gunnar leaped at his man, smashing down a shield and using his shoulder to barge him to the floor. The second man in the formation, thrown back by the force of Gunnar's attack, just sat down in the sand, shocked at what had happened. The rest broke like dried tinder under an axe.

'Ha!' I slapped my thigh in joy, then pumped an emphatic fist in the air. 'That's how you do it!' I called as I ran across the beach to congratulate the victors, the burning wound in my back forgotten.

This time, I joined in with the back slapping and bear hugs, so enthused I was at what I had seen. 'A few more days of this and we may just stand a chance,' I muttered to Hilde when I thought we were out of earshot of the others. But a few more days we did not have.

Just as the celebrations were dying down and the losers had ceased their arguments over where the blame lay, there was a call from the fortress behind us. Lookouts stood and watched out to sea at all hours of the day, such was the constant fear of another attack. And they were shouting at us then, waving frantically and jumping up and down.

'What are they saying?' I asked, to anyone who was listening.

'Ships, Lord Alaric,' Hilde said. 'They are saying there are ships on the eastern horizon.'

And just like that, all my good humour faded away.

16

'Quickly now! Shields, helmets, armour!' I roared to the scampering men, who streamed back through the northern gate and into the fortress of Tastris. Men were shouting that we should stay behind the high wooden walls, but I wanted them back out on the beach, formed up in a wall of shields, ready to face their enemy.

'Should we not stay?' Sedric murmured in my ear. 'This lot make me look like a veteran.'

I shook my head. 'The walls are rotten, and the men's courage is thin. To hide behind crumbling walls will do them no good. We need our feet planted firmly in the sand, a wall of spears and shields. Trust me, my young friend, we will fare much better out there.'

I stalked the mud-made alleys, screaming, bellowing, harassing every man I came across. The chests we had brought north from my hall were thrown open, and desperate men wriggled into ill-fitting mail. Blades were handed out, helmets fastened, shields hefted.

Loki the dog followed me to my sleeping chamber, where he wagged his tail in excitement as I threw on my mail, the wound in my back burning in protest. The pain was so great I could almost feel the knife in there once more, tearing through flesh, seeking my death. It gave me pause, the pain, as I wondered once more who it was who had sought to bring me down. Would I be standing in line next to that man? Fighting shoulder to shoulder with a faceless enemy, awaiting their chance to strike once more?

I shrugged the thought off; there was little I could do about it. Eadger appeared at the door, dressed in mail, helmet fastened. 'We are ready, Lord,' he said with a nod, stooping down to stroke Loki.

I doubted the men were ready. They may have been dressed for battle, but they had proven to me that morning they were far from ready for war. But it seemed the gods were not willing to grant us the time to prepare them further. If we were to win that day, we would need the Sly One at our side. I too stooped and ruffled Loki's mangled fur, murmuring to him softly. 'Bring us luck today.' I shut him in the small hut, and he howled in anger as Eadger and I made our way back to the northern gate.

Hilde was overseeing the warriors as they filed out of the northern gate, slapping shoulders and calling encouragements. She was clad in her war gear, her bone-made breastplate fastened around her slim torso. Of Chief Wilhelm, there was no sign. 'Do you have a plan?' she asked as I walked towards her.

'Not as such. Let us see what our enemy are about, and we can plan from there. Have they beached yet?'

'They'll be doing it now. Whatever tricks you have up your sleeve, Lord Alaric, now would be the time to bare them.'

I smiled at that, walking under the archway of the gate. It wasn't the first time a warrior I had allied myself with assumed I had some cunning trick, or hidden knowledge, ready to spring a trap on an unwitting enemy. At times, I had. I once had my second in command, Ruric, dig vast ditches across a seemingly innocent field, then cover them in loose grass and leaves. We were facing a horde of enemy horsemen, and their commander had recklessly ordered them to charge our shield wall. Not many horses made it to us, and those that did died on our spears. But that day I had no hidden tricks, had not had time to prepare the ground. But I hoped that once I had sight of the enemy, something would spring to mind, some spark of cunning sent from the gods, and I would be able to lead these men to victory.

That hope flickered in my chest, right up until the moment I saw the vast horde of warriors filling the beach.

There must have been three hundred of them, and their ships' hulls filled the horizon. They clambered from the boats, feet splashing in the shallows, before running forwards to join the ever-growing wall of shields that stood between us and the sea. 'Bollocks,' I groaned, wondering, not for the first time, what *exactly* it was I'd done to offend the gods so.

'Orders, Lord Alaric,' Eadger said to me. I was in a daze, lost in the sheer scale of the wall of wood, metal and bone that faced us. I was suddenly aware of a hundred pairs of eyes fixed on me. Snapping from my reverie, I turned my head left and right, meeting every gaze I could, judging the men's morale.

'Shield wall, Gunnar in the centre. Eadger, you have the left flank, Hilde, you will command the right. It is imperative that no one gets around our wall; if we are surrounded then it is over. Understand? Good. We will form three ranks deep. Come men, into line!'

I beat the men into formation, and already there was a distinct smell of excrement and urine in the air. It had never been uncommon for a man to void his bowels in the moments leading up to battle, and I have always ridiculed those who poke fun at the men who feel the need to do so. For nothing quickens the blood more than the prospect of near certain death, nothing makes you feel more alive. If it helped a man fight better, then he could shit where he wanted as far as I was concerned.

It seemed to take an age to get the men into a shield wall. Some men literally fought to not be in the front rank, forcing their way back through their comrades, so they could stand in the relative safety of the third line. I did nothing to stop those cowards, for I needed willing men in the front rank, men with stout hearts and firm resolves. It pleased me to see Sedric on my left, Gunnar to my right. Red Beard was there, alongside Rolf, and even Rudi and Mellow stood shoulder to shoulder with Eadger on the left flank. They were warriors, proud men, who all had their flaws, but their courage had been tested once before, and none had shirked the challenge.

'We advance at the walk!' I called to the men when eventually everyone was in place. We could hear the roars of support from the walls behind us, the cries of desperate wives and mothers who begged their men to return to them alive. I heard the thud of the gate closing and turned to see Wilhelm on the balustrade above, watching on in stoic silence as his warriors marched to war. I despised him even more then, for how could a leader do nothing when his people were under attack? I knew that if I looked right, just around the bend where the beach curved off to face the east, I would see the ruins of the town of Tastris, the home that Eadger had once shared with his wife and daughter. How could a chief do nothing when the people he was charged with protecting lost everything? And how could that chief still rule?

I felt Wilhelm's eyes on my back, and we trudged further down the beach. 'Keep those shields straight!' I called as our line began to waver, as some men increased their pace, eager to meet with the enemy and get it over with. We were perhaps sixty paces off them, and I could hear the shouts of their commanders, see the bone armour they wore on top of wet trousers, the bone-tipped spears and bone-bladed swords. Eadger, it seemed, had not exaggerated their lack of iron, and I wondered if perhaps even the infamous merchants of Rome had not managed to dock their ships on the shores of this foreign people and force upon them treasures the uneducated tribesmen could never have dreamed of.

At fifty paces it became horribly clear that our line was too narrow, and the only way I could lengthen it was to take the men of the third rank and dispense them to the flanks, which is what I did. Twice I had to use the flat of my sword to force the damn cowards to depart their place of safety, but by the time we were thirty paces from the enemy, our line matched theirs. Our enemy, though, had a battle line five deep; ours was just two, and for the first time that day I felt a twinge of doubt seep up my spine. I remembered the fear that had gripped me when we had beached my Celox on this very beach, and the same warriors that flanked me then had fought the enemy to our front. I remembered seeing Ruric, his big wet eyes staring at me accusingly.

And then I felt it, the spasming, tingling knife edge grate up and down my spine, and for a moment I thought I would lose my footing. My breath was suddenly shallow, my knees buckled and I leaned into Gunnar, desperately trying to keep my footing. Hands grabbed my shoulders, and I felt Sedric's breath hot in my ear as he whispered. 'It's okay, Lord. It's going to be okay. Breathe.'

I obeyed. I closed my eye a moment, the cacophony of impending battle drowning out as my mind sought refuge. It brought me back to the small farmstead I had been raised on. My mother and father sharing a jug of ale, a waning sun bleeding out on the horizon behind them. I was young, maybe four or five, and I skipped through a field thick with weeds, dancing and twirling, doing anything I could to make my mother laugh. My parents broke from their embrace to applaud my antics, and the pride I felt in my little chest could have burst a beaver's damn.

And then I was back. I felt the warm sun on my face and wished it was the same waning sun that had set that golden night when I was a boy. I was thrust back into the noise of war, the snarling enemy crouched behind their shields, the hiss of the waves that lapped at their feet. Our own men were spitting and cursing, hoping words and taunts would fill their hearts with courage. It was not unusual for men to drink before battle. I'd known seasoned warriors that needed the strength found in the bottom of an ale jug to charge an enemy wall, for it was the hardest thing to do. And it was something I was certain my men would not do.

'Halt!' I called, and clumsily, our line stopped. The men on the flanks were too far away to hear my command, but they stopped and shuffled back as soon as they saw their comrades do the same. We stood there, dressing our line. I walked along the front of the men of the Cimbri; my men, as they were that day. My Ravensworn. I straightened shields and shared the odd joke, shouted encouragements and prayed to every god that would listen that these men would stand firm.

Our enemy was howling. We had not even allowed them the time to reach dry ground, and that too had been part of my thinking. The beach was far from ideal. It was too wide and too flat, no landmarks we could form our line between to protect our flanks. But it was the same for our enemy. And we had not allowed them the time to prepare, the time to form a plan and for their own courage to grow. Those men had just rowed across the sea; their arms would be tired, their backs sore, numb spots on their legs from sitting on the oar bench too long. I told all this to the men of the Cimbri, promised them an easy victory if they could just hold their nerve.

A promise made in battle is a futile thing though, as any veteran could tell you. I returned to my place in the line, heart still thumping, a waning sun still flickering in the corners of my mind. 'Lock your shields! Show them nothing but the whites of your eyes and your spears!'

I could feel the man behind me leaning into my back, feel the warmth of his breath on my neck. Our enemy were moving forwards now, wary in their approach. The waves lapped at their calves, and I could hear their leaders haranguing spearmen in their guttural tongue, urging them to spring forwards and break our feeble shield wall. My heart had steadied, my breathing slowed. This was what I knew, what I had dedicated my life to. Some men were born to be farmers, or smithies, to grow crops or make fine objects from molten metal. I was born to take lives, to lead men into the chaos of war. This was where I was in my element.

Finally, they charged us. I just had time to yell 'shields!' before they were on us. I winced as a warrior with an axe of bone crashed into my shield. I was rocked back, arms heaving with the pressure of the man's weight. But the man to my rear stood firm and within moments I was back up right, hacking my sword through his bone breastplate, which broke like a twig under the weight of my blade. The axeman fell from sight and I just had time to wonder how old those bones had been when I was once more under attack. A bearded warrior, spitting and cursing, leaped onto my shield and used his bare hands to try and wrench it from me. I spat in his face, roaring my own challenge, before lunging forwards with the shield, smashing it into his face then sweeping my blade underneath the willow board to slice through his bowels.

Two down. And I hadn't even gotten warmed up yet. Sedric and Gunnar fought like titans either side of me. Gunnar had already felled three men with that great axe of his, whilst Sedric had downed one and was halfway to ridding the world of another. I panted, no longer a young man. I could feel the first wave of adrenalin already waning thin. The din of battle roared in my ears, the sea air carried an iron tang of blood and I knew it would be much worse before the battle was over. Sand flew up from the blood-marked beach to sting my eye and block my nose. I could taste it on my tongue, feel it lodging between my teeth.

I lowered my head and leaned into my shield, feeling the weight of my next target on the other side. He was a short man, bald, sickly yellow teeth and foul breath that wafted between us. He tried to slide a knife around the edge of my shield, but I moved to block it and inadvertently caught his hand between my shield and Gunnar's. He screamed as he tore his hand back, dropping the knife in the process, and I took the opportunity he gave me to reach up and hack at his exposed head. He dropped; I never saw him again.

I felt the battle slow then. Felt the collective intake of breath from the opposing warriors as everyone took a moment to regain their composure and size their enemy up for weaknesses. The pressure on our shields lessened, and I could hear the leaders of our enemy shouting at their men once more, I assumed ordering them to throw themselves at us.

But it was then I heard the warning call from Hilde on the right flank, and craning my head to see, I saw my biggest fears coming true. The enemy flank was not attacking Hilde and her men who had so valiantly held them back, they were simply running around our thin line and streaming up the beach, straight for the defenceless people inside the fortress.

'Hold your positions!' I called, fearful that my men would lose heart and feed their natural urge to run back to their families. 'Gunnar, remember what you did earlier today?'

The big man nodded, sweat and blood trickling down his face. He was still grinning though. 'I need you to do that now. We are going to charge them!' I called, for there were still men opposing us. Their leader seemed to have sent men from his flanks around our wall to attack the fortress, but had left enough men to our front to prevent us from turning and giving chase. It was a clever plan, something I might well have done had I been on the other side. But we needed to break the men left on that beach as soon as we could, for every man of the Cimbri standing had people they loved behind the rotting walls of Tastris, and I didn't know how long I could persuade them to hold their ground.

'If we turn and run we are dead!' I called, and I was gratified to hear my words being repeated down the line. 'We break these men, then we get back to the fortress! On me!'

We took five steps forwards. Our enemy had retreated back into the shallows, and there they formed their new wall and awaited our attack. I waited a moment more, every moment aware of the screams from the walls back up the beach, the terrified howls of the defenceless women who could do nothing but hug their children tight as death loped towards them.

I cursed myself. Cursed myself for being arrogant

enough to think these men – who were not warriors – would be brave enough to march down the beach and face their enemy man to man. I remembered leaping from the prow of my ship, fighting my way up the beach to where a half circle of men fought around their mould-ridden gate. I should have done the same; maybe fighting in the shadow of their families would have given the men a desperate courage. But if the enemy had any sense, they would have sent men to our right and left and ordered them to scale the walls. Hell, that's what they were doing anyway.

I ground my teeth in impudent frustration, then roared a wordless war cry at the top of my lungs and ran at the enemy shields. My men followed. If it had been the Ravensworn at my back, they would have been a heartbeat behind me, already anticipating my move. But these men were not the battle-heartened warriors I had once led into war. But they showed their bravery, their desire, and with their own battle cry, they streamed after me.

I hit the enemy line with all the force of a charging boar. I crashed into a circular shield, sending the man behind it flying. With a swipe of my sword, I took out the man to his left, then smashed my shield into the face of the man to his right. And just like that, I had broken their wall. Gunnar bel-

lowed and jumped, landing almost on top of his star-
tled opponent, who fell from an axe blow he never
saw coming. Sedric was suddenly at my left shoulder, leaning his weight into his shield as he forced
two men to their knees in the sea. And then all was
chaos as the rest of the warriors of the Cimbri battered into the remnants of the shield wall, slashing
and hacking their way through until nothing stood
between them and the empty boats that rocked in
the shallows.

'Eadger!' I called as I staggered out of the battle. It
had lasted mere heartbeats, the remaining enemy not
strong enough to hold us, not brave enough to stand
and fight us. They were being slaughtered like dogs,
and in my mind I was already moving on to the next
step.

'Lord Alaric!' Eadger said as he approached. He
had a savage-looking cut under his left eye and blood
streamed down his right arm, but he seemed uncon-
cerned by both. 'We must get back to the fortress,
Lord.' He pointed up the beach, to where there were
men clambering up the timber walls.

I made a mental note to reprimand Eadger for
building such shabby walls, then refocused my
thoughts. 'I need you and four men to set these ships
alight. We need those enemy warriors to come back,

and threatening their only way of escape is the way to do it.'

'Fire?' He frowned. 'How am I going to get a fire going down here?' He waved his hands at the damp sand and the lapping waves.

'Think of something! Pick four men and get on with it! Hilde!' I turned to find her spearing a kneeling man through the chest. 'We need to get back up the beach!' She nodded, leaving the spear in the corpse's chest and moving off to get the men moving back towards the fortress.

We ran then. It was two hundred paces at most from the waterfront to the north gate, but it felt like miles. The wound in my back had split back open; I could feel warm blood and sweat running down to my legs. My lungs were on fire, legs like stone and every step was such an effort I feared I'd have no wind left in me to fight once we reached the fortress. I looked up, saw the sun still high in the sky and cursed. Surely these tribesmen would not want to be rowing back across the sea in the darkness? It had been late morning when the sentry on the wall had first alerted us to the ships in the water. How long had it taken them to row over? Three hours? More? Another half hour for them to disembark their ships, then we were marching down the beach to meet them. I cursed again, reckoning there were a good five hours of daylight left. Five more hours to stay alive.

The enemy were swarming the walls when we reached them. Eadger and his fellow carpenters had put no real thought into defending these walls when they had built them. For on the outside, they had left beams running left to right all the way up the wall, with convenient foot and hand gaps in between each one. These horizontal beams should have been on the inside, with the vertical beams on the outside. So the enemy warriors made little effort of scampering up the side. Even weighed down with bone breast-plates, helmets, shields and spears as they were, it took them a matter of moments. 'Open the gate!' I yelled with all the breath left inside my lungs as we reached the fortress. But there was no one left on the balustrade to hear my call. 'Hilde,' I said, panting. 'Get some men up the wall and get the gate open.'

'Is that wise?' she asked, but she ordered men up the wall anyway.

'It will make it easier for us to get in, and for them to get out. So yes, I'd say it's wise.'

The screams coming from behind the wall were sickening. The first black plumes of smoke were rising to the deep blue sky, and I had a sudden vision of Loki the dog locked inside my sleeping quarters.

And then I heard barking; could have been any dog, could just have been my mind playing tricks on me, but I swore I could hear the desperate yelps of a scared and lonely Loki. I growled to myself under my helmet, my tiredness all but forgotten. We stood there, the survivors from the beach, unable to do anything as the fortress burned in front of our eyes. Looking round, I saw men in tears, fearful for their families. And they had every right to be.

With a groan, the gates were finally pushed open and, like a pack of wolves entering the sheep pen, we cheered as we stalked inside. All was chaos. Enemy spearmen rampaged through the huts. Women and children were being herded into the open area outside Wilhelm's feasting hall – the doors to which remained closed. The spearmen were out of control, leaderless and fixated on rape and plunder. I'd have never allowed my men to get so out of control, not knowing there was still an enemy warband fighting a few hundred paces from where we were. But if the enemy had a leader within those walls, he was doing a piss-poor job at controlling his men, and that made life a hell of a lot better for us.

'Split into five groups of ten!' I called to the remaining men who had not run off to search for their families. I'd wanted to call them back, but there was no way I could stand over them all inside the mudded streets of the fortress. 'Discipline is our only hope now! I know you are worried for your families, but if you all run off on your own then you will die, and your wives and children will spend the rest of their lives as slaves on a foreign land. Five groups of ten, now!'

They obeyed. 'The first group will go left and stick to the wall. Make your way around the outskirts of the fortress, kill any resistance you meet. The second group will go right and do the same. Third and fourth group with Hilde, and you will take that ground outside the hall and keep those people safe. Fifth group, with me. We go through the alleys, work our way through the huts, clear these stinking rats out into the open. Is everyone clear on what they are to do? Good. Remember, stick together, work as a team, and kill as many of the whoresons as you can!'

With that, we were off.

17

We stalked through the myriad of alleys that shadowed Wilhelm's feasting hall. Smoke filled the air, choking us, and the roar of flames could be heard over the howling of terrified screams. I had ten men at my back, two of whom were Rudi and Mellow, the other eight I did not know. We went from door to door, kicking them down, hacking at any enemy spearmen we found inside before moving on to the next one. It was bloody, tiring, repetitive. By the time we had kicked down the sixth door, my right arm was bloodied to the elbow and I was once more panting like a dog.

That it was a dog we were aiming for kept me focused, kept the desperate need for water at bay. For we were getting closer to my hut. 'Fan out,' I said to the men as the mud street widened. It seemed quieter to the east of the feasting hall, and the quiet gave me a sense of unease. Up until now all had been noise and chaos, but in noise and chaos a warrior can find comfort. For this was his home, how he earnt his keep. But it was quiet in that alley, the din of sword on shield distant. And I didn't like it.

We shuffled up to my hut. It was one of the few that had a proper wooden door, rather than a canvas flap. I could hear no barking from inside, but just one look at the door told me it had been opened. I crept up to the left-hand side of the door, motioning for one of the warriors to take the right. The other men, Rudi and Mellow among them, made a ring of shields around us. Whoever came out when we opened it would find themselves trapped. Gently, slowly, I reached up and grasped the handle, and with a nod to the waiting men, ripped the door open.

In an instant the quiet was gone. A barrel of a man with a red beard and tattooed arms charged out of the hut, but he charged with such conviction he was unable to slow his momentum, and he staggered right on to a waiting spear. A shorter man came next. I caught a glimpse of a wiry frame and thinning grey hair before Mellow stepped forwards and slashed his throat with a neat cut. Another came hurtling out after, and as one of my men cut him down, I wondered just how many warriors had been holed up in that tiny hut. But that seemed to be the last of them, and it was with a sense of trepidation that I took a step inside.

The small hut had been ransacked. The pallet was on its side, my full chamber pot had been knocked over and the brazier that smoked in the corner had been upended. But I had no care for any of that; it was the bloodied furball on the floorboards that captured my attention. Loki had been stabbed four times, three in the torso, one through the neck to finish him off. Funny how a man who has often struggled to care for other people can care so much for an animal he barely knew at all. But I did care. I remembered Loki's howls as I had locked him in that very morning, and wished I'd had the sense to let him roam free. But what would he have done? Follow me onto the beach? Charge the enemy with me? He had been no great war hound to strike terror into the hearts of our enemies. Just a normal dog, who longed for someone to love him.

I lowered myself to my knees and picked him up. I mumbled to him, telling him I was sorry again and again. Old hurts resurfaced in my mind. Ketill leading a doomed charge across a lost battlefield to try and save me. Ruric cut down in a shield wall, that double-headed axe of his bloodied to the hilt. Them and so many more. I thought of Saxa and our boys, then felt another surge of guilt as I realised it was probably the first time I had thought of them all day. I stepped out of the hut and looked at the men around me. Why was I there? For a few carts of amber? What was I going to do with it all? Sell it? I still had chests of silver buried underneath my hall. I had a family; what need did I have of more coin?

'Looks like he made them pay for what they did.' It was Mellow that spoke, probably the most he'd spoken to me in the entire journey north. I followed his pointing finger to the bite marks that riddled the three corpses in the alley. The three men were covered in them – hands, legs; one even had a giant gash in his cheek.

'He was a good boy,' I said quietly. 'You men finish the search through the alleys, kill every enemy you find.'

With that, I left them to it. Tears rolled down my cheeks as I carried Loki back to the feasting hall. A sense of calm had descended. Our enemy had outnumbered us three to one or more when they'd landed on the beach. But they had been badly led, had split their forces too thin. The survivors were streaming out of the north gate; couldn't have been more than sixty of them. Some had captives over their shoulders, young women and children mostly, for who sees the worth in enslaving the old? I could see smoke and flames through the north gate and knew Eadger had managed to rustle up a fire and get their ships burning. I nodded, too drained to be satisfied.

One of the huts closest to the feasting hall was ablaze, the fire a raging torrent that would have to be left to burn out of its own accord. Hilde was already organising warriors to tear down the nearest buildings to it and create a fire break, and I paid neither her nor her men any attention as I walked up to the burning building, not bothered by the searing heat on my cheeks, and placed Loki's body onto the flames as gently as I could. 'Be at rest now, my friend,' I said quietly.

'Lord Alaric! Lord Alaric!' came an urgent call, and I ground my teeth in anger as I recognised the voice. 'Chief Wilhelm,' I said, turning to greet the man as he approached.

'Care to explain yourself, Lord?' he raged. 'I have fires inside my fortress, women and children captured, taken to be slaves across the sea! How can you have led our men to such a calamitous defeat?'

'Defeat?' I was numb. Suffering from blood loss from my open wound, exhausted from the day's fighting. And this worm, this *whoreson*, who wasn't even man enough to bed his own wife, dared to speak to me of defeat?

'Yes, Lord Alaric! Defeat! Utter defeat! What were you thinking, marching my men off down the beach like that? Why did you not stand here and defend our walls?'

'Defend your walls?' I repeated. I sighed. I had no energy for this, for a war of words with a man not fit enough to tie my boots. 'I am sorry, Lord Chief, if you are unhappy with our performance in battle. And I am sorry the enemy got inside the walls. But you have barely a hundred warriors. To defend these walls I'd need to spread them out so thin you'd maybe have a warrior every ten paces. And what good would that do? I've had half a day to train—'

'You have been here much longer than half a day! If you had spent less time fighting your own individual duels and coercing with my *wife* then you would have had more time to train my men! That *is* what I am paying you for, after all!'

I breathed deep, slowing myself down, controlling my rage. 'Again, I am sorry, Chief Wilhelm. Clearly, I am not the man you thought me to be. I shall be gone with the dawn, and I do not expect payment for the services I have given thus far. Now, if you'll excuse me.'

He raged at my back, cursing me to the gods and spitting every insult he could think of. Nothing he said made me halt in my stride though. I was weary of people and needed some time alone to gather my thoughts. 'Check on Kai,' I muttered to Sedric as he made to follow me, and the young warrior, sensing my mood, had the common sense to nod and be on his way. I walked back out the northern gate, turned east, away from the flaming ships and fleeing enemy, and went to find some solitude.

* * *

A flame flickers in the corner of my vision. I blink, unaware of where it has come from. Above me, a purple sky is ablaze with twinkling stars. The moon is half full, its light sheening over a slate-grey sea. I sit up, trying to remember how it is I have come to be lying down. There is sand in my hair, on my face and arms. And blood, so much blood.

I am cold, and I shuffle closer to the fire, pale skin shiv-

ering as I reach out with unsteady hands to feel the heat. I am not alone. I see no evidence of this, but something inside me tells me there is another presence here. I turn slowly from the fire. To my left sits a man. He is tall and well built, if a little run to fat. His iron-grey beard shines in the moonlight; his hair would do the same if it were not hidden by a drooping hat.

'So, you are awake at last,' the man says.

'Who are you?' I choke out the words, my throat as dry as charred timber. A water skin is thrown to my lap and I drink greedily, before trying to return it to the man.

'Keep it,' he says. 'Your need is greater than mine.'

'Who are you?' I ask again. I feel the fire's warmth seeping through me, feel the shivering in my jaw and hands cease.

'I have had many names over the years,' the man says. 'None of which are important now.'

'What do you want from me?'

'Nothing,' he shrugs. 'Everything. You were a great man once. A man with a reputation.'

'I was.'

'But you have fallen. Fallen so low you cannot see the light any more.'

I study this stranger who has disturbed my solitude. 'You are Him?' I ask, my voice a hoarse whisper.

He gives me a cracked smile. 'Yes, you know who I am.

I am one with whom you used to share your thoughts, your prayers, your dreams. Though it would seem the man that sits beside me now is a pale shadow of the one who schemed his way to power.'

'The sun has set on my glory days,' I say, looking down to the sand in dismay.

'No, Alaric. There are many different ways to measure a man's success. Wealth is one, glory another, and these are the tools you used to forge your path. But another one awaits you, a simpler one, and, I think, a more rewarding one.'

'Family,' I say, almost before the man has finished speaking.

'Yes. The simple life, the pleasure of seeing your children grow, the smile of your wife greeting your return from a hard day's work on the fields. You are a changed man, Alaric, and you think that change has made you weaker. It has not. The man that sits beside me has a good few years left in the sun, I would think.'

'Why are you here? To tell me what I already know?'

'To show you what it is to truly fall. These people you fight for, what have you made of them?'

'They are brave in their way, but they are no warriors. They lack any real leadership and are in desperate need of military aid.'

'And why is it, do you think, that in their desperate

hour of need their neighbours will not lift a finger to help them?'

'I do not know. There are many things about their situation I have not been told.'

'And this makes you feel uneasy.' He didn't ask, but told me, as if he could already see into my soul, or read the answer in my mind. 'You are right to feel uneasy, Alaric. Answer me this: have you seen a priest in your time here? Any sort of man of the gods at all? Do the people pray? Do they worship the same as you do?'

I chew my lip as I think, and realise the answer is no.

'There is a reason for this, Alaric. A secret the people of the land thought they could conceal in darkness. There is a pit to the south of their tired little fortress. When the sun rises, walk to it, look inside. I can promise you will find the answers to your questions. Although I cannot promise you will be happy to have them answered.'

I nod. 'I will. Why are you here? Why are you telling me this?'

'One of the names they call me, here on this middle earth, is Far Wanderer. And wander I do. I have seen many things over the long years. Few things have disturbed me as much as what I have seen here.'

He turns to face me for the first time. I see his missing eye, concealed by a black eye patch. Lost in the pursuit of knowledge. I feel lesser then, knowing I sacrificed mine in *a feeble quest for power. We stare at each other in silence for a long moment, before I feel an overwhelming need to sleep.*

'Rest now. And come the dawn, seek out the pit and find your answers.'

I lay back down, face to the flames, unable to keep my eye open. I have so many questions to ask this man, this god. But I struggle to concentrate on anything, and I drift back off into a deep sleep.

* * *

I was awoken by the red glow of the rising sun. I lay awake a moment, content to keep my eye closed. Then in a flash of remembrance I surged to my feet, throwing my head from left to right as I sought the god that had come to me in my dreams.

A dream. That was all it was. There was no grey-beard sitting with me on the sand, no evidence he had been there at all. Embers smouldered from a dying fire to the left of where I had slept. That much had been true then. I sat back down, trying to re-member what it was He had said to me. The pit, south of the fortress. I had seen it before, from the ruins of the town where Eadger had poured out the contents of his shattered heart.

Craning my neck, I looked that way, then back to the fortress. On the beach, the remains of the burnt-out ships smouldered away in the dawn, and I thought I would not be missed in Tastris a while longer. I rose, brushing sand off my armour and skin, wincing at the searing pain caused by my reopened wound.

It was only when I went to place my hand on the wound that I noticed I was carrying a half-drunk water skin.

18

I skirted the dilapidated walls of Tastris in a daze. My eye kept reverting back to the water skin in my hand. I was certain I'd not had one with me when I'd stormed out of the fortress the day before. Maybe Sedric had passed it to me as I'd left? But I did not think so.

The wind changed as I walked, and for the first time I noticed the stink coming from my blood-stained body. I needed to wash, to rest properly for a few days, a week maybe. The thought of putting my ship to sea cheered me. At sea I would find some solace, lounging on the steering oar, the wound in my side free to heal.

But first I had to see what was in this pit, whether

I had been told by a god or not. Thoughts flashed through my mind as I trudged, so many threads I still needed to bind together. Who was the man who had tried to kill me on the beach? Was it the same man who had sabotaged the equipment on the ship? It had to be, surely? And why? Why did someone want their tribe to be defeated so badly? Why did they want me to fail?

Also, there were the questions surrounding Wilhelm and his leadership of these people. Why did they put up with such a weak chief? I had seen better men usurped for lesser reasons before. To be a chief you had to be strong, brash. You had to know you were the most fearsome warrior in your tribe, that you could put down any challenger. You had to rule with a lingering fear, especially over your warriors. Wilhelm certainly did not do that. And when I thought about it, he had so few fighting men left I supposed there was no one to challenge him. Hilde could, though she seemed content enough to bed her chief's wife. Maybe that was her form of revenge on a man she despised? Though I had seen no evidence of that.

I thought so much my head began to ache. Drinking greedily from the water skin, I stopped as I reached the higher ground at the edge of the pit. It was more sand than grass, though a few stubborn patches of green fought a losing battle for dominance over the small ridge. Looking around, north to south, I saw this was as high as the ground got on this flattened peninsula. I could see the fortress, a few hundred paces to the north, and make out the tops of the heads of the men guarding the southern gate. To the east and west there was the sea, to the south just flat green land, as far as the eye could see. The sky was clear again, the sun not long risen, and already it beat down a fearsome heat.

Emptying the last of the water skin, I threw it to the ground and walked gingerly forwards, suddenly nervous at the edge of that dark abyss. It was cut into a rough square, the banks of earth and sand it had been dug from piled high around its edges. Looking back to the fortress once more, I saw the same heads, unmoving atop the southern gate. I wondered briefly if there would be a runner searching for the chief, alerting Wilhelm to my whereabouts. Was this pit something I was not meant to be looking in? Eadger had stared at it repeatedly when he and I had walked back from the ruins of Tastris. I had not wanted to ask, thinking it a mere burial pit.

But the man in the dream was haunting me, his words repeating in my head. *There is a pit, to the south of their tired little fortress. When the sun rises, walk to it, look inside. I can promise you will find the answers to your questions. Although I cannot promise you will be happy to have them answered.*

And he was right, this dream god. There were no holy men in Tastris. And that *was* odd. Why had I not thought of it before? Every tribe had priests, old men in tattered robes that thought themselves close to the gods. I'd never held much stock in them, though we'd always had a couple in the days of the Ravensworn. They had proven themselves useful to me once or twice, building the odd ghost fence from the heads of men we had slain, putting fear of a curse into our enemy if they risked a charge at our line. But on the whole, they were worthless. They put more fear into their own men than they did the enemy half the time. They stank like piss, took food and clothing they never earned, and I even had one who demanded he be allowed to sacrifice one of my own men before a battle, in honour of the great Donar. You can imagine how well that went down.

As a people, though, we were a god's fearing bunch. Even I, lost soul that I am, have spent much of my adult life worshipping Loki, and I still have a fine golden torc depicting the Allfather with his two ravens buried in a chest by my hall. As my mind wandered, I found myself hoping that the torc could still be there when I returned. Though I had doubts that even the hall would be. What a fool I had been, leaving no one to defend so much.

I was at the pit's edge now, atop the mound of sand and earth. The stench was mortifying, like a battlefield at day's end. My hunch had been correct, I was certain; this was a burial pit. So why then did I need to look inside? Dead people all look much alike when it comes down to it. Strip away our armour, our clothes, cut our hair then shed us of our skin. Bones are bones. Rich, poor, Roman, German; it doesn't make any difference. We all go to our gods on equal footing.

I edged closer, the ground loose underfoot. One hand over my nose, my one eye squinted, I peered into the darkness. What I found will stay with me for the rest of my days.

It was a burial pit, no question. But the poor souls buried there were no innocent victims of war. I saw bare bones tied together with threadbare rope. Grinning skulls loped from torsos, ribcages with yawning holes. I suspect if I had looked hard enough, I could have made out the edges of the spear blade that had punctured through bone and flesh.

It was too much. Even I, a veteran warrior of a

hundred battlefields, did not have the stomach for it. Reeling away, I wretched, gagged, then threw the contents of my stomach up onto the sand. I stood there a while, hunched over, panting like a dog. Suddenly I knew. I knew why there were no holy men left. I knew why the population was so sparce. It had little to do with war.

'You should not be here,' a voice said. I was queasy, a little dizzy, and I staggered a couple of steps, seeing double.

'What did you do?' I spat, hauling in air as I tried to regain my focus.

'I did what I had to do. For my people.'

'Murderer!' I screamed. Wilhelm didn't so much as flinch, just fixed me with that eery calm of his. I hauled free my sword, still bloodied from the previous day's fighting. 'You will pay for what you have done here.'

'Perhaps one day I shall. But it will not be today.' He made a casual gesture with his hand, and before I knew it, I had two swords pointing at my neck. Rudi held one, Mellow the other. 'You bastards,' I hissed at them, before throwing my sword to the ground.

'I shall tell you what happened here, Lord Alaric, if you have the decency to listen.'

'Spin whatever tale you wish. There is nothing you can say that will make me feel lesser of you.'

He smiled, a tight smile that didn't reach his eyes. 'I shall tell you the truth. Once I am done, you may ask me whatever questions you wish.'

'Awfully good of you, Lord Chief.' I spat again. 'Speak then.'

He took a moment to compose himself, running a small hand across his lips. The wind kicked up a stir, blowing lank hair into my face. I needed to bathe, to rest. But by all the gods I wanted nothing more than to pick up my sword and see this weasel dead. And then he spoke, and I forced myself to calm.

'A while ago we received a trade delegation from a people across the sea. It was a joint venture, two tribes who were merging into one. I assume by now you are familiar with their names.'

'The Sitones and the Suiones.'

'Correct. They were joining together in marriage and wanted to expand their horizons. In their country, amber is used as a form of currency, and it washes up aplenty on our shores. So in exchange for providing them amber, they would send us grain. As you have probably seen, the soil in our country is thin, and we relied heavily on trade with Haribert and the Anglii. But relations with Haribert have been' – he chewed on the word – 'inconsistent, shall we say.'

'So what happened?' I asked. My head swivelled from left to right as I kept my one eye on both Rudi and Mellow. Rudi had the decency to look sheepish, but Mellow grinned triumphantly, exalting in the experience of holding my life in the balance. I knew it had been him, then, who had stabbed me on the beach. Probably him who had broken into the chests on the ship, him who had hit Sedric round the head and put the fear of the gods into Kai.

I had suspected the sulking youth from the start, though some part of me had dismissed him as nothing but a miserable fool. I cursed myself for my stupidity.

'They sent a delegation of men. We negotiated for a while, eventually coming to terms. I promised them a fortune in amber, much more than Eadger has promised you. Alas, when they returned to our shores, they brought with them less than half of the grain they had promised.'

My eye was still wavering between the two swords pointing at my chest. 'So what did you do when you did not receive the grain you were promised?'

'I held a council with my inner circle. We had a priest at the time – Conrad. He worshipped the old gods. He advised we build a pit and make a sacrifice of them to the gods. With this sacrifice, he said, our fallow fields would bring us life. We would be able to live off our own land and cut our ties with the Anglii and the Sitones and Suiones.'

'So you sacrificed them, here.' I gestured to the pit.

Wilhelm nodded. 'We did. To Tuisto, the oldest of the gods, older even than the Allfather himself, we spilled blood onto His land, and in return we awaited his favour.'

'But it didn't come, did it?' I was eyeing my sword, three paces from my left hand, the blade half buried in the sand I had thrown it in. Could I reach for it before Rudi or Mellow struck me?

'Sadly, no. My people rose up in rebellion, cursing *me,* demanding *my* head! And what had I done other than listen to the one man who said he spoke to the gods? Did *they* not listen to the same man when he cast the runes for them? Did *they* not smile and weep tears of joy when he told them their children were blessed by the gods, that they would live to see them grow strong and hale?' He spat in disgust. 'But no, it was all *my* fault.'

'But you had a plan, didn't you? One more disgusting little trick to keep the people on board.'

Wilhelm smiled. 'The joy of it is, Lord Alaric, that it wasn't even my plan. Conrad spoke to the masses on a late autumn's day, a weak sun hovering above the clouds. He told them that we must make one more sacrifice, even greater than the previous! Surely then, he assured them, with such a glorious deed, the gods could not ignore us any longer.'

'You cast lots?' I guessed, risking half a step to the left, edging closer to my fallen blade.

Wilhelm nodded. 'Lots it was. There were more than a thousand of us back then, over five hundred men of fighting age. Conrad insisted every man, woman and child take part. One hundred souls would be sent to the gods, one hundred souls pledged so the rest of us might live. You have to understand that even then we were starving. We knew we had no grain to get us through the winter, relations with the Anglii had all but soured, and without the grain coming from across the sea, it would have been a hard winter, one many of our elders and children would not have survived.'

'You took a lot yourself?' I took another step. Rudi prodded his sword into my torso, telling me he was aware of my movements.

'I did. Over a thousand strips of wood were cut from the nearest trees. They were shaved down, levelled out into equal lengths. One hundred short lengths, a thousand or so longer ones.'

'Bet you made sure yours wasn't one of the shorter ones before you took it?'

'Of course! You think me a fool?'

'No. Just a coward.'

'The lots were drawn,' Wilhelm continued, ignoring my insult. 'The hundred with the short lengths were rounded up and brought here.'

I winced, picturing the scene in my head. 'And your priest? You have no holy men left here. What happened to him?'

Wilhelm shrugged, brushing some dirt off his shoulder. 'I had no further use for him.'

'So he got a short stick?'

'He seemed happy, actually, to be leading the chosen ones to meet their gods. I've always found men who claim to speak with the gods to be... somewhat erratic. He was going to meet Tuisto, to worship at the feet at the father of the gods. I like to think he found what he was looking for, though I do not think of him often.'

I felt sick. How could men like Eadger have stood by and watched this happen? A man who went on to lose his wife and child because of his chief's wickedness. I thought back then, to when I had first met

Eadger. The man had travelled hundreds of miles to find me, to bring me to this place. Why? Why had he done it? And why had Wilhelm wanted me here?

'Why did you send for me?' I asked. 'And why wait so long? You could have sent men for me last year, or even earlier. Why wait until all was lost, until your people were half starved and in need of a miracle?'

He didn't answer at first, just fixed me with a venomous gaze. 'We'd never met, before you arrived at our shores in your depressing little boat. But for a long time now, I have been hearing your name. The great Alaric Hengistson! Lord of the Ravensworn! Vanquisher of a thousand foes, victor of a hundred battles! Kings kneel at your feet, chiefs quiver when you ride through their land! We've all heard the stories, Alaric, and I for one have grown sick of them.

'I had an agreement with your father-in-law, an agreement set in stone, that your wife, Saxa, would be mine. An alliance with the Chauci would benefit my people greatly, sandwiching Haribert and the damned Anglii between us. What an alliance it could have been! What good we could have done! But no, *you* barged in, stealing *my* wife! And then what did you do? You rode off into the east and got your arse handed to you by the Romans!

'I tried again then to get Chief Dagr to change his

mind, but he would not be deterred. The vowels had been spoken, hands shaken; he would stand by you.'

'Seems you took that personally.' I could have pointed out that Dagr went on to wage war against me, the war that eventually brought me down, but I chose not to.

'The indignity of it! You were nothing! *Are* nothing! And yet you, the son of a nobody, leader of no one, would get the hand of a chief's daughter, whereas I would get nothing.'

'You seem to have found another bride without too much trouble,' I said.

'A woman lover! Gods break me! Another stick I am destined to be beaten with!' There was a shadow moving slowly through the grass, about ten feet from where Wilhelm stood. I caught it out of the corner of my eye, but I didn't want to alert anyone by staring at it. I looked once more at my sword.

'Sure does seem an odd dynamic, what you, Isvilt and Hilde have going on. Anyway, back to the matter in hand. Why am I here? You knew I'd been defeated out east, knew I'd no army to come and save you, though you sure as shit seem to have told your people that. So why drag me up here? I was a depressed drunken, just so you know. Couldn't have had many winters left, the way I was going.'

'I wasn't going to let you die quietly in your hall, Lord Alaric. After all, you didn't offer the same courtesy to my good friend Warin, a king no less, when you slaughtered him in his own bedchamber.'

And there it was. Once again, my past was catching up with me. I'd slaughtered Warin, killed his wife too, a woman I had once coveted myself, until I learned of her parentage, anyway. But it had been Warin that had brought about my downfall, Warin who I had gone east in a blind rage to kill. If only I had listened to the men around me, Ruric would still be at my side, chewing my ear off for getting us into another scrap.

'So you brought me here to die. That I can believe. What I don't get is where that leaves you? Your people will still be slaughtered victims of a war you started with your greed. How do you plan on getting out of this hole you've dug?' The shadow moved again, edging closer.

'Oh, don't worry about me, Alaric, I have it all worked out—'

He never got the chance to tell me. Eadger erupted from his hiding place, sword in one hand, a hammer in the other. He cleaved down with his sword, the blade biting through Wilhelm's skull as blood erupted into the morning air. Quick on my feet,

I danced around the point of Rudi's sword, knocking his arm wide as he looked on in shock as his chief collapsed to the ground. I had a hand around his throat before he knew what had happened, his sword fallen to the sand. 'Drop your weapon!' I shouted at Mellow, seeing with pleasure the smirk had been wiped from his face.

'Keep it in your hand, boy,' Eadger growled. 'I'd rather kill you in a fair fight.'

'No!' I said to Eadger. 'We need these two alive. I have questions for them, questions I need answering.'

The big man didn't take his eyes from Mellow, but he nodded after a time. 'Guess you'll have some for me too.'

'Aye, I will at that. Take his sword before he gets any stupid ideas,' I said to Eadger, gesturing to Mellow. 'And then these two traitors can drag *that* back to the fort, for all to see.'

Eadger and I watched as Rudi and Mellow picked up the corpse of their chief, and then we followed them back into Tastris.

19

'You speak first,' I said to Eadger. Rudi and Mellow had dragged Wilhelm's corpse through the mud-ridden streets of Tastris, throwing the body on the floor outside his hall. If anything, the greater feeling among the surviving citizens of the Cimbri seemed to be nothing more than disinterest.

That confirmed to me that their chief meant nothing to them. That he had been a ruler in name only and not a man his people respected. And that was good. The last thing I needed then was a revolt, a panicked population rising up and causing chaos in a time that was already drenched in their warrior's blood. What I needed was a moment of calm, to think. And to learn.

'I don't know where you want to me start,' Eadger said, his voice melancholic.

We were in Wilhelm's old bedchamber, shut away from the noise outside. Rudi and Mellow were with us, of course. Hands bound, they sat on stools in the corner of the room, and I disdained to look at them until I was ready for them to speak. Sedric was with me, stood at my right hand. He had wanted to kill the two brothers the moment we returned and I had given him a brief overview of everything I had learned. But I had calmed him for now, though I could feel the anger pouring from him. This venture north had already taken one friend from him, and though Kai was not dead, he would never be the same carefree youth who had drunk and whored freely with Sedric. For that he wanted revenge, and in good time, I would let him have it.

Isvilt and Hilde made up our little party, the former pouring wine into cups whilst the latter lounged on her dead lord's bed. Neither seemed to feel the loss of their chief greatly. Again, I was not surprised.

'Start with what you told me in the ruins of your sad little town. Begin with your wife and daughter. I want to know how much of the tale you spun me was true. It was quite a performance, if that's what it was.

Perhaps you should think of going to Rome; from what I hear there are always openings for actors in their theatres.'

Light flooded in through the room's only window, the odd patch of darkness marking the passage of clouds. It took Eadger a while to find his voice, and he picked his words carefully when he did.

'All of what I said was true, Lord.' He took an offered cup of wine from Isvilt and drained its contents in a single gulp, leaving a red stain in his beard that trickled down like blood.

'Then what *didn't* you say? What did you happen to skip over when you told me the story of your woes?'

'The offering,' Eadger mumbled, his eyes fixed on a time somewhere in the past. 'It happened before my wife and daughter were taken from me. The first one, anyway.'

'You are referring to Conrad suggesting to Wilhelm that it would be a good idea to offer up the missionaries from the Sitones and Suiones to Tuisto?'

'Aye.' Eadger nodded, his face twisting into a bitter grimace. 'Was a bad business, that. And we all knew it too. Wilhelm had people queueing outside his hall to petition against it for two days straight, but he wouldn't listen.'

'Was there anyone who really believed that slaughtering innocent people would make this sand-ridden soil you farm more fertile?' I aimed the question at them all. None of them, not Isvilt, Hilde, Eadger or the twins bound in the corner, had the courage to meet my eye.

'Conrad spoke well, he always did. Seemed to a lot of us that if he said it would happen, then it would.'

'Fucking priests.' I spat on the floor before draining my own cup of wine. Isvilt rose silently to refill it, doing her best to keep out of my line of sight. 'So what happened next?'

'There was chaos, for a while. Of course, nothing changed, our crops grew no taller, and without the promised grain from across the sea we grew hungry. It was clear to all of us that we would not last out the winter. I remember one day in the autumn, I was replacing some split wood on the granary walls; the chamber could only have been a third full. Even if it had been full to the rafters, I doubt that would have been enough to see us through to spring. Winter is tough up here. The wind rolls in off the sea, bitter cold like you wouldn't believe. And then Chief Haribert came up from the south, that brat of a son with him.'

'Sigimund?' I'll admit that caught me by surprise. That 'brat', as Eadger called him, had done me much harm already, but I had thought his part in this story done.

'Aye, Sigimund. He made quite an impression on our chief; some might say it was even him who planted the idea of another sacrifice into Conrad's mind in the first place.'

'Why do you think that?' I stood up straight suddenly, some sense within me telling me I was about to uncover another venomous snake in this pit of lies.

'Because he did. I saw it happen with my own eyes.' Isvilt spoke for the first time. 'We were in the main hall, at the top table. Chief Haribert had heard tales of a sacrifice being made to the gods, a sacrifice of innocent people from across the sea. He wanted to come here personally to see if it was true. He was concerned that his lands would be raided in retribution.'

'So what happened?' I thought back to my conversation with Haribert, of the warning he had given me. The man had known some of what was afoot here, that had been obvious, and I thought I should have taken more heed of his words.

'Haribert had harsh words with Wilhelm. He told my husband that there would be no support from the

Anglii if we ended up at war with the Sitones and Suiones. Sigimund, though, spent the evening whispering into Conrad's ear. They had not been gone two days when Conrad first voiced his suggestion.'

'Aye,' Eadger chipped in. 'By that point, Wilhelm was facing a full-blown rebellion. There were men in the streets ready to spill his blood.'

'So *how* did this Conrad manage to convince you all that *another* sacrifice was what was needed?' I rubbed my face in frustration. 'It makes no sense to me!'

'No, I don't suppose it would.' Hilde spoke. She rose from the low bed and ran a hand through Isvilt's hair, before drinking from her wine cup. 'But you never met Conrad. When he spoke, especially to a large crowd, he was captivating. He was not a native of the Cimbri, had come to us from the east, said he had been serving Agnarr, King of the Suebi.'

I cursed, throwing my now empty wine cup to the floor. That name was one I had not heard in a while, and I had no interest in hearing again. Agnarr was my father, my *real* father, not the man who had raised me. Though I had not found that out until late in life, and I was still not sure how holding that knowledge made me feel. But I did know he had been a powerful man in his day; other chiefs bent the knee too. You couldn't say that about many of the war chiefs in Germania. 'So, this priest turns up one day from the south, gives it the large about who he has served and where he has been, and you lot lap it up. Is that the right of it?'

'Aye. That's about it,' Hilde said, eyes fixed to her boots.

'He told us this had been done before, that he had performed the rights and seen first-hand the rewards Tuisto lavished on those who asked for his help.'

There was silence for a while as I digested this. I could not believe in the stupidity of it all. There I was, thinking I had become embroiled in some great conspiracy, but all there was to it was a lunatic priest, a desperate, weak chief, and a tribe of people too naïve to see they were being duped. 'You know what the Romans would call you all, don't you?' I said after a time. 'Provincials. Stupid fucking provincials. And do you know what? They would be right to. I can't believe that you lot could be so fucking stupid! Your chief, who you all knew to be a coward, saw the chance to effectively steal a ship's worth of grain, so he jumped on the chance to murder the Sitones and Suiones without paying them their amber – which, by the way, washes up on the shores of your beaches! It's not like you have to work hard to find it!

'And if that wasn't enough, when things grew desperate for him, when his people were finally starting to see the cracks appear in his leadership, he gets his priest to throw out the idea of a mass sacrifice, only this time using his own people rather than some strangers from across the sea!'

Silence and shamed faces greeted my words. 'How badly were the lots rigged by the way, for the second sacrifice?'

No one wanted to answer at first. I was close to freeing my blade when Isvilt finally broke the silence. 'None of the men of fighting age were drawn, their wives and children mostly spared too. We made sure it was the old and infirm that took the greatest risk, leaving most of the longer rods in one pile, which were drawn by Wilhelm and those closest to him, before any of the other people had the chance to draw theirs.'

'I was not aware of that,' Hilde said.

Eadger shook his head. 'Me neither.'

'Again, did no one think to question this? Was it not *at all* obvious to any of you what was happening?' Gods, I was tired. I was tired of that place, of those people. I was tired of the wound in my back burning every time I moved. I thought back to my meeting with Him the night before, if it had happened at all. I remembered what he told me, about how I had measured greatness in my past, and how I should be measuring it now. I thought of Saxa and my boys, and I yearned for home.

'I think, Lord, that we were all in a trance. All too shocked about what was happening, so desperate to believe in anything that would see our children through winter that we clutched on any straw that was offered.'

I paused then, breathed, and tried to put myself in their position. They were an isolated tribe, up there on that peninsula. They were not surrounded by fertile fields, by neighbouring tribes eager to trade and offer support to one another – although admittedly, that was a rare thing in those days. But they were lacking a leader, direction, and worrying themselves to sleep each night about how they were going to keep their children fed through winter. I thought once more of my boys. The gods knew I had been no model father, but I would have done anything to see those boys went for nothing. That was part of what drove me to go there in the first place, to that gods cursed fort on the sea. I kept breathing, in and out, nice and slow, calming myself. These people were not to blame. The man who had been was a near-headless corpse, slung to the dirt outside his own hall.

'How long was it after the sacrifice that the next ships came?' I said to Eadger.

'The sacrifice was late summer. The ships came with the spring.'

'And it was how you described it? When you spoke in the town?'

'Aye. Aye, it was.' A single tear rolled down Eadger's cheek.

'Did they not make any further effort to talk with Wilhelm?'

Eadger looked to Isvilt for guidance, unsure of what to say. Isvilt in turn looked to Hilde, who cleared her throat before she spoke. 'They only came here for war, after. But we did hear word of a ship beaching further south, and a small party of men being greeted by a group of local warriors. There was no battle fought, but words were shared. We don't know any details.'

'They beached on Haribert's lands?'

'Yes. But Haribert was away south at the time, we think with the Chauci.'

I put the remaining pieces together myself. 'So, it was Sigimund that met them on the beach. No doubt with the same group of hangers-on that had the misfortune of bumping into us.'

'Aye, that's the story,' Eadger said.

Sigimund. So the little shit had been stirring the pot this whole time. 'Was any effort made to reach out to the Anglii? To speak with Haribert when he returned?'

'Wilhelm sent word. There were a few of us who would not let him get away with not.' Hilde was filling her wine cup once more as she spoke. I was starting to get a feel for the hatred she held for her former chief, and I wondered how she had gone so long without killing the man herself.

'And what word came back?'

'You saw how he was with his son when they were here,' Isvilt said. 'He thinks the sun shines out the boy's arse. He got how many of his friends killed when he attacked you? And for what? A pointless skirmish on a nameless beach. The boy is disturbed, but cunning. I'd wager, and I know I'm not the only one to think so' – she shot Eadger and Hilde a pointed look – 'Haribert did nothing to punish him, even after you told him what happened on that beach. He just laughed and watched on as you killed one of his most valued men. There is a sickness in the boy, but he is his father's only son, and Haribert remains blind to his flaws.'

I nodded, thinking of Haribert's reaction when I had told him his son had had the nerve to attack my shield wall. For all that though, Haribert struck me as a decent man who led his tribe well. I thought again of my sons then, and whether I would be able to see through my love for them if they ever grew to be as poor a man as Sigimund had. I thought I would, but until you've had to face it, I guessed no man really knew. 'So Sigimund meets them on a beach and tells them what has happened to their men. He then promises them what? What do they gain from attacking you? Apart from the obvious revenge. And to keep coming back the way they have been? There's more than blood lust driving them, I'd wager my life on it.'

'Land,' a voice said from the corner of the room.

No one spoke for a long moment as each of us in turn craned our necks to peer into the corner of the room, where two forgotten brothers sat with their hands bound. 'Say that again?' I said.

'Land. It's obvious when you think about it.' It was Rudi who spoke. Mellow sat with his head to the floor, trying to rub some life into his bound wrists.

'Is it?' I moved towards him, lowering myself to a crouch when I reached him so I could look the lad in the eye. 'Seems to me you might know something we don't. Speak now, boy, and you might have a chance of getting out of this room alive.'

Rudi sighed, his eyes roaming around the room, giving each of us a weary look in turn. 'The Suiones and the Sitones, they need more land. Think about it. We know nothing of their country, of what other peoples dwell across the sea. There is a reason these people are reaching out west, across the water. Why would they not look east? We've all heard tales of the great eastern steppe, of the endless sea of grass that stretches across the horizon. Why can they not gain land there? Why could they not provide the grain they promised? Something, *something* is driving them away from the east. There is more to their needs than we know, of that I am certain.'

I considered this a moment and found myself nodding in agreement. I had no knowledge of these people from across the sea. Perhaps they never intended on trade between them and the Cimbri? Perhaps they'd had eyes on something else all along. Whether they had or they hadn't, I couldn't bring myself to care. From what I saw, they were an innocent people, wronged by Wilhelm, and now hell bent on revenge. That was a sentiment I could understand.

'Was it your chief who told you those pretty lies?' I asked Rudi. 'What did he tell you about me?'

'You? What do you mean?' Rudi scrunched his nose up at me, as if the mere thought of me offended his nostrils. In truth, it might have. I was still covered in blood from the previous day's fighting.

'When he sent you south with Eadger to find me. What was it he told you to do? I know it was you two little shits that broke open those chests of weapons and mail, no point denying it now, lad. You've shown all of us your true colours today.'

Eadger growled in agreement, and I could feel the energy building in Sedric, the man desperate to be the one to end their lives. Rudi and Mellow shared a look, Rudi still with his face scrunched up. 'What are you talking about? I told you that had nothing to do with us!'

'One of you little cunts did this to me!' Sedric suddenly bellowed, his simmering rage finally boiling over. He pointed to the scab on top of his head, still red and livid from the blow he had received below deck on our journey north. 'And I want to know which one of you it was.'

'That wasn't us! I told you, Alaric, on the bloody ship when you threw my brother overboard that we had nothing to do with it. I wasn't lying then, and I ain't lying now.'

I remembered the earnest look on Rudi's face that day, the honesty I saw in his eyes. My gut had told me then that they were innocent, and it was telling me the same thing now. 'So why did you agree to come after me with Wilhelm today then, if you weren't secretly in on his little scheme all this time?'

'Because you threw me into the fucking sea!' Mellow yelled, his voice shrill with emotion. 'You threw me in there to die! All because you didn't like the look of me!'

I had to admit, he had the right of it there. 'Came in for you though, didn't I? Not like I left you there to drown.' It was a weak come back, and I knew it. 'Guess I know who gave me this wound on the beach, though,' I said, still looking at Mellow.

'That wasn't me.'

'It wasn't him! On our honour, it wasn't him,' Rudi added, and once more I reluctantly agreed it might not have been. 'So tell me what you know. Why were you out there at the pit with Wilhelm today? What did he offer you for my death?'

The brothers shared another look before Rudi shrugged, seemingly not seeing the point in holding back. 'Gold.'

'Gold?' Isvilt snuffed. 'Wilhelm had no gold, you fools!'

Rudi shrugged. 'Said he did. Said he had a hole chest, buried under the back of his hall, beneath the rushes where the cattle wintered.'

I puffed out my cheeks, leaning back on a stool to take the weight off my back. 'Know anything about this?' I asked Hilde, who had laid silently on her dead lord's bed throughout this exchange.

'News to me,' she said. 'Guess there's only one way to find out though?'

20

We made Rudi and Mellow dig. Seemed only fair. The rest of us stood or crouched in a semi-circle around the deepening hole, eating watery oats and drinking ale. I was bone tired. My brain, though, was wired, and I could not stop thinking about Wilhelm and Sigimund, and Him, the god that had stalked my dreams the previous night.

I'd asked Sedric if he had passed me a water skin the previous day when I had stormed out of the fortress and away from Wilhelm's lashing tongue. He'd just shrugged, but the lad looked as knackered as me, and for that I couldn't blame him. Sedric was no veteran; he was just a kid from the country who, until a few days ago, had never seen the horrors of war. He'd seen enough now to last him a lifetime, and if he made it home, I wouldn't begrudge him if he decided to pack up and go back where he came from. In my youth I had despised young men who chose the plough over the sword, but right then I was envious of my father and his little patch of land in the middle of nowhere. The simple life. The peaceful life.

'Sedric,' I found myself saying, 'when this is done, when we go back south, I want you to go home, back to your family. Leave all this' – I gestured to the dried blood on my tunic – 'behind. Go back to your family, learn a trade, do anything. But don't spend your life doing this.'

He said nothing for a moment, just chewed on his soggy oats. 'You are my family, Lord,' he said. 'I had nothing when I came to you. My parents were killed when I was still a child, and I roamed from place to place, doing what I could to earn my keep. No one gave me a home though, until I met you. You took me in, fed me, trained me, and treated me well. You are the great Alaric Hengistson! And it is my honour to serve you and call you Lord.'

I'm not ashamed to admit I felt hot tears on my cheek then, and an overwhelming urge to reach out and hug the lad tight. I thought of Batur, the poor youth lost to the sea, and thought he would have probably said something similar to me, right up until the moment he was flung down my ship and propelled to a watery grave. Young Kai, too, still healing from life-changing wounds in a small, lank chamber, just down the hall from where I sat. Would he say it was all worth it? Worth the blood, the loss?

An image of Ruric flashed through my mind. My trusted old right-hand man in the Ravensworn. He had tried to warn me once – no, he had flat out told me that I had gone too far, that I was letting my men die for my need for revenge. If only I had listened. Maybe I still would be the great Alaric Hengistson, lord of five hundred battle-hardened warriors. I certainly wouldn't have ended up there, on that sun-drenched peninsula north of nowhere, digging for a fool's gold.

I pictured Saxa and our boys, and sent a swift prayer to the gods that they were well. I was sure they were, being with her father and his people. Dagr and I may not have always seen eye to eye, but he had given me his daughter in marriage all the same, and I knew he thought the world of her. I wondered if Saxa had indeed ventured to my father's small farmstead and given the old man the opportunity to spoil his grandsons rotten. I smiled at the thought, tears still leaking from my one good eye.

'Lord?' Sedric said, and I realised I had been silent a while.

'You're a good lad, Sedric. No, a good man. You are far more than I deserve. If I've never told you before, then let me tell you now that I value you more than you could ever know. You, Kai, poor Batur; you lads stood by me when I had nothing to give. I never questioned why. Maybe I didn't want to hear your answers. But whatever drove you three to my door, I am grateful that it did.'

'As am I, Lord. You taught us all so much; you just didn't realise you were doing it.'

Eadger moved towards the pit the brothers were digging, squatting down to get a better look. The Cimbri still had a few half-starved cattle that lived in the cramped space at the back of the hall. My guess was they had judged a small supply of milk daily was worth more than butchering the beasts and giving the tribe one good meal. Though for what it was worth, I doubted there was enough meat on the cows to feed fifty men. We had eased the animals out into the open, then closed the back doors to shut ourselves away from prying eyes. Rudi and Mellow had swept back the lank rushes to expose the floorboards, and Rudi had not hesitated when asked which ones should be prised up.

And so we had set them to digging, and it appeared they had almost reached the required depth. 'A chest!' Eadger called as Mellow's shovel thumped onto something with a clank. The brothers eased the last of the dirt from the top to reveal an unremarkable wooden crate, no bigger than a newborn babe. I confess to feeling a little underwhelmed. In my mind, the chest would be four foot long, and at least two deep. For that was the size of the chests I had dug under my own hall, filled with mail and weapons, a few remaining with silver.

But everyone else was elated, whooping and cheering as the chest was wrenched from the earth. 'That sly bastard,' Isvilt had muttered, and I'll admit to being surprised she had no knowledge of it. Though in truth their marriage had been nothing but a sham, so in hindsight it did not surprise me in the least that Wilhelm would have held something back from her.

Rudi dropped it onto the floorboards and we all huddled around excitedly, impatient to see what we had discovered. The chest was fitted with a simple lock, easily smashed off with the hilt of a knife. Eadger tore the broken lock away and threw open the chest... and we all groaned in disappointment.

Three sodding coins sat at the bottom. Three

coins. Cursing, I picked one up, turning it over to see the image of Emperor Nero on the reverse side. Old coins then, and Roman ones at that. Intrigued, I tossed it back to the chest and turned on Isvilt and Hilde. 'You two ever heard of the *frumentarii*?'

'The what now?' Hilde said with a frown. I turned from her and stared at Isvilt, seeing the doubt wash over her face. She didn't speak, but nodded.

'When were they here?' I asked, rising to my feet. I could feel the anger building within me, once more faced with my old nemesis: Rome.

'A long time ago, seven or eight years maybe?'

I focused on my breathing, feeling a slight tremble in my hands. Seven or eight years, so around the time I myself had come across a *frumentarii* agent. That agent had been lurking at the home of a minor chief of some inconsequential tribe, Wulfric, if I remember correctly, chief of the Fenni, not that they were much of a tribe. He had been the man to gift me the golden torc of the Allfather, twinned by his ravens, Huginn and Muninn. Thought and memory. How very apt. I wondered briefly if the ravens had been present when He had met me on the beach, if He had even been there at all. I wasn't sure they had been. But that agent had been real, and he had followed me north and west, to the home of my good friend Ketill. There we had slaughtered him together.

I was pacing up and down, lost in my thoughts. 'Alaric?' Eadger asked. 'What is it? What are the *frumentarii?*'

'How long were you and Wilhelm married?' I asked Isvilt, ignoring Eadger for the moment.

'Six years,' she said.

'And did you come here before the marriage?' She shook her head. 'So how do you know of the *frumentarii?*'

'For the gods' sake, Alaric! Will you please tell us what is going on?' Eadger was on his feet now. I cast a look at the others and saw all their eyes on me.

'They were here a year or so before Wilhelm and I were married. I know this because I remember Wilhelm and my father discussing the man's proposal together when the marriage was agreed.'

'Do you remember his name?' She shook her head again, fear in her eyes, and I realised that I was visibly bristling with anger. 'To answer your question, Eadger, the *frumentarii* are Rome's network of spies. Grain men, they call them in the empire. Officially, they operate in and around a marching legion, tasked with ensuring the soldiers never go hungry. Unofficially, they are spies. They walk foreign lands, whispering in ears, making false promises. They are half the reason our people will never be able to rise up and defeat Rome. For when any one tribe becomes too powerful, the *frumentarii* pay two others to go to war with them.'

Now I'll be the first to admit that for a few years, Ravensworn and I profited handsomely from this. We would take one chief's coin, help him win his war, then ride off into the sunset, chests filled with silver. It wasn't until I'd been doing that a while that I started to realise where the silver was coming from.

'It wasn't long before my downfall, before I lost my men and my status out in the east, that I came across one of these agents. His name was Ambrosius Trajianus Valerius – quite the mouthful. He had been tasked with bringing me down and was scouring our lands, putting gold in chiefs' pockets, trying to or-ganise a war against me.'

'Why would Rome want *you* dead so badly?' Rudi scoffed, and Mellow joined in his mirth.

I smiled, one of my wolf grins to let the pup know that I was still a dangerous man. 'I wasn't always an old drunk, young Rudi. I once commanded an army, an army unrivalled in our lands. I was a threat to Rome, openly hostile to them. They wanted me gone. To cut a long story short, I killed the fool who thought he could walk our lands and set my own people against me. Then I travelled south, across the Danube, and killed the man who controlled the *frumentarii*. To my knowledge, Rome haven't sent one north of the river since.'

'So why does it matter if this Valerius, or whatever his name was, came here eight years ago?' Eadger asked. 'And what does it have to do with us fighting off the Sitones and Suiones?'

I had to admit I didn't rightly know. But there was something bothering me. Why would Valerius have come all the way up here? I'd had no quarrel with the Cimbri back in those days. Sure, we had fought on the opposite side of a conflict once or twice over the years, but if I counted every tribe I'd fought against as an enemy then I'd have no friends at all. Oath breaker, that's what they had called me back in the day. A title I knew I'd earned.

'Just seems odd that Rome would bother to send an agent all the way up here. I don't mean any offence to you people, but you are a small tribe, tucked out the way. What did Rome think they were buying with gold?'

'It had something to do with your wife, I think,' Isvilt said in a small voice. 'Wilhelm was raging to my father, saying how insulting it was that he had been unable to marry into the Chauci – that he would have to marry me instead.' She spat on the rushes, her disgust evident in her tone.

I felt for her then, that poor young girl forced into a marriage with a cretin like Wilhelm. But then my thoughts turned to my own wife, Saxa, and I wondered if she had held me in as much contempt when we were wed. I thought I knew the answer to that, but didn't want to linger on it. 'He told me that, up by your burial mound. I had no idea of his prior agreement with my father-in-law, though it still does nothing to explain why a Roman agent bothered to venture this far north. Or what interest he would have in the marriage of Wilhelm.'

'I think I know,' Hilde said. She stood suddenly, her eyes wandering to the small chest and the three gold coins within. 'There were twelve coins in there originally. I was there, holding a shield for Wilhelm, when the Roman came.'

I gave an exasperated sigh. 'Why are you just mentioning this now?'

She shrugged. 'I'd forgotten all about it. To be honest, I wasn't even sure the man was a Roman.'

'Wasn't sure he was a Roman?' I spat. 'They look completely different to us, smell completely different!

Plus there's the small fact that they speak another fucking language!'

'Well, how am I supposed to know? We don't live near the border. I'd never seen a Roman before,' she said in a sulking tone.

Allowing myself a moment of calm, I reasoned she was probably right. Most of our people probably couldn't tell you a Roman from a Saxon. It was only the tribes that lived bordering the Rhine and the Danube that had any cause to interact with Rome, and then usually only to shed blood. 'Tell me what you remember,' I asked.

'A man came to see Wilhelm. He cleared the hall, which was rare enough, but me and one other stayed and stood over him, each carrying a shield, looking as menacing as we could. This man came in. He was short, thin, no beard, spoke through a translator. Have to admit I wasn't paying much attention to what they were saying, but I do remember Wilhelm being offered a bride and something about the Chauci.'

'Kind of you to tell me this!' Isvilt exclaimed, though I saw the playful smile she threw her lover. I found myself momentarily distracted, wondering how these two came to be together. Figured that was a question for another day.

'I'm sorry. I was young, my only interest was the sword. I had no care for tribal politics or strategic marriages.' She was silent a moment, her face scrunched up in thought. 'I think the marriage between Wilhelm and Saxa was a building block in relations between us and the Chauci. The Roman wanted an alliance between the northern tribes. An alliance against you.'

She looked right at me, and I nodded. That wasn't news to me. That alliance had existed. I'd fought it, and I'd lost. If that's all there was to it, then Rome's scheming had already done its worse. I had the scars to prove it.

'None of this explains one thing though,' Eadger said, closing the chest and pushing himself to his feet.

I arched an eyebrow. 'What's that then?'

'If it wasn't these two who broke into the chests on the ship and knocked Sedric out with a rock, then who was it?'

That brought me back to my senses. Talk of Roman conspiracies and battles long lost was all well and good, but Eadger was right. That *frumentarii* agent was long dead, as was my army. What was happening now could surely have nothing to do with them. 'Let's talk through your men. Start with Rolf. How long have you known him?'

Eadger puffed out his cheeks. 'Years. He was a carpenter, same as me. We worked together on the walls, this hall even. He's Cimbri through and through.' I thought of the man diligently stitching Kai's wounds after our skirmish with Sigimund on that beach. I found Rolf to be a good man, if a bit unremarkable. But then he had one of those faces that could disappear in a crowd, an unobtrusive nature. Two traits that would serve a spy well.

'And Gunnar?' I did not want to suspect the big man. He had fought by my side, and fought well, and his smile was infectious. It would have been a blow if he had been deceiving me this whole time.

'What you see is what you get,' Eadger said. 'He's a simple man, but an honest one. I'd wager my life on that.'

'You might just have to,' I muttered, but I was relieved to hear him say it all the same. 'That just leaves Red Beard.'

Eadger nodded. 'Aye, Red Beard. I've not known him as long, and he isn't native to the Cimbri. He came north five years ago, part of the escort that came with Conrad. He was a warrior, never held sway by any other craft, and the gods knew we needed fighting men. He's never given me reason to doubt him though,' Eadger added quickly, holding up his hands.

'But if it isn't these two pups' – I gestured to Rudi and Mellow – 'and it isn't Rolf or Gunnar...' I let it hang in the air.

'Well, it damn well isn't me!' Eadger said.

'Then...?'

Eadger sighed. 'Aye. What shall we do?'

'Find him, bring him to me. Sedric, would you go and see if Kai is up? Bring him here if he is.'

Eadger and Sedric walked off into the main part of the hall, and I found my eye wandering through the slits in the wood by the rear door. I moved towards it, thinking of opening it and letting in some fresh air, for there was nothing there that needed to stay hidden from the people of Tastris, when I saw a shadow flicker between the gaps in the door. I drew my sword, took three giant steps forwards and ripped the door open, pouncing out into the open, hoping to catch whoever had been spying on us before they could escape.

But there was no one there, just a hint of wind rolling down the muddy street. I stayed there a long while, looking left and right, but nothing moved. Eventually, I turned back to the hall, and it was only then that I saw the footprints on the mud. Footprints that forged a very distinctive pattern. And then I realised where I had seen them before.

21

'And you can't find him anywhere?' I was in the main hall, seated on what should have been Wilhelm's stool, drinking ale and thinking. Outside, the sun was bleeding out in the west. I heard birds call and dogs bark, which made me sad as I just thought of Loki. Wilhelm's body was still in the dirt outside the front door, which was fine by me. There were maybe thirty other people in the hall; each had walked past the body of their chief, though so far, none had asked in my hearing how he had come to be dead.

'Nowhere, Lord. I've got men out on the beach, as well as going through every hut left standing inside the fortress. He's just vanished.' Eadger was opposite me, rubbing tired eyes with his hands. Gunnar stood behind him, eating, as always. Wouldn't want to let the small matter of a traitor keep him from his dinner.

'And you're sure about the boots?' This I directed to Gunnar, who swallowed his bread before replying. 'Aye, sir. Said he took them from a dead Roman soldier a few years ago.'

'Hmm.' I nodded. It was the boot prints on the floor outside the hall that had me thinking. See, Roman soldiers wear studded boots, or sandals, depending on the time of year. But those iron studs made a certain imprint on the ground. I'd seen it a thousand times before – the last time being on a wet deck in the hold of my ship. No German boot made that print; our boots were poor things in comparison, as admittedly were our swords, helmets and armour. We had established earlier that day that Red Beard was the traitor, and now I was wondering just how far back his treachery went. For a moment, I regretted the death of Wilhelm, for if there was anyone to help us unravel the mystery it was he. The man had been a weasel, and a coward. I was certain he would have told me all I needed with just the threat of a burning blade. Smiling at the thought, I turned at a flicker of movement from the corner of my eye and saw Kai enter the hall, and my smile widened.

I rose to meet him, almost crushing him with my embrace. He was stick thin, but there was more colour to his face, and his hair had lost that lank, sweaty look that bears all the signs of a man lost to fever. The wounds on his cheeks looked healthier too. The swelling had receded and the wounds scabbed over. I didn't think the lad would ever be handsome again, but it was nothing a good beard could not conceal – when he got old enough to grow one, anyway. 'You're looking better, my young friend. How do you feel?'

'Okay,' he said with a slur, then held out a wavering hand, tilting it from side to side. 'Hunwey,' he managed to say, and immediately Eadger was on his feet, on the hunt for soup. Kai and I sat down and I poured the lad some ale. He drank greedily and messily, the ale spilling down his cheeks and soaking his tunic. I made no comment, the lad had been through enough, and it was good to see him out of his small room. Eadger came back with soup and spoon, warning Kai it was hot before sitting back down.

'So what do you want us to do?' he asked me once Kai was tucking into his first proper meal in days.

I pinched my nose and forced myself to think clearly. In my fixation with Wilhelm and plots and traitors, I had all but forgotten that our last battle with the enemy had only been the day before, and we'd had to fight them through the streets of the fortress. 'How are the people? After yesterday. How many warriors did we lose?'

'Ten dead, three injured, but not badly. Not disastrous, I don't think. By the gods Alaric, but we were holding them down on the beach! I never thought I'd see the day.'

I nodded, sucking my teeth. It seemed so long ago, felt as if so much had happened since then. 'So how many fighting men does that leave us?'

'Around eighty. Not many, I'll grant you. But they're your men now, Alaric, no question of that.'

'What of the people who were taken by the raiders yesterday? Do we know who they are? And how many civilians were killed when the enemy got over the walls?' It came back to me all of a sudden. Women slung over warriors' shoulders; children ripped from despairing mothers. I had thought we had fought well, all things considered. But I worried there would be discontent among the men at the people we had lost. Understandable, of course. But selfishly I was hoping that discontent would be aimed at their dead chief and not me. It wasn't just the fighting men I would need on side if we were going to prove victorious.

'Seven women gone, eight children. Five of the women were widowed, two still have husbands fighting with us.'

'And how are those men today?' The wound in my back chose that moment to spike in pain, and I thought back to my charge along the beach, running with my comrades at my side, and one of them plunging the blade into my back. I could not have anything like that happen again. It was bad enough having one traitor in Red Beard; I didn't need to be keeping my eye out for another threat within my own ranks.

'Desolate, heartbroken. One of them lost his two daughters yesterday too, one to the fire and the other to the raiders.'

'Gods below,' I muttered, before draining my ale. How would I react if it were me? Saxa taken, my boys with her. I would be blinded by my rage, ready to plunge my blade into whoever I thought responsible. I needed to see these two men, and quick. I had to judge them for myself. 'How bad was the fire in the end? Did you get it out without much trouble? That reminds me, you did a great job setting their ships alight. I doubt they'd have scarpered off if you hadn't.' Such had been my rage when I had returned to the fortress that morning, Wilhelm's bloody corpse dragging behind me, I hadn't even thought to check on the blazing fire I had laid Loki to rest on the day before.

'Aye, they went up a treat! Was Rolf that did much of the hard work though. He's a useful man to have around. The fire in the fortress was contained to one building; we lost three people in total to it. I'm only thankful they didn't get into the granary.'

'True. Not that there's much grain in there to be had.' I swigged my ale, swishing it around in my mouth, thinking. 'Eadger, I want you to do something for me. I want you to organise a meeting, with everyone, outside the hall at dusk tonight. Can you do that?'

'Aye, I dare say I can. What are you going to say to them?'

'I'm still working on that,' I said, and I downed the rest of my ale. Eadger gave me a thoughtful nod before taking his leave, off to spread the word of the meet. I sat in silence a while, Kai finishing off his soup at my side.

'It was Red Beard, wasn't it? The one that attacked Sedric on the ship and emptied the chests?' I said suddenly, unable to hold it in any longer.

Kai's cheeks reddened, his eyes falling down to his soup, but he gave me a sullen nod. 'You tried to tell me, on the ship, but I couldn't understand what you were saying.' It all made sense in hindsight. *Re ear,* Kai had said. I'd thought it just delirious noises, but Kai knew what he had been about. 'Did he threaten you, once we reached here? When I came to see you, the day after we arrived, you wouldn't say anything, and it wasn't because of your wounds. You were scared.'

He nodded again, eyes still fixed on his bowl, spoon prodding its watery contents. 'Listen to me, lad.' I moved closer to him, put an arm around his shoulder. 'Never be afraid to speak the truth, especially to me. That whoreson Red Beard near on killed me on the beach, a knife in the back. The gods only know how he missed all my important parts. I need you to remember who you serve. Hell, maybe I need to remember who I am. I'd wager you, Sedric and Batur wondered what the fuck you were doing serving me, back in my sad, lonely hall. You came to serve under the great Lord Alaric and found a lonely, bitter old man drinking himself into an early grave.

'Well, you listen to me, lad, and you listen good. I was a great man once, a feared man. And the Trickster himself knows I'm never going to be that man again. But I will have my reputation back. You know how I'm going to get it?' Kai shook his head, wincing at the pain it caused. 'I'm going to save these poor people, with words if I can, and my sword if I can't. I swear this to any fucking god that still thinks me worthy of their attention.

'You and me, and Sedric, we're going to beat these curs from across the sea, and then we're going to go home, with our heads held high and our pride intact, with a ship full of amber too. And when we get home, you'll be able to tell every pretty girl you meet that you fought under the great Lord Alaric, that you held an indefensible outpost against an innumerable enemy, and you won. What say you to that?'

Kai grinned, and for a moment his face was that of the happy lad I had known back home. 'Gooo,' he slurred, and I beamed back at him. I'd have grabbed his cheeks and kissed him if I hadn't thought the pain would have been too much for him to bear.

* * *

It was under a bruised purple sky that the citizens of the Cimbri gathered outside the chief's hall. I stood on a raised wooden dais, my wound re-stitched and bandaged, mail cleaned and polished, hair still damp from my bathe in the sea. I had my sword at my waist, helmet tucked under my arm. I wanted to project a confidence I did not feel, and that started with how I looked.

We'd had men out looking for Red Beard all afternoon, but none had seen any sight of him. They had, however, found a flock of ten sheep grazing on the sparse grass to the south of the fortress, just past the pit. On balance, I considered that a bigger win than finding our traitor.

'People of Tastris,' I called, holding out a hand for quiet. The mutterings ebbed out, and gradually every one of them turned to face me. 'I stand here today, not as a warlord, or some conquering hero that has come to right all your wrongs. I speak as a father, and as a husband. What you have gone through, everything you have suffered, is far worse than any of you deserve. You want to raise your children in peace, to grow crops and tend to your animals. You want to sing and dance around a fire, the stars watching over you. I know this, as this is too what I want.

'I want to return home to my wife and my sons, to set my ship out to sea and point the prow south. But I find I cannot do this. I cannot, and will not, abandon you to a fate you have done nothing to bring upon yourselves. In my short time here, I have seen you for what you are: good, honest people who have been badly led. The man who has done these wrongs to you, the real enemy, lays dead on the ground behind me, rotting outside his hall. It was Wilhelm who set you down this bloody path of war and ruin. The raiders from across the sea came to you looking for trade, and Wilhelm, greedy, cunning, sought to rob them when they did. That is the cause of this war you have been raging, that is the cause of the losses you have suffered. I want you to take a moment now to think on those you have lost. Husbands, wives, sons and daughters, all gone before their time.'

There was utter silence when I stopped speaking; you could almost taste the remorse in the air. A lady standing in the front row, a toddler clutching at her skirts, sobbed and was consoled by an elderly man next to her. Gods, but my heart went out to her, to all of them. I believed in what I was saying, even if I'd laid it on a bit thick. They *were* good people, and they'd certainly done nothing to bring on the doom that was coming for them. Or wouldn't be coming for them, if I had anything to do with it.

'I've gathered you here tonight to ask one thing of you. This war is far from over. The raiders will come again, once they're done licking their wounds. They'll want more blood, more slaves to carry back across the sea. We've few enough warriors left standing, and if we are to be victorious, I'll need every one of them focused on the task in hand, without worrying about the family they've left hiding behind our walls.'

I took a breath, taking in the tear-stained faces before me, bracing myself for the inevitable backlash once I had finished speaking. 'And so I would like every woman and child to leave Tastris, to head south to the lands of the Anglii, take shelter with Haribert and his people.'

It was like I'd asked them to bury a spear in their mothers. An eruption of noise that hit me like an avalanche, people screaming in fury, all their anger and fear, bottled up for so long, released in one murderous roar.

'We'll never survive the journey!'

'Haribert can't be trusted, he'll turn us all away!'

'We've no horses! You can't expect us to travel by foot, it will take weeks!'

'I'll not let my wife and daughter leave without me! Who'll protect them on the road?'

'We've no food! What will we feed our children on the journey?'

All valid points, and ones I had no real answers to. 'Please, quiet down!' I called, but it had as much effect as throwing a stone in the sea.

'SILENCE!' Eadger roared, a cry echoed by Hilde

and then Gunnar. The cacophony died away, and I slapped a grateful hand on Eadger's shoulder.

Clearing my throat, I started again. 'We don't have the manpower to defend the walls of this fortress, and even the greenest amongst you must be able to see what a state they're in. We've no allies riding to our aid. We stand alone, and as yesterday's battle showed us, I cannot keep you safe here. The best thing for you all to do is head south and leave the warriors here to fight. With a small, mobile force, we stand a greater chance of victory. Without having to worry about protecting these mouldy old walls, we can strike out, use the terrain to our advantage, and do more damage to our enemy. Believe me, I would not be asking this of you unless I thought it necessary. I know I am not one of you; I know many of you would never have heard me speak before this night. But you have all seen me fight. I have shed blood for you, killed for you, and when it comes to war, I have some small experience.' That drew the smatter of laughter I was hoping for, as all there would have been aware of my reputation, heard the tales told around the fire at night. I was a man to be feared, a good man to have on your side.

'We have ten sheep, found today by one of our scouts. I'll have them slaughtered tonight, the meat salted and wrapped. It isn't much, but it should see you through to Haribert's hall. Take some time, speak amongst yourselves. Once you come to a decision, you let me know.'

I stepped down from the dais and walked towards the hall, Sedric, Eadger, Hilde and Isvilt hot on my heels.

'A good speech, Lord,' Sedric said when we were inside. Isvilt put a cup of ale in my hands and I sat down, suddenly weary. 'Aye, but will they go for it?'

'They will,' Eadger said with a certainty I didn't feel. 'You'd won the warriors over by the end, they'll persuade the rest.'

'Good.' I nodded, draining my ale. 'Can you get me quill and parchment? I assume Wilhelm could write? I've three letters I need to go south. Eadger, I need a messenger, a reliable young lad. One letter will be for Haribert, begging him to take our women and children in, the other two to go on south then west. I hope Haribert will be kind enough to lend us a mount, as you've eaten all your ones here.'

'Who are the other two for?' Eadger asked.

'One is for my wife. The other for the one man that might be persuaded to aid us.'

Though if I was being honest, I held out very little hope at all.

22

They agreed, just as Eadger said they would. I ordered everyone unable to wield a spear to be ready to depart at dawn. The ten sheep were slaughtered and roasted, though their blood was collected in four giant cooking pots and left in a barn. I wouldn't tell anyone why.

The sun was casting its first shadow when everyone was gathered on the road outside the southern gate. There were tears, many tears. I found myself quashing down a few myself, watching on as fathers kissed their children goodbye, and couples embraced as if it would be the last time. It may well have been, after all.

It was with great reluctance I sent the women

and children, the elderly and the infirm on their way. What that left was eighty fighting men, though that description was optimistic. In truth, they were made up of untried boys who stood shivering with nerves, spears gripped in pale hands. I had veterans, men who had survived campaigns fought when even I was a boy. They stood hunched but proud, wispy grey hair billowing in the summer breeze. Around forty of them were what I would call prime fighting age: between twenty and forty, and it was these men who wore the chainmail I had brought north with me. I made sure they all had good swords and stout helmets to go with them. It was these men who would form the core of my shield wall, and I was relying on them to stay alive long enough to give me a victory.

We stood together, an unlikely alliance of youth and experience, and watched the southern road until our people passed out of sight. With them gone, I ordered my warband to the beach, and we got to work.

'You want us to dig?' Gunnar asked with a frown.

'Aye,' I said, a small smile dancing on my lips. 'That's what I said. Let me tell you, more wars have been won with a shovel than they have with a sword, and that's a fact.'

'Bollocks to that,' Mellow spat, looking at the

shovel in his hand with all the disgust one gives a stray dog that's just pissed on his boots.

I have spoken already of the time my Ravensworn had beaten a column of Batavi by digging pits and forming our line behind them, watching with glee as the horsemen rode to their unseeing doom. So I shall not repeat it now. But I told them, all eighty of them, as they gathered around me in a circle on the sun-drenched beach. Slowly but surely, I could see I was winning them around. We were outnumbered, hopelessly so. But our advantage was the battle would be fought on our ground, and we could manipulate that.

And so whilst Eadger and three picked men went to the fortress to cut down great lengths of timber from the rotting walls, the rest of the men dug trenches. As tall as a man, and half as wide. Until the sun waned in the west I had them digging, and when our work was done, and only then, I gave them permission to down tools and seek an evening meal.

Isvilt had one ready for them, for she had outright refused to seek sanctuary in the south with the other women. I had given up trying to persuade her, but that night I was grateful for her skills in the kitchen, as each of my men wolfed down a hearty meal of oats mixed with whatever was left in the granary.

That done, I gathered the warriors in the open

space in front of the main hall. I'd had Eadger and Sedric build four huge fires in the clearing, one on each corner, and it was between those my men huddled. The cooking pots full of the sheep blood were brought out, and I ordered each man to place his shield on the ground in front of him.

'A lifetime ago,' I said to them when all were still and quiet, 'I led the deadliest warband our lands have ever seen. We unseated chiefs, toppled kings, and gave the cursed empire more than one bloody nose. We were *feared* the land over. People would lay awake at night, terrified that the next day would be the day when Alaric and his Ravensworn came for them. You've all heard the stories, have you not?'

I smiled as a chorus of 'ayes' echoed back at me. 'And how was it, do you think, that I came to garner such a reputation?'

'I heard you killed twenty men fighting the Quadi, and by the end of the day they refused to take the field against you,' one unseen voice piped up.

'Aye. Good day's work that,' I said with a wink.

'You fought a Roman legion down on the Danube, and beat the bastards with five hundred men!' another called.

'Well, it wasn't a whole legion, and we didn't exactly win, but aye, we fought 'em.'

'You took on the Lugii and won, forcing their chief to run off into hiding!'

'That was the Frisii, and to this day I don't know what happened to their bastard chief!'

'You took Ulpia Noviomagus from the Romans and stole three of their ships!'

'Aye! One of which sits proudly on that very beach,' I said, pointing out to the north. 'But what I asked was *how*? How was it I was able to form such a band of warriors? What was it that had them flocking to fight under my banner?'

'Coin!'

'Reputation!'

'Women and plunder!'

'Victory!'

I held up my hands for silence. 'Yes, all that and more. But most of all, it was for this.' I brought forward my own shield, sliced and battered as it was. The black raven on the red banner. 'Men came to me because they saw something, an idea, a collective, and they wanted to be a part of it. The men who fought for me were landless men, outlaws, driven from their tribes, with no friends, no family. But when they fought for me, when they stood in line before a battle, do you think they were thinking about scoring some easy plunder, or finding a nice plump ale wife to keep their bed warm at day's end?

'No. They fought for this.' I thumped the shield. 'They fought for their brother next to them in the line, for their comrade standing behind them. The Ravensworn were not a tribe, not connected by blood. What bound us was our devotion to the cause, what drove us was the desperation to not be the one man in the line to let his friends down when it mattered. And that, men of the Cimbri, is what I need from you in the coming days.

'If you believe in something, if you *truly* believe, and strive to make it happen, then it will be so.'

'Hence the sheep blood,' Eadger said, a knowing smile spreading across his lips.

'Aye, now you see it, my friend. Each of you will smear your shield in the blood, and when it has dried you will make the raven mark upon it. And then we will be one. Gone are the defeated, tired, weary warriors of the Cimbri. We will be the Ravensworn reborn, and I promise you, brothers, I will lead you all to victory.'

'Just one thing you missed out,' a voice said, and Rudi stepped into the firelight, the chatter around him fading away.

'And what's that then?'

'Oath breaker. That's what they called you, back in your glory days, when you had the world at your feet. You'd start a day fighting on one side and be cosying up to your enemy by the time the sun set. That's why you never lost, I reckon. It's not because you're some great hero, old One Eye back from the dead, leading your army to glory. You're a traitor, willing to turn your back on your allies at the slightest whiff of a better offer. What's to say you won't do the same to us?'

It was a fair question, I supposed. And by the sound of the muttering of the men, I guessed they thought the same too. Who was I, after all, to expect these men to put aside their love of their tribe and fight under my banner? But I had thought only to inspire them, to drive them on to be better fighters than they thought possible. I weighed the answer in my head before responding. 'Aye, I've been called that before. Was a time when I revelled in the name. But I'll tell you who I never abandoned – men who held this shield.' I thumped it once more. 'Because the men who carried this symbol into battle were my brothers, come what may. And if I took the odd bribe, if I turned my allegiance when I saw a battle not going our way, then I did it for my men. To see them live to see another sunrise, to see them home to their families, to their loved ones. I will make an oath to you now, young Rudi, to all you men.' I raised my voice, my battlefield voice.

'Me, Alaric, the oath breaker. I swear to you that if you fight under my banner, I will never turn my back on you, never sell you out. I didn't have to come here, to the most northern tip of our land. I could have stayed at home, snug in bed with my wife, watching my boys play in the river. But I heard of your strife, of your desperate need, and I came, did I not? I have armoured you, armed you, and stand here today ready to embrace you as my brothers. You have all seen me fight, seen me bleed. Join me in this, men of the Cimbri, and I promise you, I will lead you, until your enemies are thrown back to the sea for good.'

There was a pregnant pause, followed by a deafening roar. I had them. I walked up to Rudi and held out a hand. The youth took it after a moment's thought, and we embraced. I saw Hilde, her eyes twinkling in the firelight, and she gave me a mischievous wink before organising the men into lines so we could begin the process of transforming their shields. I walked away from them then, out the northern gate and onto the beach. It was quiet, peaceful, cool after the heat of the fires. I breathed in deep and allowed myself a small smile of satisfaction. Turning at footsteps behind me, I saw Sedric and Kai approaching. I'd tried to tell Kai to go south with the others, but much like with Isvilt, he had refused. He might not have been able to speak, but he was stronger, eager to fight. I put an arm around each of them, and we stood in companiable silence, the stars shining down upon us.

23

'Ships to the east!' Mellow called from the top of the mast, and at once we burst into action.

'Get the sail raised, oars to bank east!' I called, at once a man of action.

It had been five days since the men had painted their shields with the raven mark, and in the days since we had been digging and training. That day I had left Hilde with the warband, drilling the men on the ways of the shield wall, ensuring each among them knew their role until they could do it in their sleep. I had taken the small Celox and pushed her hull back out to sea. I'd swam in the morning, the wound in my back still burning, but not quite the fireball it had been before. It had felt good to be back on open water, the wind in my face, the tang of salt on my tongue. I had Eadger with me; Gunnar, Rolf, Rudi and Mellow too. Kai worked an oar like a man possessed, desperate to make up for all he had missed out on. Sedric was adorned once more with a damp rag around his sun-burned head. It had been good to leave my troubles behind, if only for a short while. On shore I had been on constant alert, sure Red Beard would appear at any moment, another knife to hand, ready to finish me off. At sea, though, I felt a freedom a land lover would never experience.

There had been another motive, of course. We were in a constant state of anticipation, awaiting another attack from the raiders. I'd figured if I put my ship on the waters between our land and theirs, I would get a chance of seeing them before our lookouts atop the walls of Tastris did. I also thought I could do them some damage before they'd had a chance to make land.

'Come on, lads! Put your backs into it!' I bellowed at the rowers before lowering myself into the spare oar bench and heaving on an oar myself. There were only eight of us on the ship, so when we were all rowing, it left no one to steer or watch the sails. But for the next few heartbeats, speed was all that counted. Rudi was down from the mast and once more at his bench, and as a team we strained at the oars, Gunnar calling out the strokes. I lost myself to the rhythm for a time: *stroke, stroke, stroke*. There is a solace in manual work, a welcome break from the mental strain of being responsible for the lives of a whole tribe, and I embraced it, clearing my mind.

'I can see the bastards!' Eadger called from his oar bench. 'Northeast of us!'

'How many ships?'

'More than I can count!'

I grinned; it was going to be a bloody day. My favourite. I leaped from my bench, ordering Eadger to do the same. Running to the steering oar, I scanned the horizon and, sure enough, saw a multitude of small ships, rowing their way across the sea.

'Gunnar, slow it down a bit,' I said to the big man, who rowed with a hunk of bread on his lap.

'What's your plan?' Eadger called to me, making his way unsteadily to the rear of the ship.

'I'll get us as close to the bastards as I can. We'll ram a few, and I want you and the lads throwing spears when we're close enough.'

Eadger nodded. 'If we can stop them here, there'll be a few less widows amongst our women.'

Our men rowed. I watched the enemy grow, more and more ships appearing across the horizon. Their ships were tiny, more like row boats used for rivers than ships built for the open sea. Eight men sat squeezed in every ship, oars dipping into the grey water. They had no sails, and for the first time I saw the genius of it. They were very hard to spot. Out on the open sea, a sail acts as a beacon of sorts, visible for miles if the conditions are right. These ships could sneak across the sea without being spotted at all if you weren't looking for them. Unfortunately for them, we had been.

As the distance grew shorter, I could see the panic in the crews. Men were shouting, their voices carrying across the waves. Two ships tried to back oars and turn back, but they had no cohesion and ended up floundering in circles. Others bent double to their oars, straining to break away from the pack and hide in the open water. I let them go. If four or five ships made it past us to our shore, Hilde would deal with them, no problem. I tried to count the ships, got to thirty and gave up. Even thirty ships carrying eight men would outnumber my warband three to one, and they were not odds I wanted Hilde to have to face. I aimed my Celox at the closest ship and called for Gunnar to up the speed. We flew across the water, and as we crested a wave, I caught a glimpse of terrified faces, a bearded man roaring in terror, and then we smashed into their hull, snapping it in two. 'One down! Up oars!' I called, not wanting my men to get their oars caught in the wreckage.

We had ships to our left and right, and Eadger had the men up from their benches, loosing spears into the hapless warriors who had nowhere to hide. 'Back to your benches!' I ordered, seeing a group of eight ships off to our left, who had the sense to group together and row towards us. The wind had picked up, a strong easterly gale that filled our sail and carried us away from the imminent threat. Gunnar once more called the strokes: 'With me, stroke! Stroke! Stroke!' and we carved another hull in two, feeling the timber snap under the weight of our heavier ship.

I heaved the steering oar to the left, and the nimble Celox turned to the north, and once more the men were up from their benches, spears raining down on helpless warriors. Leaving Eadger to command the men, I found my eye roaming to the group of ships that still held some formation. There were twelve of them now, and even as I watched, another two rowed up to their flanks. They had turned with us and were once more rowing right at us. For the first time, I considered how low in the water our own ship was. It wouldn't take much effort for a determined group of warriors to board us. One man on one of their row boats to give a leg up for the other seven, and they would clamber aboard. Despite the imminent threat, I grinned at the thought, my fingers finding the hilt of my sword. *Let them try.*

Wrenching on the steering oar once more, I turned us back so we were head-on with the enemy group. There was a man in their central ship, standing where others were sitting. He wore mail that shone in the sunlight, a drawn sword in his right hand. He was screaming at the men in the ships around him, ordering his ships into a wedge. I thought back to the men I had fought on the beach. There had been very few in good mail, even fewer with decent swords, and I thought I had found their king, or battle chief at least.

'Cut the head from the snake,' I mused to myself, and I ordered Eadger and the others back to their benches. 'See those ships ahead, formed together in a wedge?' I called to the men. 'We're going straight for them!'

'Leave them be!' Eadger called back. 'There's plenty of easy pickings to be had!'

'I don't want easy pickings, my friend! I want that bastard in the mail!'

Gunnar called the strokes once more and everyone bar Eadger heaved at their oars. We picked up speed, the Celox skimming the waves as Eadger quickly lowered our sail that was straining against the oncoming wind. 'Keep going!' I called, though I had no need. Eadger ran to the prow of the ship and loosed a spear at the clutch of rafts that opposed us. Their leader still stood in his boat, heedless of the doom that rushed towards him. He waved his sword in arcs around his head, bellowing words that were lost on the roaring wind.

I showed my teeth with a savage grin as we came upon them, certain we were about to put twelve ships' worth of men in a watery grave with one furious charge.

I was wrong. Just as we were on them, just as our prow was metres away from splintering their ships, they split. They pushed their oars on each other's ships, propelling themselves to the left and right, leaving a gap for us to power through. Cursing, I could do nothing as my men had their oars wrenched from white-knuckled palms. Rudi was thrown into the side of the ship with such force that when he rose, the right side of his face was bloody. Gunnar had fared better; Rolf too. They still gripped their oars, and I watched as Gunnar drew his back as far as he could, before ramming it forwards, knocking six men into the sea with one blow.

But my focus was on him, and not what was happening to my right. Four men clambered aboard our ship, propelled up by their mates below. Kai was the first to see them, and his mangled tongue let out a shrieking war cry as he rushed to meet them. He buried his sword in the first man, twisted the blade and wrenched it free, before using the hilt to pommel the next around his head. Then Sedric was with him, the damp rag still tied around his head. He felled a balding axeman with a jab to the throat, then ran through a bearded spearman without breaking stride.

I just stood and watched the two of them fighting a moment longer, pride welling in my chest at the warriors they were becoming. And then I was off down the deck, sword in hand, the wolf grin back on my face.

Three more men forced their way aboard, one with decent mail and a fine longsword. I'd not put my own mail on, fearing the weight of it dragging me down beneath the waves if the worst happened. The others all wore theirs though, as none of them could swim a stroke. If they went overboard, they were dead either way. I charged the man in mail. He wore his beard cropped, grey nestling amongst his black hair like a touch of frost. He parried my first blow well, turning my sword out wide before stepping in to finish me off. I saw it coming a mile off though, and had already danced away before he could land a blow. I could hear the clash of swords around me, and was nervous as to how many enemy warriors had managed to climb aboard our ship, but I had no time to look. I swiped away a lunge at my throat before missing with one of my own. We circled each other, each trying to get a measure of the other. My enemy was panting, sweat leaking into his beard. His eyes were a dark green, sweat-soaked hair plastered across them.

To my right, I made out Gunnar charging two enemies with his oar, knocking them screaming overboard with his power. My opponent saw it too, and was momentarily distracted. Taking my chance, I stepped in, feinting high to his right before bringing the sword back down and hacking at his calf. He fell for the feint, my blade hacking into his leg with a great spurt of blood. He roared in agony, and I pulled back my sword and kicked him in his mailed chest. He took two staggering steps back before falling over the rail.

It was me panting now, sword scraping the blood-soaked deck as I took in the carnage around me. Kai and Sedric still stood back-to-back. They were fighting off three men between them, and I saw Kai's sword snake out to take his opponent in the throat. Gunnar still fought with the oar. Using it as a giant club, he swatted men aside like they were flies. I was only surprised he wasn't eating whilst he was doing it. Rudi and Mellow fought in a three with Eadger. They were hacking at men still trying to clamber up the rail, and I made a mental note to thank Eadger for having the sense to do so.

Suddenly the ship lurched beneath me, banking left. Staggering, I turned to see a mass of enemy warriors clambering over the rail. 'Ravensworn, to me!' I called as I stumbled towards them, but all my men were still locked in combat. Snarling, I charged them myself, knocking two back off the rail before they had a chance to get a leg over, and they fell screaming to their deaths. Five men did get over though, and I saw one of them was the leader I had seen in the midst of the enemy ships. He was tall and broad, short hair hidden by a gleaming helm. His mail seemed to be trimmed with gold, and he had fine-looking leather boots that came up to his knee. I went straight for him.

He had no shield, but carried a sword two-handed that was nearly as tall as me. I thought the weapon too heavy, that it would slow him down, be cumbersome in battle, but he wielded it like a man born to sword craft. I jabbed low at his calf, and he brought his sword down quickly to block. Turning my blade wide, he stepped forwards and swept his sword up with a blow that would have taken my head clean off if I had not jumped back just in time. I was shocked, a little scared, and tired. I was no longer a young man, and I felt the wound in my back protesting with every movement. I roared, hoping to drown out the mounting dread building inside me, and charged him once again. I thought I saw the hint of a smile under his dark beard before he leaped to his right and once more sent that great sword in a savage arc at my head.

I fell to my knees, the sword singing above my head, and I used my own blade to cut at his boots. The sword cut through the leather but then hit something with a metallic clang, and I cursed, realising my foe had lined his boots with armour.

Rolf had answered my call for help and was off to my left, shoving one man over the rail and cutting into the shoulder of another. I could make out Gunnar in the corner of my eye, his oar now split in two, but he still held one half in each hand and was using them as clubs to batter his enemy to the deck. Of the others I saw no sign.

I rose back to my feet unsteadily, the deck slick beneath me. The wind picked up once more, throwing salt air in my face, and I winced as I saw that great sword snaking out to me once more. I managed to block the blow, gritting my teeth in desperation as I used all the strength left in me to push the sword back. My opponent was tireless, elegant in his movement, and he wrenched his sword away from mine then swung it over his head, aiming a savage blow at me from above. I'd no energy to retreat, my legs dead beneath me, so instead of moving backwards, I allowed myself to fall forwards into him. We crashed together and fell to the deck, his sword bouncing off the timber boards, mine still clutched to numb fingers. I was atop him, and he snarled and roared, trying to get his arms around me as I fought to get a proper grip on my blade.

We tussled and rolled, me on top, then him. He managed to clamp his thighs each side of my waist and pressed his thumbs on my throat. Gasping for air, I lost the grip on my sword and could do nothing but flap at his unwavering grip. I writhed and wriggled, desperation kicking in. My enemy smiled above me, eyes locked on to mine, and I could think of nothing but Saxa and my boys, standing on a distant shore, awaiting my return. What would they be told? That I had died a hero, fighting for a noble lost cause? I doubted it. I hoped they would never hear the truth, that I'd died on a fool's errand, trying to fight off thirty ships with my one.

The gods had truly abandoned me.

But then, just as the light was fading from my one remaining eye, there was a flash of movement above, and Gunnar smashed an oar into the back of my attacker's head, knocking his helmet off and revealing a short crop of brown hair. Another hit with the oar and the grip around my throat loosened, and I gasped in a lungful of sweet sea air. One more hit and the man slumped over me, dark blood gushing on my face.

'Took your fucking time,' I managed to croak out, heaving the dead weight of the body off me.

Gunnar just shrugged. 'Had to stop for lunch,' he said, and took a bite from his bread.

24

The sun was bleeding out when we made land on the beach. I felt every bit the old man I was, with my throat burning, wounded back aching, plus a hundred other old wounds resurfacing to register their complaints.

Word soon spread of our battle out at sea, and the men cheered as I limped through the north gate, desperate to shed my armour and lie down. Isvilt took one look at me and tutted, before ordering I strip in Wilhelm's old bedchamber and lie down on the bed. I didn't protest.

The wound in my back had opened once more and was leaking blood onto the straw pallet, but I couldn't bring myself to care. I had new cuts on my sword arm, one on my face I didn't remember receiving, and a long gash down my right calf. I'd been wounded before, of course, countless times. But as I lay there on the pallet, I couldn't help but feel that the wounds got worse the older you got. I pinched the leathery skin on my arm between finger and thumb, then released it. It took an age to settle back down. I remembered doing the same thing to Ruric once, and teasing the old man, saying I'd be able to wrap his skin on my shield. Seemed funnier then.

Eventually, Isvilt finished fussing over my broken body, and I rose from the pallet with a sigh, throwing on a tunic and heading out into the hall. The warriors were jubilant. They had won a major victory without having to draw their swords. Without even knowing they had fought. I smiled to them, shook hands and mingled my way through the crowd. I felt oddly melancholic, my thoughts drifting to my wife and children.

'He's awake,' Sedric said to me as I passed him.

'He said anything?'

Sedric shook his head. 'Eadger and Gunnar are with him now.'

'Guess we'd better get there before they kill him then.'

Outside, the air was warm with a cool sea breeze. The sun a memory, lost over the western horizon. Thick cloud hung low in the night sky, and as I walked back out to the beach, I wondered if the morning would bring rain. Kai joined us, skulking out of the shadows. He had not taken the opportunity to bathe since the battle and dark blood was splattered over his face and mail. He grunted as he came alongside us and I smiled to see him and Sedric embrace. They had become men on this doomed trip to the north, and if I could get them both home alive, whatever the outcome, I would consider it a win.

We boarded the Celox in silence, hearing nothing but the sigh of the wind over the rippling waves. Clambering down the ladder to the hold, flickering torches formed the outline of three figures. Two were standing, one sat hunched on the deck. 'How's our friend?' I asked.

Gunnar's teeth flashed in the dim light. 'He's got a bit of a headache.'

'Can't think why.' I grinned back at him. Lowering myself to a crouch, I took an offered torch from Eadger and shined it in our captive's face. It was my attacker from earlier in the day, the man with the fine sword and mail. 'Can he understand us?'

Eadger shrugged. 'He's not said anything, but I'd wager he can understand us well enough.'

He looked awful, that nameless man, which cheered me up no end, feeling as bruised and battered as I was. He winced as the torch flashed past his eyes, highlighting the matted blood tangled in his beard. 'How about it then, can you understand me?'

The warrior spat at me, phlegm splattering all over my face. There was a collective intake of breath behind me, and Sedric stepped forwards, fists bunched, but I held out a calming hand before he could do any damage. I passed Sedric the torch and wiped the spit off with the hem of my tunic. 'I'm going to take that as a yes,' I said, offering him another smile. 'What's your name?'

He spat again, though this time I was quick enough to dodge it. My temper rising quicker than I could control, I slapped him with the back of my right hand, with enough force to leave him bleeding. 'Now, we can do this one of two ways,' I said, rising to my feet. 'The easy way, where I ask questions and you answer them, followed by you receiving a hot meal and some ale. Or the hard way, where we beat the answers to my questions from you, then slit your throat and throw you in the sea. I'll leave the decision up to you.'

Silence as I awaited his answer. Gunnar took the opportunity to begin sharpening the blade of his axe, the whetstone grinding up the metal proving our intent with more clarity than my words ever could.

'My name is Godin,' he said at last. Blood welled from the new cut at his lip. He winced as he licked it, clearly deciding he had taken enough punishment for one day.

'Godin! There we are, we've made a start! And which tribe are you from, Godin? The Suiones or the Sitones?'

'The Suiones. Adalwolf is my king.'

'Adalwolf? Stupid fucking name for a king. And what do you do in service of this Adalwolf?'

'I am his battle chief, his lord of war. At least, I was.' He spat again, a mouthful of blood, though this time mercifully at the floor.

'And how long have you been fighting this war against the Cimbri?'

'Since the beginning. I was commanding the first voyage sent out to find our emissaries that came to you in good faith to make a peaceful offering of trade. Good people who never returned home to their families.'

I had to give him that, at least. 'Do you know what happened to them? Your emissaries?'

'You killed them, threw their bodies in a pit. All in the name of Tuisto, a relic from a time long forgotten.'

I nodded. I was intrigued. Intrigued that this man spoke our tongue, that he knew the name of our oldest of gods. Also, that he knew not just that his people had been murdered, but how and where their bodies were buried. And why. I thought back to Isvilt saying she had heard tales of this people beaching their ships further south, holding talks with Sigimund. It confirmed to me that the stories were true.

'I'm going to talk for a while, Godin. You are going to listen, without interrupting me. Once I am finished, you may say what you will. Do you understand?' He nodded. And so I spoke. I told him of the Cimbri, a simple tribe in the far north of our land. I told them of their needs, of the poor farming this far north, of their dependence on their neighbours, the Anglii, and the frosty relationship they had with their chief. And then I spoke of Wilhelm, the disgraced chief who, blinded by ambition and greed, had sought to turn the offered alliance of Godin's people in to something he could profit from. I told him of Wilhelm's death, and finally, I told him of me and why I was there. 'You are not at war with the Cimbri, Godin. You were at war with Wilhelm, and for that I cannot blame you. But the cretin is dead, and I for one see no reason as to why your people should lose any more warriors to Cimbri blades.'

'You speak of peace?' Eadger hissed, stepping out of the shadows. 'This man admits freely to leading that first raid on our people.'

'He was coming to find his missing emissaries,' I countered.

'They didn't stop to speak to anyone on the beach though, did they? They didn't stop to speak before they murdered my wife and daughter!'

Godin grimaced, sensing trouble. Kai and Sedric put hands across Eadger's chest, keeping him back from me. I took a deep breath and calmed myself. I could well see Eadger's pain and frustration. But sometimes a leader has to do what he sees is right, detached from any sentiment. 'Calm, my friend,' I said quietly. 'How many warriors have we got left back up that beach? How many more will come across the sea? You saw the number of their ships to-day; we cannot go on fighting forever.'

'That wasn't what you told the men when you were sending their wives and children away to who knows where, and to what fate!'

'Get him up on deck for a moment, would you?' I

asked Gunnar, who simply picked a raging Eadger up and carried him up on deck.

'He has a point though, doesn't he?' I turned back to Godin as Eadger and Gunnar disappeared up the ladder. 'You didn't stop to ask questions, that day you beached your ships. You disembarked, swords drawn. Why would you do that if you were simply sent out to gather information? And how many warriors were there with you? From what I've been told, it was a lot.'

'You are Alaric?' he said, ignoring my question. '*The* Alaric? Lord of the Ravensworn?'

Well, I couldn't resist a smug little smile. 'That I am.'

'Then where are your warriors? Where is this army you lead that I have heard so much about?'

'That, my friend, is a long story, with a rather shit ending, for me at least. But put it this way. I am the man who routed your forces at sea with a single ship. I think that is proof enough of my credentials. Now, back to the question. Why is it you came to our beach that day with your swords drawn?'

He studied me a moment longer, as if seeing me for the first time. 'It was clear to me that our people had been slaughtered,' he said, just a little too quickly.

'Was it? Storms happen at sea, ships get wrecked,

people drown. Those boats of yours are awfully small. Why was it "clear to you" that your people were dead at Cimbri hands?'

I knew I had him. Knew he would be forced to reveal his truth. I gave him all the time he needed, just picked up Gunnar's axe he'd put down to carry Eadger and calmly ran the whetstone along its blade. 'It was all an accident really,' he said eventually, sighing. 'There was a strong southerly blowing us off course as we rowed. We'd been rowing for a whole day, the sun waning in the west. Finally, we sighted shore. Pulling the ships onto the beach, I knew we'd missed our mark, but I wasn't sure by how much. I told my men to bed down for the night, that we'd head out north come the morning. Didn't think it would be that far. Turned out we were in the lands of the Anglii. Some whipped up puppy by the name of Sigimund came across us, his little entourage in his wake. Said we were in his father's lands, and if we wanted to spend the night on that beach, we'd have to pay a tax.'

I shared a look with Kai and Sedric. 'Sounds familiar. What happened next?'

'He told us a story. One of sacrifice and old gods, of a long-gone power returning to their lands. Said our people had been slaughtered in the name of progress, that soon he would be the ruler of Jylland, and that I would do well to do his bidding.'

'The ruler of Jylland,' I said with a smirk. 'What ambitions he has. So, what did you do? You had an army with you, no? How many men did Sigimund have with him? Twelve? Fifteen? You should have slaughtered the fool where he stood.'

Godin shrugged, wincing as his shoulders creaked. 'Me and my men were rattled. We had just been told our people were dead, murdered, in the most brutal way. Sigimund gave me gold to take back to my king and said there would be more rewards if we took the fight to the Cimbri. Not that we needed any encouragement after what we had learned.'

'Gold?' I asked, my curiosity well piqued now.

'Aye, not that it's much use to us over the water. We trade in furs and cattle; we have no use for coin.'

'So, what did you do with it?'

'There are a few coins in my pouch at my waist. I'd show you, but...' He trailed off, nodding down to his bound hands. I reached forwards and tore the pouch from his waist. Opening it up, I reached in and pulled out a coin, holding it up to the nearest lantern. I saw what I was expecting to see – Roman gold, with the image of the emperor Nero on their side. The same coins we had found under Wilhelm's Hall. 'How many of these do you have?'

'Thirty? At a guess. The rest are with my king. These he gave to me before we set off, in case we had to buy provisions if we got held up.'

I mused on that. Thirty pieces of gold was more than Wilhelm had buried under his hall, little good it did him in the end. And then I mused some more. What Godin had said of his homeland was as true in Germania as it was here. As a people, we had very little use for coin. We traded with each other, cattle and furs, amber and grain. All these things had a use to us. Even the tribes that bordered with Rome took no coin from their tradesmen. They swapped amber for wine, or iron to forge swords, boots and tunics to wear. What use was gold for us? 'What does your king expect to do with this gold?'

Godin puffed his cheeks. 'Don't rightly know, he doesn't seem that interested in it. Guess it can't hurt to have though. Once we knew it was your people that had slaughtered ours, we did not attack for the coin.'

I reckoned that true enough. 'So I have told you my story, Godin, and the dark and bloody tale of the Cimbri. Do you think there is any chance that we could broker a peace between our people? That we could bring this war to an end?'

His eyes narrowed, and for a few heartbeats he fixed my gaze, saying nothing. 'What sort of trick is this? There is no way you will let me leave alive. I know that already, and I have made my peace with it. Just kill me and be done with it.'

I shared a look with Sedric and Kai, then turned back to Godin. 'I don't want to kill you, friend. I will if I have to, don't get me wrong, but that isn't my intention. Do you have a family, Godin?'

His eyes widened at the question. 'Yes. A wife and five children.'

'Five! Gods, you need a hobby. You want to see them again, right? To go home and lay with your wife, play with your children in the shallows? Watch them grow into adults, have families of their own?'

'Yes. I want all these things.'

'Then let us talk of peace. What is it your king and his new queen want? Is it land they are after? What is your situation at home?'

Godin took a breath, weighing his answer before responding. 'The offer for trade was a genuine one. We are not friendly with our neighbours. Our land is tough to farm, the soil thin, winters so cold your breath can turn to ice. My tribe had been at war for ten years with another tribe from our north. Back and forth it would go, losing ground one summer, gaining the next, but neither side ever won a decisive victory. The hope was that by joining with the Sitones, we would make ourselves stronger, and just the threat of our combined forces alone would stave off the threat of renewed war with our neighbours.'

'Feeling a but coming on here,' I said.

'But on the day of our king's marriage, we were attacked.' Godin hung his head in shame. 'I should have had more scouts out, should have organised our warriors better, but...'

'But you were too busy getting pissed at your king's wedding,' I finished for him. 'Bad defeat, was it?'

Godin nodded. 'They took nearly half our land, camped their warriors on it. They dug in, ditches, wooden walls, hidden pits to snap a man's ankle. We were not able to take it back. We lost our best farming land. Away from the sea, next to a forest of pine. We had three bleak winters after.'

'And your queen's people? The Sitones? Have they not been able to support you?'

'Bah,' Godin scoffed. 'The Sitones barely farm at all. Their land is further south than ours. They have many cattle, but they struggle to grow much. Even with the support of their warriors we were unable to retake what was ours.'

'So you built ships,' I cut in.

'Aye, we did. Only simple craft. Well, you've seen them for yourself. We're no sailors, but we can row. We figured the narrows between our lands weren't too wide and we could get across them easily enough. And as you know, we did.'

'And what is your situation like now? Is it land you seek, or trade?'

Godin lowered his head. 'Land. It is the only hope for our people.'

I nodded, chewing on it a moment. 'I have told you, as honestly as I can, of Wilhelm's intentions towards your people. And now I need you to do the same of your king's. You sent men here with grain, offering that and much more in exchange for amber. You offered peace and trade and fellowship to a fellow people from across the sea. Is that correct?'

Godin nodded, eyes downcast, staring at his feet. He knew where this was going.

'But you had lost your best farming land? Seen your fertile fields taken by your enemy. How did your king expect to make good on his promise to the Cimbri? When he hadn't enough grain to feed his own people, let alone offer out more to another tribe.'

Godin sighed, eyes still studying his boots. 'There was some hope that we could buy off our enemy with the amber.'

'But your people see no use for coin; why is amber any different? You trade in furs and cattle, you said so yourself.'

He didn't reply, he didn't need to. We both knew how the conversation would end.

I left Godin. Clambering down the ladder back onto the beach, I saw Gunnar and Eadger awaiting me. 'Don't!' I held out my hands before Eadger could speak. 'I have made no peace.' We walked back to the fortress. I asked Gunnar to quietly fetch a bowl of stew and some ale for Godin, for no one outside of the men who had fought with me that day knew he was there. I marched through the hall straight to the stable at the back, where Eadger and his men joined me with Isvilt and Hilde. I filled them in on what I had learned, then asked for their opinions.

'Gut him and throw him in the sea,' Mellow said.

'Agreed,' Hilde added. Rolf just rolled his huge shoulders, quiet and thoughtful as ever.

'Maybe we should take him back to his home,' Rudi ventured, sharing what he hoped was an encouraging look with Mellow before continuing. 'Taking him back would be a sign of good faith, then he could relay your story to his king. Maybe then he will see sense and stop his warriors coming across the sea.'

There was uproar. Hilde bellowed that he was a coward, Isvilt hissed he was a *nithing*. Eadger raged about his lost wife and daughter, whilst Rolf just rolled his shoulders once more. 'I confess I had considered it,' I said as Gunnar walked in, hunk of bread in hand. He gave me a nod to say he'd seen Godin fed, then sat down on the floorboards. 'I mean, what are we fighting for? We don't want this war, didn't ask for it. Maybe there's a chance.'

'But you said yourself, Alaric, it's land they want. *Need*. There will be no peace,' Hilde said.

My shoulders sagged, acknowledging the truth in her words. I wanted to go home, so very much. 'Any news from the men on the southern road?' I asked Sedric. I'd had him place five men on the road, two miles apart, extending to five miles to the south. I'd no horses to mount them on, so I figured each man sprinting a couple of miles to pass a message on to the next one would be the quickest way of news reaching me.

'Nothing,' Sedric said. 'What are they looking for, anyway?'

'Don't worry.' I waved a dismissive hand. 'Too

soon anyway, I reckon,' I muttered to myself. Sedric and Eadger gave me questioning looks but I left them unanswered. 'There is one other problem that remains unsolved,' I said to change the subject.

'What's that then, Chief?' Gunnar asked through a mouthful of bread.

'Where the fuck is that murderous bastard Red Beard?'

25

Daybreak saw me walking alone along the beach, about half a Roman mile south of the ruined town of Tastris. The grassland to my right was denser, with small green knolls rising up from the flat land. I hummed as I walked, enjoying the peace. Hilde was once more drilling the men on the beach outside the fortress, and I could hear the distant clash of metal on wood as the men sparred.

My mind chewed over everything I had learned in the last few days. Roman *frumentarii* venturing this far north, whispering in ears and handing out gold coins. I hadn't thought it possible. And to what end? My best guess was that at the time they were wary of the Suebi, under the command of my father, growing too powerful. An alliance of tribes – which is what the Suebi really were, rather than one people – could have caused Rome real trouble. Had they seen my father's tribe grow, migrating as they were ever west? They'd have reached the Rhine at some point, and then Rome's troubles would have intensified. It was the only logical reason I could find. The Anglii – and certainly the Cimbri – offered neither any threat nor any help to Rome. They were small tribes, far to the north of Germania. Why waste good coin on them?

But then there was Sigimund, heir to the chiefdom of the Anglii. The self-styled future ruler of Jylland. If ever there was a man playing a game, it was him. What was it he hoped to achieve? By allying himself with a king from across the sea, did he really think he would be able to win himself more land to rule? And to what end? Sigimund, Wilhelm, both with their own schemes; how was it I had become mired in them both? The Norns were playing with me, cackling as they weaved me into this bloody tale.

And then there was one more mystery that needed solving. I'd walked off the beach and up one of the grassy knolls, the long grass brushing against my knees. I was just squinting up into the sun, enjoying the warm breeze on my face, when there was a sudden impact on my back, my breath driven from my lungs, and I was face down in the grass, a great weight upon me. I writhed and kicked, throwing my body to the left and right, but I could do nothing to break the hold on me. 'Finally, I have you,' a voice said behind me. I heard the hiss of a blade freeing itself, and I closed my eyes, pictured Saxa and my boys.

The death blow was not to come though. I could hear the thudding of feet on the grass, feel the vibrations in the earth. Then there was a war cry, taken up by another, and the weight from my back released as my attacker was thrown off me. I rose quickly, baring my blade, watching on as Gunnar and Eadger circled Red Beard, the rat finally caught in a trap.

'Drop your weapon,' I said to him. 'I can promise you a quick end if you do.'

'Your promises are worth shit!' he spat at me, lunging forwards with his blade with a blow Gunnar couldn't sidestep, the sword burying itself in his gut.

'No!' I cried, or Eadger cried, or we both did, and together we ran at Red Beard. I lunged high, looking to take him in the throat. Red Beard neatly stepped aside and swatted my blade away. Overstretched, I stumbled and tripped on a rock, my body hurtling into Eadger, who could do nothing to get out of the way. I smashed into his flank, and together we hit the ground, rolled, and by the time I had risen, panting, to my feet, Red Beard had smashed his sword onto Eadger's helmet, and the big man's knees buckled as he fell, his own sword flailing to the grass.

'Why are you doing this?' I said through ragged breaths. Gunnar lay crumpled on the floor to my right, whining like a starved puppy, knees up to his chest, bloodied hands pressed tight to the gaping hole in his belly.

'You always were a self-absorbed cunt! I'm not surprised you don't remember me.' He waved his blood-slicked sword in my face, his eyes a dark pit of menace.

We circled each other as I tried to block out Gunnar's cries. I knew this man, or at least, he knew me. That meant I'd either fought against him before, or with him. 'You were Ravensworn?' I asked, certain I had it. My men were the hardest bastards north of the Danube. Cutthroats, outlaws; I didn't question where they came from, who they might have been running from. If they could kill, they were in. And Red Beard was certainly a killer.

'Four years,' he said. 'Fought in Baldo's Hundred.'

Baldo. Baldo the Brave, his men had called him. Baldo the Reckless, I had. He'd commanded one of my Hundreds back in the day, and largely done a good job. I remember once setting him the task of provoking a small Roman auxiliary patrol into following him. When I had met him and his men on the road, the stupid bastard had a full five hundred horses chasing him over the horizon. Still, we'd beat them in the end. 'A good man,' I said. 'One I miss very much.'

I'd not given Baldo a thought in years, but it felt like the right thing to say. 'He died for you, just like countless others I could name, in that shitty little town out east. I came to you because I had no one, nothing, and for a time I found a cause I could believe in, brothers to fight for. And then you saw them all dead, all in your quest for a fucking crown!'

'And here I was, thinking you just another mercenary along for the coin and women. Don't give me that shit, Red Beard. You joined up because you had nowhere else to go and were unlucky enough to be one of the few left alive when it all went to shit. So then you had to start again, find another lord to fight for. Guessing you couldn't just go home? What had you done to force you to come to my door in the first place?'

'None of your fucking business! Your recruiters didn't stop to ask when they made me sign my mark.

Made no difference then and it sure as fuck don't now!'

I was still circling, Gunnar behind me. He'd stopped his crying, and I worried the man was already dead. Eadger hadn't moved, though I reckoned I could make out his shallow breaths as his chest gently moved up and down. Just unconscious then, though I could have done with him waking up. 'Aye, fair enough. How did you end up here then? You can't have been here long when the first ships appeared from across the sea?'

'I'd been here a while when that happened. Came up here with Conrad from the Anglii.'

Aye, well, I knew that well enough. 'Spend some time with Sigimund, did you? What did the pup promise you?' I tried to think back to the fight on the beach. There was no way Red Beard could have known the little lordling would appear that night. And to my memory he'd fought well enough in the battle. Guessed he wouldn't have had much choice, though. Doubt Sigimund even realised he was there.

'He might have greased my palm with the odd coin. Sent me up to the Cimbri with Conrad, said he was going to cause some mischief, and that soon there would be new neighbours to the north, and by the time his father was back to the mud and he was chief of the Anglii, there'd be riches enough for every man who stood with him. Never thought I'd bump into you again, though.'

'Did you even know I was still alive?' Red Beard shook his head. 'Were there many others from the Ravensworn that survived?'

'Aye, a few. Most drifted off back to their own people. I travelled north with a small band, but left them when I came up to the lands of the Anglii.'

Eadger was awake, lying behind Red Beard, groggily rubbing his head. Red Beard hadn't noticed, and I willed Eadger to get up. Gunnar was still as stone, and I reckoned him a goner. 'So why come south with Eadger when he came to recruit me? Why not come clean, tell Wilhelm I was dead?'

'Wanted to see if you really were dead, I suppose. When we reached the Anglii on our journey south, I told Sigimund what Wilhelm's plans were. He just laughed; said you were still alive but that you were finished. I thought of killing you in your own hall; would have done, given half the chance.'

'So you decided to jeopardise me any way you could. Neat trick, hiding the mail and weapons in the ribs of the ship. Wouldn't have found them if it wasn't for the footprints.'

Red Beard grimaced. 'Wasn't much I could do

about that; I was more concerned with that little brat Kai giving me away. Luckily for me, that kid's a coward.'

'He's got more stones than you, I'd wager. He took his wounds to the front and recovered to fight again. Your dirty little knife in the back was cowardly. Even now, hiding out here in the wild, waiting for a chance to finish me off. Why not come and face me like a man?' I spat at him. 'I'm just surprised you haven't run back to Sigimund, cowered in his father's hall.'

Eadger had sat up. Rubbing his eyes, he squinted at Red Beard and me, a frown fixed to his face, as if he were trying to work out who we were.

'No need for that. Sigimund will be here in a day or so, as will our friends from across the sea. You'll have an enemy to your front and back. What will the great Alaric do then, I wonder? Hide behind your crumbling walls? You've no great army to save you this time. You're finished. Might be I'll pay that wife of yours a visit when I head back south. She'll be needing a new man, after all.'

I roared in anger, took five quick steps forwards and swung wildly at him. He raised his blade to meet mine and they clashed with a flash of sparks. Still screaming, I pushed against his blade with all the strength I had left to me, heedless of the pain from my wounded back. I swung left to right, Red Beard backtracking, off balance, bringing his own blade up once more in a desperate block. The weight of my attack forced him back three more steps into a bewildered Eadger. Red Beard cried out as he fell back, his sword falling from his grasp. I leaped over Eadger, raising my blade over my stricken enemy. And then I stopped.

For all his faults, Red Beard was a man who had once served me faithfully, without me even realising. He had gone to war on my orders, risked his life when I told him to. And he had a point about me betraying him. Isn't that what I had done to him, and all the other men who had fought with me on that doomed march east to Parienna? I'd led them there blinded by greed, and lust for power. I'd thought myself invincible, that there was no warband or Roman legion that could stand against me and my Ravensworn. I pictured the friends I'd lost that day. Ruric, my trusted second, who had just a few weeks before berated me for the ease in which I sent our men to their deaths. Ketill, and his feared Harii, all slain because of me. I lowered my sword.

'What's the matter? Lost your nerve?' Red Beard mocked me from the ground.

'No. Just trying to remember the man I used to be.

You're right, I wronged you, you and the others who looked to me for leadership. It is a burden I will carry with me for the rest of my days. Go now. If what you say is true, then I will see you on the battlefield soon enough.'

I turned my back on him and, sheathing my sword, helped a blubbering Eadger to his feet. With his arm around my shoulder, we walked over to Gunnar, and together kneeled at his side. When I looked back, Red Beard had gone.

26

We burned Gunnar's body the following night. The gods knew the men of the Cimbri had seen enough burial pits; they didn't need to dig another. We built a pyre of wood salvaged from burned out buildings, and under a purple sky awash with stars, we sent the big man off to the Hall of Heroes. He was a great man, Gunnar. An easy charm, a winning smile, and utterly ferocious in battle. I wished I had met him ten years sooner, for he would have been an ideal commander in the Ravensworn. Men would have flocked to him like bees to their queen, and he would have led them to victory after victory.

I drank as his body burned. I drank to his memory, and I drank to forget. I was consumed by guilt, old wounds that would never heal. Once more, I slipped into the despair that had gripped me for six long years. How many men were right then sharing a bench on the other side with Gunnar? Men who left behind wives and children. Men who had fought for me and against me. All gone too soon, and all because of me. I looked around at the sombre faces of the men of the Cimbri. They were no hardened warriors, just ordinary men who, until not long ago, had led ordinary lives. Cooks and farmers, carpenters and blacksmiths. They had no business in this fight for their very survival, and I had no business leading them. I should have just stayed at home, drinking myself into an early grave.

The sun rose, though I felt none of its warmth. I was still on the beach, the pyre a smoking ruin beside me. I looked down the beach and saw my ship, sitting on the sand. Godin was still in the hold, unbeknown to the mourning men around me. Absently, I wondered if Sedric had bothered to go and feed him. I should have probably gone to check. I didn't. Birds squawked overhead, their screeching offending my ears. 'Thought you could do with this,' a voice said behind me, and I turned to see Eadger with a steaming bowl of oats.

I grunted and took it, too tired to speak. Forcing

down my tasteless breakfast, I kept my gaze out to the sea. 'They'll be here tomorrow, if Red Beard spoke true.'

'Reckon he did,' I said, scraping the spoon around the side of the bowl to gather up the last of the oats. 'Then Godin's mates will come from across the sea. I'm assuming Sigimund is in contact with them somehow. We didn't sink all their ships at sea the other day; some made it home. Their king will probably know we have Godin.'

'He'll assume we've killed him,' Eadger said. He sat down next to me and for the first time I saw the huge lump on the side of his head. Someone, Isvilt presumably, had cut his hair short around the wound, and to be quite frank, he looked ridiculous. I burst into laughter, giddy from the wine and lack of sleep, tears weeping from my eye. 'The fuck you laughing at?' he asked with a frown.

'If only you could see what you look like,' I said, wiping my face dry. 'Why didn't you tell her to cut it all the way around?'

'I didn't tell her to do anything, wasn't in any state to. But all things considered, I'm feeling much better this morning. Thanks for your concern.' We shared a look, my eye drawn to the purple lump on his head, before I burst into fits of giggles again. This time, he joined me.

'What are we to do then?' he asked once our mirth had settled.

'About what?'

'About the two bloody armies that are about to descend on us! What else?'

I shrugged. 'No point dwelling on it. We set our lookouts, prepare our kit, and when the time comes, we fight.'

'Aye. Guess so.' Eadger scoffed a laugh, reached down and scooped sand in his hand, watching as it was carried off on the breeze.

'What?'

'Just thinking of the mess we see ourselves in. How could it have come to this?' He upturned his hand and the last of the sand trickled out.

'Greed? A lust for power? A need to move your people on and see them safe? Depends which side you're looking at it from. Wilhelm was driven by greed, that much is obvious. He saw an opportunity to make himself rich from the tribes across the sea. Take their grain, feed his people and sell the rest in the south. He sought status, I think, from the tribes south of here. Don't forget, he was supposed to marry the daughter of Dagr and ally himself to the Chauci, a much more powerful tribe than the Cimbri. But that fell apart. So he grasped the next opportunity that came his way.'

'Sounds like you're defending him.'

'Not at all! The man was scum. What he did to those people, to his own people, was unforgivable. But I can see what he was aiming for, even if how he went about it was rotten to the core. Sigimund is driven by power. He saw the *frumentarii* come to bribe his father and no doubt rebuke them. So he made a little deal himself, bagged some gold that he hoped one day he could put to good use. Then before you know it, a boat full of foreign warriors washes up on his shore with a grievance against his northern neighbour, and he has a motive, and a way of paying them to see it through for him. Again, I can't stand the little brat, and I'm hoping his father will knock some sense into him before I have to, but I fear that ship has already sailed. He'll be here, warriors paid for with Roman gold at his back, looking to clear this beach for his newfound friends from across the sea.'

'Newfound subjects, more like. King of Jylland my arse.' Eadger spat in disgust.

'And then there's Godin's people. They're not the enemy, not really. Wilhelm murdered their emissaries in cold blood, blinded by his greed. What were they supposed to do? Come back with more grain, shake his hand and say no hard feelings? No, they have been wronged as much as you and the rest of the Cimbri. They have a king and queen who seek nothing but the refuge of their people, and the only way they can get that is with the sword. That I understand.'

'And then there's you,' Eadger said, fixing me a look. 'The fabled mercenary whose name, whispered around a fire, can strike fear into the hearts of the stoutest warrior. You have been wronged in this, perhaps more than anyone else. This was never your fight; you were brought here under false pretences, and yet when all hope is gone, when your army is on the cusp of defeat, you, the man they call oath breaker, is staying to see it all out. What is your motive?'

I sighed, rubbing my tired face. 'Maybe I'm just tired of always being the bad guy. Or maybe I've just found a cause I feel is worth dying for. I have made friends on this journey, people I would see live to tell the tale of these dark times. Maybe I just want to stay to make sure you do.' I clapped Eadger on the shoulder and rose unsteadily, standing upright and waiting for my blood to get to all the right places.

'Where you going?' Eadger called to my back as I walked off.

'To do the right thing,' I said without looking back.

* * *

Godin winced as I cut the rope from his wrists. He rose slowly, warily, eyes never leaving mine. 'What is this?' he said.

'It is me, setting you free,' I said with a smile. 'No catch. Your people will be here tomorrow, or the day after. When they come, before the battle starts, you will be free to go and join them. But before then, you're welcome on the beach, get some fresh air and the sun on your face. There'll be food for you, and you can sleep out in the open.'

'You're setting me free? Just like that?'

'I am. You are not our enemy, Godin, not really. We have both been betrayed in this. There would never have been a home for you here. You were goaded into fighting, told that you were fighting for your freedom, told so much that you started believing in it. Whatever happens tomorrow, I wish you luck, and I would offer my apologies for the way you have been treated these last days.' I held out a hand. Godin eyed it with suspicion a moment before taking it in his own.

'I would rather an apology for the all the men and women we have lost in this war. But there are no words to make up for that loss.'

'There aren't, so I won't say any. We have lost people too, as you well know, and we feel our losses just as keenly as you. I would ask but one thing from you.'

'Ha! I knew there would be a catch!'

I smiled. 'Nothing you cannot deliver on. When your king lands on this beach tomorrow, and I feel sure he will come himself, speak to him, try to drum some sense into him. Sigimund is not your ally. He will betray you the first moment he gets, maybe even tomorrow, when my blood still drips on the sand. There is no future for your people here. There never was.'

Godin rubbed his wrists, then his face. 'After all you have told me, I think you speak true. I can promise I will speak with him, if he makes the crossing himself. I cannot promise he will listen, though.'

'I would just like you to try.'

We left the ship together, and I introduced him to warriors we passed on the beach. Godin ate in the sun, slept on the beach, and I sent more lookouts south and doubled the watch atop the northern wall. Hilde drilled the men one last time as the sun bled out across the western sea, and we all tended to our kit, sharpening blades and polishing mail. And then we slept, and just as the sun crested the eastern horizon, the first lookout shouted from atop the battlement. 'Ships! Ships to the east!'

And just like that, the battle of our lives begun.

27

I watched Godin walk along the beach. He had seemed confused when I had asked him to take a specific route, walking east to the old town of Tastris before cutting back to the sea, but he'd not asked too many questions. I was no fool, and I hadn't quite told him all we had been up to whilst we waited for his king to come and finish us off. Our men had been digging pits, this I have already told you, and I was banking on those pits saving a few of my men's lives.

'I hope you know what you're doing,' Eadger said to me, eyeing Godin's back as he fingered his sword hilt.

'So do I,' was all I said.

Hilde had the men in a shield wall, one hundred

paces away from the northern gate. The sand was firmer there, the sea reluctant to come that far inland, and I hoped it would give the men a more solid foundation to fight from.

'Any news from the southern road?' I asked Eadger, who just shook his head. 'What about the runners we sent down the east coast?' Another shake of the head. 'Well, not the worst news, I suppose.' I had a team of ten men watching the southern road spread out across the peninsula. They had paired up, each pair having one man two miles from the fortress, the other venturing a further two miles away. We'd no horses, and if Sigimund was indeed marching north, I needed as much notice as I could get. Two men running two miles each rather than one man running four would ensure the news reached me sooner. I hoped. I'd sent another four men down the eastern coast. When the women and children had left Tastris, I'd written three letters to take with them. I hadn't told a soul what they said, or even who one of them was for. But I was Alaric, a disciple of Loki. And I reckoned I'd a little cunning left in me.

Our enemy were off their ships now, their own shield wall forming in the shallows. I was counting ships, stopped when I got to fifty. Fifty ships, eight or so men in each; the maths made me dizzy.

Our wall was twenty men wide, four deep. It was too narrow, and very thin, but it was all we had. I was out in front of them, clapping shoulders and offering encouragement. We were missing the men on the southern road, though I'd made sure those scouts were taken from the youngest of us, the greenest. I didn't have a host of battle-hardened warriors, but I had men with stout hearts and courage, and I knew that whatever was thrown at them, they would meet it with everything they had.

'You don't need to be here,' I said as I reached Kai. He stood shoulder to shoulder with Sedric, the two young men as inseparable as ever. He couldn't speak well still; it hurt him to try. The wounds on his face were unbandaged and looked just as raw and swollen as they had when we'd first landed on that very beach. He didn't reply to me, just unsheathed his sword and banged it on his shield boss, giving me a nod as he did. Sedric laughed and mimicked the gesture, then Rudi did, and Mellow. Rolf joined in, Hilde too, and then all the men were doing it. Eighty swords on eighty shields, making a racket to wake the gods. I smiled. 'Then today, my young friend, we fight for Batur.'

'And Gunnar,' he replied.

I clasped hands with Sedric and Kai, and I'd have

hugged them, kissed them, if I thought it wouldn't have made them look daft on the cusp of battle. *Whatever happens today*, I prayed, *let them be spared*.

I took my place in the line, right in the centre, Hilde on my left flank, Eadger the right. 'One more battle!' I called. 'One more battle and this lot will be done! Send them back to their ships today, and I promise you we have beaten them for good!' I didn't know that to be true, didn't even think it. But sometimes you have to tell a man what he wants to hear, and that usually doesn't mean telling the truth.

Clang. Clang. Clang. The men continued to beat a rhythm on their shields, and I closed my eye and savoured the moment, feeling the wind on my face. It was a clear day, warm but not muggy. As good a day to die as any. I felt none of the weakness that had appeared the day we beached my Celox, none of the sudden loss of breath. I was ready. Whatever happened, I had chosen to stand by my men to the end, and doing the right thing rather than the most profitable for once had left me feeling at peace. *Just see me home to my children*, I prayed silently, hoping the One-Eyed Wanderer was still keeping his eye on me.

The Sitones, or Suiones, or both, had left the shallows and were making their way towards us. They had a banner aloft, blue on white, that looked like the image of boar flapping in the wind. Their king was there, I was certain, though I could see no sign. I looked intently for Godin; would he keep his word? Was he even now speaking to his lord, begging him to send his men back to their ships, to leave us in peace? Either he was or he wasn't; there was nothing I could do about it.

'Make ready to advance!' I called. 'Men with spears to the front row!' Hilde had drilled them from dawn to dusk more times than they could remember. They all knew what to do. We moved forward as one, men with spears gripped in their right hands in the front rank, the others still beating swords on shields behind us. *Clang. Clang. Clang.*

We moved twenty paces, then stopped. There were rocks on the beach, innocent enough looking things, sticking out of the sand at intervals to my right. No one from the enemy would even bother to remark on them if they noticed, and that was the whole point. If you can't win, cheat. I was still the famous Alaric, after all. Hilde called the halt and the beating stopped. We stood silent as the rocks, the enemy coming for us in a disorganised rabble.

'Shields up!' I called as I felt the familiar twinge from a suddenly full bladder. Sweat-sheened palms slick on the grips of my sword and shield. I licked dry lips and reminded myself I had done this a hundred times before and lived to tell the tale. Wasn't sure the odds had ever been stacked so thoroughly against me though.

The enemy picked up the pace as they came for us. They saw nothing but open beach and a thin line of shields. In their minds, they would crush us in one overwhelming charge, hacking their way through our inadequate wall and butchering the last of a decimated tribe that dared to stand against them. There was no doubt in their minds, no second thoughts. I could see men smiling, shouting jokes and challenges. Their war, their desperate struggle for survival, was almost over, and they were going to win.

That was when they met the first of the pits my men had dug. Thin strips of wood had been placed above it, strong enough to hold a spattering of sand, quite inadequate at holding the weight of a host of charging men encumbered with weapons and mail. There was a loud *crack* and the wood gave way. Men fell in their droves, screaming as they landed on the sharpened wooden stakes at the base of the pit. The lucky ones, those who avoided the stakes, were crying out with the pain of snapped ankles and legs; others, no other injuries than that of their pride, clambered desperately over stricken comrades, trying to claw their way free. I grinned my wolf grin, looking past them to the tide, which was on its way in. If the fall hadn't killed them, the sea would finish the job. I doubted many, if any, of them could swim, and no one floats in mail.

Our men cheered, a vicious, merciless war cry that had those in the rear ranks of our enemy recoiling. I could see their fear, smell it, and it took all my discipline to resist the urge to charge them there and then. I looked back over to the rocks, those innocent rocks, and reminded myself why they were there. 'Hold!' I bellowed, for the men of the Cimbri felt the same bloodlust I did. But discipline was our greatest weapon. Eadger was edging forward on my right, his urgent need to wet his blade evident as he snarled through ragged breaths.

'Easy, my friend,' I said quietly. 'There will be time enough for us to fight yet.'

I watched with glee as the enemy stood confounded. The pit wasn't wide, four feet maybe. Most of the men stranded on the other side would be able to jump it no problem, even with sword, shield and mail. But – and this was what held them back – what was on the other side of that pit? Nothing but the open beach they could see? Or something else?

I was grinning again.

As we watched on, hurling insults at them, calling them cowards and whoresons for not daring to charge us, I saw a group of men flock to a man standing under their banner. He was not tall or broad; nothing in the way he dressed distinguished him from any other. He wore plain, serviceable mail and a dull iron helmet. But he was undoubtedly their leader. He used his sword as a pointer, ordering men left and right, sending them out probing for a safe pass around the pit. Two men did make the leap of faith. Together they edged forwards, eyeing each other and the sand at their feet. We laughed as they shuffled forwards, each step a careful probe, careful not to put their weight down until they were certain.

They reached the second of the marker stones off to my right, and inevitably that was where they both stopped. They felt the wood beneath the sand, the give in the thin planks. A man off to my right launched a spear at them that hissed past one of the probers as he was scanning the sand. That was enough for them, and they scurried back to their king.

'What will they do?' Hilde asked, jogging back to me. She'd wasted no time in heading off down the line in search for the man who had wasted a spear. I hoped the tongue lashing he'd received would be the worst beating he got that day.

'What choice do they have? They'll go left or right, try and circle around us and come at us where they think it's safe.'

'And us?'

I gestured to the rocks, all around us at different intervals. 'Stick to the plan, Hilde. Trust me, one last time.'

She nodded, though I could see she was uncertain. We had been through this a hundred times, me, her and Eadger. I was asking a lot of these men and I knew it. It isn't easy, standing idle whilst an enemy warband manoeuvres towards you, but that was precisely what I needed from them today. They would have to fight well enough, and soon. But first, we held our ground and waited.

'Tell the men to down shields. They can eat, drink, piss, shit, whatever they need. But every man keeps his place in the line.' Hilde and Eadger split and ran off, each passing on the order. I took off my helmet and ran a hand through my long, lank hair. The wound in my back was itching, though Isvilt said that when it started doing that it was a good sign. Looking back to the fortress, I could see her above the northern gate, flanked by two men I'd left to guard her. There was one doubt to my plan, and that was our own inability to move. We were surrounded by pits, to our front, left and right, with just a path back to the fortress open to us. What happened if the enemy figured this out for themselves? What if they left us to our holes and charged to take the fortress? They'd done that before, of course, just a few days ago. But this time I didn't think they would.

By then our women and children would have reached the Anglii, and Sigimund would have had time to pass that information on to his new friends. There was nothing of worth in the fortress, and if they did charge it, Isvilt would have time to scurry through the alleys and out the southern gate. She'd be long gone before they got there. No. Those men had come for us, not our rotting walls.

The enemy, it seemed, had made a decision, and it was to their right that they moved, our left. I gave no orders to the men, just left them to rest. I drank greedily from a water skin and pissed where I stood, feeling much better for both. By the time I was done they were formed up once more on our left flank. Back to our front I could see men trying to claw their way from the pit. The tide was coming for them, slowly, creeping its way in to engulf the land. I reckoned the survivors had an hour to get themselves out. One man managed it, lying flat on his back after clambering out. Eventually, he rose and waved a fist to his compatriots, angry none had bothered to stay and help him. I'd thought the same myself, guessed their king was reeling with the shame of watching his men fall into such an easy trap. If there was any division in their ranks, that could only help me.

Back to our left they were moving once more, ten men out in front of the rest, probing for another pit. 'Right then, best make it look like we're ready for them.' Men in earshot laughed, and together we refitted helmets and hefted shields. We turned our line, so I was once more front and centre.

'Same again?' Eadger asked. 'Surely they won't be so stupid this time.'

'One way to find out.' I shrugged. 'Ready to charge!' I called, holding up my sword. 'With me!'

All at once, we moved off at a slow jog, keeping our shields tight together. I allowed myself a small moment of pride, seeing no one rush ahead of the others. Discipline was prevailing, the men were focused, sharp, and I wished only that I had the black raven on a red flag flying over my head. We kept up the jog, no more banging on shields, no more shouting at the men come to kill us. Silent as the wolf we were, and just as deadly. I kept an eye on the rocks, to our left this time rather than the right, and let out a war cry when we were twenty or so paces away.

The men of the Cimbri joined in. It's amazing the noise just eighty men can make, even in a wide-open landscape with the wind buffering in from the sea. I widened my stride, increasing the pace of our charge, my one eye fixed not on the enemy in front but the planted rocks to our left. Our enemy were screaming back at us, and their rage was plain to see. They had been tricked by us, had stood powerless as friends and brothers fell to their deaths, and they were keen for their revenge.

In ten paces, a mass of warriors outran the probers to their front. I thought amongst the cacophony I could make out an authoritative voice, ordering them back. Though the voice may as well have tried to control the wind. 'Hold! Plant your shields!' I called, getting as close as I dared to the rocks. As one the men of the Cimbri stopped, hunching down behind round shields, a bristle of spears stuck out from the wall. Still the enemy charged us, blood up, sure that this time they would reach us, break us.

They didn't.

The second pit did its job just as well as the first. The first two ranks of warriors were hurled down with a thunderous crunch of breaking bones and shattered mail. We were cheering then, spears held high in the air as we roared our defiance. We had killed a third of their strength and were yet to wet our blades.

It was then I saw Godin. He was standing at his king's right shoulder, speaking urgently in his ear. I imagined what he was saying, pleading with his lord to stop this fruitless assault. But, I reasoned, that king had seen hundreds of his warriors perish, without the battle even starting. I did not think he would be in the mood to listen. And so it was.

They rallied around their king once more, and off back around us they went, circling the new pit and the old, without, I noticed, stopping to rescue any survivors from their fall. I ordered ten spearmen to run over to the second pit and finish off any man trying to climb to safety. We would be fighting to the east, and I did not want any nasty surprises coming from our rear. It was grim work, but necessary, and this was a fight for our very survival.

In no time they were formed on our eastern flank. We had a pit there, but it was a shallow thing. It would turn a few ankles, maybe snap the odd leg, but it would not stop a determined charge. But I didn't need it to. Lining up on the east, the tide coming in, the men on the right of their flank were now standing in the shallows, the men on their left up against a sharp bank of grass that formed a knoll at the beach's end. They could only come at us ten men wide, or risk losing men to the tide. The first pit had vanished now, and I sent a swift prayer for the poor souls trapped beneath the lapping waves. Drowning always seemed to me such a horrible way to die, one of the reasons I had willingly learned how to swim.

They took their time, coming for us the third time. They were weary; adrenalin can only carry a man so far, after all. I felt it myself, the bloodlust in me thinning, leaving an ache in my legs and arms. 'Do we charge again?' Hilde asked me. She looked nervous, licking her dry lips in anticipation.

I shook my head. 'We go to the rock and hold our line there. With luck they'll charge the last few steps and lose a few men to the pit. Should cause a bit of confusion, then we pounce.' She nodded, licking her lips once more. 'Try and relax,' I said to her. 'Think what they're thinking. They've lost men already, they'll be tired from their crossing, hungry, thirsty. They might still have the numbers on us, but they won't count for much once we get down to it.' I hoped I was right.

'Shields up!' I called to the men. 'This is what we

trained for! You all know your roles, fight now and live to see another sun rise! Fight now for your wives and children, let us give them a victory today!'

We formed our wall, five paces back from the rocks that marked the last remaining pit. I hunched down behind my shield, my eye roaming the enemy. They were cautious, uncertain, the wind taken from their sails. I smiled. I thought we had them. But their king ordered them forward regardless, and at us they came, at a steady shuffle if not a charge. Ten paces from us they hit the pit, and the thin planks split with an audible crack, and men fell, turning an ankle or jarring a knee, their comrades behind them unable to stop their forward momentum tripping over their heels.

'Now or never, I reckon,' Eadger muttered to me.

I turned to fix him a look, seeing the eagerness in his eyes. 'Reckon it's now then. Forward!' I bellowed in my best battlefield voice, and we charged them, spears held out before us.

And my world turned to bloody chaos.

28

An axe came at my face and I jerked right, the blade hissing past my ear. I reached out with my sword and felt it punch through bone and muscle. As I heaved, the blade came back reluctantly. The axeman fell, just another bleeding corpse on the sand, and I was looking for my next opponent. A giant with a spear was probing at Eadger. A savage cut from my blade and the spear was knocked from his hand, Eadger on him before he could react.

'Step forwards!' I called, hearing Hilde repeat the cry and others take it up along the line. Together we pushed forwards with our left feet, planting them once more in the sand, our right legs trailing behind us. I was sweating like a pig; it poured into my eye and I was constantly blinking, trying to keep some semblance of vision. A sword crashed into my shield, sending the rim up to my face with such force I could do nothing but block it with my chin. Which hurt. My head snapped back and for a moment I was looking up into the clear sky, seeing the black dots of carrion birds already circling. How was it they were always there? Circling, lower and lower, just waiting for the easy pickings at battle's end.

A shove in my back returned me from my brief daze, and my vision cleared enough to see the sword coming back for me, this time a blow aimed to my left. Eadger raised his shield and took it for me, and quick on my feet, I ducked and stepped forwards, jabbing my sword into a bare leg.

The melee was all around me, a maelstrom of blood and iron, and I was lost in it. I followed my low jab with a thrust to the groin and my latest opponent fell, howling to the ground. He would never rise again, the men behind me in our formation would see to that. I stepped over him and, leaning my weight into my shield, I pushed back their second line, then took the man to my left in the flank. Twisting round to my right, taking a blow on my shield I hadn't seen coming, I hacked at a helmet and pushed its owner back into his comrades. Suddenly I had space.

I danced forwards two steps. A sweeping blow from low to high took one man out, a jab to the face the next. 'Forwards!' I roared. 'Ravensworn with me!' I was lost to the battle joy, to the simple pleasure of blood and death. I'd quite forgotten that it wasn't my own warband that followed me, that those men were quite dead. I charged forwards, seeing the figure of their king not ten paces from me. Godin was with his lord, holding shield and sword, ready to defend him.

My eye fixed on him, on his grim expression beneath an iron helm. It looked as if he were shouting, at me or someone else I didn't know, didn't care. I smashed my shield into his, and we both rocked back, staggered, but kept our feet. I sent a probing lunge to his right; he moved his shield and blocked it easily. My blade still moving, I whirled it over his head and sent a backhand slash aiming for his shoulder. Two quick steps to his left, a twist of his torso, and once more my sword rattled off his shield boss. We paused a second, two old warriors, panting at each other across the sand. The beach itself had come alive. I could hear the tide over the din of battle, crashing into men's ankles as they fought for their lives. Sand was spraying up from the floor. Catching the breeze, it twirled and arced around us, forming a cloud that might have concealed the entire battle from Isvilt and her guards watching from the fortress walls.

Godin took the initiative next, dancing forwards and jabbing low to my left. I got my shield down but only just, his blade scraping the bronze on the bottom rim. I hacked at him whilst he was stretching, but lithe as a cut purse he danced back out of my reach, my sword cutting nothing but sand on the air. 'He will not yield!' he called to me as we stood again three paces apart.

'Aye, I gathered that much! If you will not yield then you will die here, surely you can see that?' I respected Godin, for the stoic calm he had shown upon his capture and for the way he fought me then for his king. That respect was returned, I knew that. But that didn't mean we wouldn't kill each other first chance we got. As if to emphasise my point, there was a change in the battle behind me. Godin's comrades were pushed back, and turning my head a crack, I saw Sedric and Kai at the point of a wedge, driving their way through to me. I smiled. 'You're late!' I called to them, before turning back to Godin.

His head was swivelling then, wide eyes roaming from me back to his king, who had taken three big steps back behind him. 'We still have the numbers!'

he called to me, though I think he was trying to convince himself of that more than anything.

'Numbers count for little in battle, friend. Stout hearts and courage win more often than not.'

'Aye, as does digging holes in the sand, it would seem.'

I showed him my teeth and came for him once more. I feinted high and right with my sword. When he moved his shield to block the blow, I stopped midswing. Stepping forwards on my left foot and changing the momentum of my body, I rammed my shield into his face, snapping back his head and sending a torrent of blood gushing from his nose. I stepped in quick, not allowing him to reset, and plunged my sword, hard and true, in a straight thrust through his heart. He gasped, mouth hanging open, eyes bulging in shock and pain. With my sword still in his chest, he sank to his knees, blood bright on his lips. 'I am sorry, Godin,' I said quietly as I knelt in front of him. 'But we both knew it could come to this.' I wrenched the sword free, blood puddling down his front, and he collapsed silently to the ground.

Standing, I could feel the presence of the Cimbri around me, their shields bristling with spears as they closed up on either side. Hilde was still there, blood spattered all over her face. Sedric had lost his helm, with a nasty looking cut above his left eye that he seemed not to have noticed. Kai was with him, seemingly untouched, though his face was such a mess of raw wounds it was hard to tell. Eadger was to Hilde's left; he appeared to be missing a tooth or two, gore matted in his beard, but he grinned at me when I met his eye. I saw no sign of Mellow or Rudi, nor Rolf, but I hoped they yet lived.

To my front, the men of the Suiones and Sitones, two proud tribes from across the sea, were in disarray. Their king was haranguing them, forcing them back into lines and raising shields, but it was clear to all that their courage had failed them. The sun was still high in a clear blue sky, a beautiful summer's day. A fine day for a victory. I raised my blade, as I had at the battle's beginning, and whirled it in the air. 'Men of the Cimbri, with me!'

And we charged them one more time. There would be no need for another.

29

I could say more of how that battle ended, but when it comes down it, killing men is much the same. We pushed them back into the sea. A few got away in their little boats, their king included, but by the time our slaughter was done, there were countless bodies floating in the shallows.

I was stooped, leaning on my sword as we finished the last of our bloody work, feeling every one of the many winters my sore back had seen. The wound was aflame once more, and I wanted nothing more than to strip to the waste and plunge into the water, red as it was. But a leader's work is never done, and before I knew what I was doing I was calling back the men, organising them once more into lines and ordering them all to drink and tend to their wounds. I sent a swift prayer to The Hanged One, for truly Wotan had watched down on me. I thought back to the dream – if that was what it had been, and for a moment I truly felt the presence of a god at my shoulder. I thanked Loki too, for the Trickster had surely been involved. Our pits had worked a treat, as they had that distant day I'd fought the Batavi in the south. What need was there for an old dog to learn new tricks when the classics worked just as well?

Sedric and Kai were huddled together, Kai holding a bandage to the wound above Sedric's eye. I squatted down next to them, clamping a hand on each of their shoulders. 'How bad is it?' I asked Sedric, and I couldn't stop myself from wincing when Kai pulled the bandage away. 'Well, you never were much to look at,' I said through a grin. The cut was deep enough, but once the bleeding had stopped, I thought it was nothing a few stitches wouldn't fix.

'At least I've still got the eye,' Sedric said to me, and the three of us were soon chuckling together.

'And how about you?' I turned to Kai, who was wincing at the pain laughing caused in his wounds. He just shrugged and gestured to a few superficial cuts on his arms. He was clearly reluctant to talk, and I marvelled at the strength of the lad's willpower.

Every step must have sent a wave of pain racing through his face, but he had stood and fought with us through that, and just the fact he was still there standing in front of me told me he must have fought well.

'You should have seen his speed with a blade, Lord,' Sedric said, holding his own bandage to his face now. 'I'd wager he could even take you one on one.'

'I should think he could! I'm not quite the man I was.' It was harrowing to realise how much I meant that. I rose unsteadily back to my feet, knees aching, calves burning, back a ruin. Moving off from them, I felt new agonies rising, my right shoulder first, then my left. I was too old to be clad in mail, lugging a sword and shield into battle. Looking around, I could see more than a few weary faces nestled under grey beards. Those men were the true heroes in my eyes – well, eye. We fought and ran and fought and ran, matching our young comrades every step of the way. When I was a young man, war had been an adventure, a way to test myself against my peers and see if I had what it took to win. It was a game, that was how I had seen it. But in my ageing years, I began to see it for the utter waste it was. A waste of coin and metal, and more importantly, a waste of good men. I thought then of Godin. I hadn't wanted to kill the man; he had seemed good, honest. But for me, he was honest to the wrong man, and I had needed him out the way. He'd said he was a battle chief for his king, and I saw the truth of that when he slumped to the sand. The men around him had given up, as if my sword had snatched out and taken their own hearts.

Sighing, I left the men to their victory cheers and boasts and trudged back up to Tastris. The decaying walls we had fought for all day looked no grander; if anything, the sight of them disgusted me more than when I had first laid my eye on them. The northern gate hung open, and I passed into the shade and paused, revelling in the cool. 'Still alive then,' Isvilt said as she approached. She had a jug of ale in one hand, a cup in the other. Feeling no need for the cup, I took the jug from her and drank greedily, ale spilling in my beard, mingling with the dried blood. 'You *stink!*' Isvilt said as I handed the jug back.

'Thanks. And you are most welcome, by the way,' I snapped, moving past her.

Isvilt laughed. 'Allow me to pay homage to the great Lord Alaric! Saviour of our nation, vanquisher of foes! I kneel at your feet.' She knelt, blocking my path, and all I could do was join in with her mirth.

'Everything hurts,' I said once we had finished laughing. 'I'm not sure I'm cut out for this life any more.'

'Come in and strip off. We have plenty of water for washing, even if we have little else.'

I did as I was instructed and soon found myself neck deep in a barrel of ice-cold water, which was fine by me. Pleasingly, the wound in my back hadn't opened, though Isvilt tutted at the stitches nonetheless. She fussed and scrubbed me, causing so much pain at times it felt worse than the battle, but once the chill had settled in my bones and I rose, teeth chattering, from the barrel, I felt a new man.

I dressed in the only tunic I had that looked even remotely clean and left my mail to be cleaned by one of the guards that had been left in the fortress. Isvilt handed me a bowl of steaming oats and I devoured it in moments, tasteless as it was. Taking my leave of her, I walked through the fortress and out the southern gate. There was a lone guard stationed on the battlement above, and it was with a mixture of relief and disappointment I heard he had seen no sign of the scouts we had out roaming the southern land of the peninsula.

For the first time since the battle's end, I allowed myself to think of what happened next. Red Beard was coming back; at least he had said as much, but when? Sigimund would be chomping at the bit to reach to me, I knew, but how fast could he mobilise a force to march at us? And what would his father do to stop him? If anything? And then there was the matter of the other letters I had sent south with our women and children. I could only pray they had reached their intended destination.

As it happened, I had my answer soon enough. I heard the scout before I saw him, boots scuffing on the dirt road as he ran. He stopped before me, leaning on his knees and painting. He was a callow youth of no more than sixteen, a pox-marked face beneath a quiff of dark hair. 'Men... are... coming,' he said through ragged breaths.

'Who's men? How far away?'

'Don't know who,' the lad said, recovering his breath at last. 'But I was told no more than five miles south, coming up the western beach. My brother reckoned there were two hundred of them.'

I nodded, remembering the system I'd put in place. This lad would not have seen the enemy, but the man who had run a mile or two to him – his brother, it would seem – had. 'You've done well. Go inside and get yourself some food.'

Needing no encouragement, the scout scampered off into the fortress. I stood a moment longer, closing my eye and hearing the sighing of the sea off to my left. Looking up at the sun, I saw to my dismay there were four or maybe five hours of daylight left. They would be here today, whoever they were, and we would have to fight again.

I walked back inside the fortress, climbed the southern battlement and ordered the guard there to run to Hilde and let her know the news. I stood there when he had gone, squinting off to the southwest. I thought I could make out the faint haze of a dust cloud, though I couldn't be sure.

Returning to the hall, I threw back on my mail and fastened my helmet, seeing with surprise a new dent on the top. I didn't remember taking the blow, but such is war. My shield was half bent with a great chunk taken out where I had painted on the raven's eye, but I figured it had seen me through one battle, it could last another. Hilde and Eadger appeared at the front of our band of men. They cantered into the open ground with a mixture of surprise and dismay written on their faces.

'Is it true?' Eadger asked.

I nodded. 'Aye. Seems our day's work isn't done yet. Come, we'll go to the southern gate and see what we can see.'

The sun had moved a finger's breadth to the west,

I reckoned as I stood once more on the southern battlement. To my alarm, the dust cloud was visible now,
easily so, and it didn't appear to be further than a
mile away. Another runner reached the southern
gate, just as breathless as the last. 'Men coming,' was
all he said, throwing an arm in their general direction.

'How are they so close?' I demanded of him. 'The
boy earlier said they were five miles south!'

'Aye, they were. But that was two hours or more
ago.'

Cursing, I walked to the southwest point of the
battlement and squinted.

'They'll be here in an hour, no more,' Hilde said
in a grim tone.

'Are there any more of you out there?' I said to the
boy, whose cheeks flushed redder.

'There was me and my brother, Lord, though I
reckon you've already seen him. Ain't seen any others
for a couple of days now.'

I cursed again. Cursed the lazy scouts for their
tardiness, cursed myself for putting too much faith in
them. My gaze roamed the southeast, hoping, praying, I'd see a runner come from that direction, but
there was none.

'Shut this gate,' I said, turning to Hilde. 'The men

need to eat and drink their fill, then come here ready to fight. How many have we got left standing?'

'Twenty dead, ten wounded,' Eadger replied with a heavy frown.

That was a blow. We'd no more than sixty fighting men left, though I reasoned that we'd killed four times that and more in a fight with the raiders from across the sea. In any other circumstance I'd consider that a fair result, but we were in dire need of men. I made my face a mask and nodded. 'Bar this gate.'

The men ate their oats in grim silence. Some muttered to each other. There were solemn hugs and a few tears for wives and children who would never be seen again. But by the gods they were a proud bunch. Every man stood tall, chests puffed out, ready to go to the Heroes Hall if it meant his brothers could fight on a little longer. I'm not ashamed to admit that a tear or two pricked my eye as I stood watching them. They had been through so much, suffered such a cruel fate. And they hadn't seen the worst of it yet.

The gate was barred and I stood atop the battlement when our newest enemy came into view. Sigimund rode a fine grey horse at their head, his flushed face already carrying the spark of victory as he rode up and down the mud road in front of his men, mail glimmering in the late afternoon sun. 'Is

that the great Lord Alaric I see up there? Hiding behind his rotten walls?' His voice was high and thick
with mirth.

'Just having a little rest. We've had quite a day of
it. Slaughtering men is tiring work,' I said to a ragged
cheer from the men of the Cimbri. 'Give us an hour to
rest up and we'll be more than ready to do the same
to you, insolent pup!'

'I crossed blades with you once before, old man. I
have a war host at my back now, rather than twelve
boys. I would not be so confident.'

I didn't reply, but looked out at the men he had
brought to bring my death. They were two hundred
strong, or thereabouts, and every one looked a hardened killer. I saw gnarled faces, scarred and weath-
ered, armoured in good mail with swords at their hips
and spears in hand. We couldn't beat them, not in
open battle. I would have to lean on the Sly One once
more if I was to lead my men to another victory.
'Ludwig thought he had the better of me, as you did
when you came across our crew on that beach. I
stand here, one eyed, greying, with aching bones and
lines on my face. But how do you think it is I came to
be so old? I'm a hard man to kill, young Sigimund. I
have fought Rome's cursed legions in the south, faced
the Batavi in the west, and waged a war against the

Suebi in the north. Men call me the *great* Lord Alaric because that is what I am! I've earned my name, boy, and if you come to take this gate, you'll find out why.'

My men roared at that. Eadger thumped me on the back as I turned away from Sigimund. Showing him my back, I made my way down the stairs, out of his sight. Red Beard would be down there somewhere, though my one eye hadn't spotted him. It did no harm to remind him who he was facing, or the men who had marched north for the promise of Roman gold from Sigimund's hand. I was old, yes, certainly past my prime. But I have always been a proud man, and that pride would not let me bow down to some pup with thoughts high above his station.

I stood at the bottom of the rickety wooden steps and basked in the cheers of the men. Smiling at them, feeling a renewed purpose, I called for Hilde and Eadger, and together we moved away to make our plans.

'We can't face them in open battle,' Eadger hissed, not wanting to be overheard.

'Neither can we stand behind these walls,' Hilde retorted. I looked from one to the other, a half-smile dancing on my lips. Sedric was making his way towards us, Kai not far behind. I saw Rudi and Mellow leaning against a wall, blood-stained faces huddled together as they shared a small moment of privacy. Rolf came over, grinning, his smile revealing three missing teeth from the top of his mouth. 'Never been much of a chewer, Lord,' he said to me with a shrug, and I could only laugh in return.

'So what are we to do?' Sedric asked, the cut above his eye still leaking blood.

'You are going to go to Isvilt and get that eye properly seen to,' I said to him. 'The rest of you are going to get the men to gather as much firewood by the southern gate as you can. Have we any oil left?'

There had been a few amphorae of oil in the hall when I'd first arrived, and they'd still been there the day Wilhelm was killed. 'Think so, I'll check with Isvilt,' Hilde said. 'Why?'

* * *

It took an hour to get enough wood to the southern gate. We dumped it on the mud under the battlement, and Isvilt brought the last of the oil out to us. 'Won't be any left for cleaning your kit,' she muttered, handing it over to me.

'If we get through this,' I said to her, 'I'll never need mail again.'

I was back atop the battlement, watching with something close to admiration as I saw what our enemy had been about. Sigimund was building a ram. Four small trunks had been cut down and fastened together with rope, and even as I watched, a team of men were lifting their creation, testing its weight and how fast they could move encumbered with it. 'Wotan's eye,' I muttered. 'But he might actually turn out to be quite good at this.'

'Only if we let him live long enough to learn,' Sedric said at my side. His head was wrapped in blood-stained bandages, and he squinted out of his left eye. I thought once more how stupid it had been of me to bring the young man here, of all the things he could have been experiencing instead.

'We'll get through this,' I said to him, with more confidence than I felt.

'You've seen us this far, Lord. We'll follow you to the Heroes Hall if need be.'

I sincerely hoped it wouldn't come to that.

It seemed they were ready with their ram, and I was cursing our lack of archers when I saw movement off to the southeast. A lone figure appeared from behind a clutch of bushes, waving manically to us on the wall. 'Look, Lord!' Sedric exclaimed, pointing out the man.

'Put your hand down,' I hissed. 'We don't want our new friends down there to spot him.' It was one of the scouts I'd had posted on the eastern coast, it had to be. He waved to us once more, frantically pointed back the way he had come, and disappeared back behind the bushes. 'Your eyes are better than my one,' I said to Sedric. 'Can you make anything out in the southeast?' I was squinting, my mouth suddenly dry as my heart thumped with anticipation.

'There's a dust cloud, Lord. Small, maybe five or six miles off?' He turned to look at me. 'Who could it be?'

My face split into a triumphant grin. 'My dear father-in-law. Who else?'

I'd written three letters when I'd sent the women and children south. One to Haribert, begging he take our people in, and also informing him of my suspicions of his son. I hadn't expected him to act on it; in fact, I thought he'd have read the words with glee, learning what plans his son had put in motion. The other two had gone further south. One to Saxa, my wife. I had explained our dire situation, told her where to dig to find the last of my silver should I not come back, and also asked if she would perhaps put in a word for me to her father, Dagr.

Dagr was chief of the Chauci, the tribe into which

I had been born. I considered myself an exile of the Chauci, though in reality that was more self-imposed. I'd had no need to cross blades with the men of my own tribe until Dagr had allied himself to the Suebi, and I had waged war on that formidable tribe. A war that would end in defeat, embarrassment, and six years of shame. Not to mention me killing Dagr's son.

But nonetheless, my last letter had been to Dagr himself. I had begged on behalf of his daughter and grandsons, and promised I would serve him in war if the need arose, if only he would march north in force and save my worthless arse. It seemed my letter, coupled with his daughter's pleas, had been enough.

'There's another one, Lord. Southwest. Look.' Sedric once more held out a hand, and I followed his pointed figure to the horizon where, sure enough, another dust cloud kicked up in the sea breeze.

'Shit.' Who could that be? Only Haribert. 'Who's closer, do you think?'

Sedric took a moment, head craning left and right. 'Neck and neck,' he said after a while. Below us, Sigimund's men were readying their ram, men surrounding them with shields. They were coming.

'The carts that had the amber in, where are they?' There had been four carts of amber, the promised payment for my services – in that Wilhelm had at least been honest. We had unloaded the amber on to the Celox, and although I feared the extra weight may have been too much for the small ship to bear, I'd reasoned that if the need for me to leave in a hurry arose, I would at least be getting away with the amber.

'They're in an alley, Lord, just the other side of the hall.'

'Grab a couple of men and bring one up.' I vaulted down the steps, throwing on my helmet and fastening it as I called for Hilde and Eadger. 'They're coming, get the men ready.'

'Should we not have men on the battlements?' Hilde asked.

'To do what? Assault them with colourful language? We've no artillery. It is a waste of time and men. And anyway, I have a plan.' I didn't tell them about Dagr, didn't see the point unless the old rogue got his men there in time to save us.

Just as the men were finishing their preparations, there was a roar from outside the gate, and then an almighty crash. The crumbling gates baulked under the weight of the ram, and for a moment I was sure the walls themselves would come tumbling down. But they held. Every man took an involuntary step back, heads swivelling over shoulders, making sure their escape routes were clear. 'Hold your positions!' I called. 'I want a wall of shields facing the gate here.' I drew a line in the mud with the end of my sword, and Hilde soon had them in a line of sorts, though none of them looked too keen to my eye.

Sedric appeared with Kai, Rudi and Mellow, pushing the two-wheeled cart up the street. I ran to the pile of wood just inside the gate as the ram smashed into it once more, sending splinters flying to me like daggers. 'Quick, load it on!' I said to them, and the five of us hastily loaded the cart with the firewood.

'What are we doing this for?' Rudi asked, gasping for breath from his exertions.

'Get me a flame and I'll show you.'

Kai covered the wood with the last of the oil. There wasn't as much as I'd hoped, but it covered the majority. Rudi came running back with a flaming torch. The gate was struck once more and it seemed the wood groaned on the impact. One more push and they would be through. Let the bastards come, I thought.

'I'll let you do the honours,' I gestured to Rudi, and I saw his eyes light up the moment he realised my intentions. He threw the torch onto the cart. For a moment, nothing happened, and I feared the wood was damp or the oil had no effect. But then the flame roared and spread, licking up as the fire consumed all it could touch. I grinned and gestured for Kai and Sedric to join me. 'When the gate gives way, we push this through the gap. There'll be two hundred warriors pouring through behind it, expecting nothing more than a thin shield wall to hold them back.'

'They'll shit themselves,' Sedric said through a grin. Kai made a growling noise from the base of this throat, then grimaced as his smile caused his wounded face to spasm in pain.

I hunched down behind the cart, sparks flying around my face, engulfed in a wave of heat. I felt the tremors in the ground as Sigimund's men ran up to the gate once more, and with an almighty bang, it finally gave way. There was a ragged cheer as warriors dropped their cumbersome ram and began to stream through the opening.

They didn't get far.

We pushed off, the two-wheeled cart light enough, even with the flaming inferno on top. We heaved as hard as we could, ran five, six steps, then let its momentum do the rest. It smashed into a wall of men and metal, hurtling them aside. It bumped its way through, rolling down the mud outside the fortress before finally toppling over and coming to a stop. It had done its job.

Sigimund's men recoiled, some crushed by the weight of the cart, and were lying unmoving in the mud. Others clawed at burnt faces with charred hands. Others stood with their backs to the wall, white faced, shocked at what had just happened to them. I didn't intend to give them a chance to recover.

With a war cry to wake the gods, I was at them, slashing a burning man with my sword before ducking under a spear and skewering a warrior still recoiling from the flames that licked at his face. Sedric and Kai flanked me, both of them snatching a life with their first action. Eadger and Hilde led the last of our men in a charge. Sixty brave men of the Cimbri, the last of a dying tribe, smashed into Sigimund's men in a devastating wave, forcing them back out of the gate they had worked so hard to break down.

It was carnage, butchery, and I was in my element. I slashed a man's hamstrings, then caved in a helmet. I battered a spear away with my shield and jabbed its owner through the mouth, my sword digging into the back of his skull. I was a lord of death once more, and no one could match me.

'Shields!' Hilde was bellowing somewhere off to my left. I was annoyed at her command, so intent on chasing down the warriors that fled before us. But then I saw what she saw. Sigimund was forming his own wall, halfway down the gentle slope that led from the southern gate. The cart burned behind them, black smoke billowing up into the darkening sky. I cursed, joined in Hilde's cry and in no time we had our own wall formed, both narrower and shallower than the one of our enemy.

Our men were panting, weary. They had been fighting all day. But Sigimund's men had been marching in their armour, encumbered by their shields and weapons, and I reckoned we could still take them. The air was full of the cries of the dying. Charred men lay in ruins in the mud. I saw one man, half his face a burned-out wreck, gurgling a stifled scream. I put him out of his misery.

'Reckon we thinned them out well enough,' Eadger said, wiping blood off his face with his mail.

Looking at their numbers, I thought maybe sixty of them were dead. That was good going, don't get me wrong, but they still outnumbered us two to one. 'We just need to buy some time,' I said more to myself than Eadger. The sun was waning now, out in the west, the sky a purple hue. How much longer until Dagr reached us? Or Haribert from the west?

'They're coming!' someone called from our line, and snapping back to the matter at hand, I watched

Sigimund lead his men up the incline towards us. I hefted my shield, planted my right foot in front of my left and readied myself. 'We hold them here!' I called. 'Let them come and meet us. We don't have to beat them; we just have to hold!'

I was looking past the enemy, hoping, praying, I would see mail-clad warriors appear on the horizon. I didn't. Surely, they would be here soon?

With a cry, Sigimund's men broke into a jog, shields held tight together. I saw Red Beard coming right for me and refocused my mind. Let them come.

We had no spears to throw or hold out in front of our shields; we'd spent them on the beach and in the first attack out from the gate. We had our shields, our swords, and our stout hearts. They smashed into our line with a rounding crescendo. I was knocked back a step, two, before I found my footing once more and leaned into my shield, grunting with the effort. 'You're a fucking dead man!' Red Beard spat at me; I could taste sour ale on his breath. 'Fucking traitor, murderer. Oath breaker!'

He came for me with a high blow. I wrenched my shield up and caught his blade on the rim, lunging low myself at the same time. Red Beard was fast. He danced past my blade and sent his own crashing down once more. This one bit into the wood of the shield, catching. I roared in triumph, twisting the shield with my wrist, trying to force him to drop his sword. He was either too thick or too stubborn to realise what was happening; he just moved around, still gripping his hilt, until he was side on to our shield wall, his back exposed to Kai.

Kai saw his chance and leaped at it. The man who had put the fear of the gods in him was at his mercy and he wasn't going to let the moment pass. He rammed his shield into his opponent's face, using the time it bought him to twist right and plunge his sword into Red Beard's back.

The irony was not lost on me.

Red Beard sunk to the mud with a howl of anguish. I pulled back my shield, and his sword dropped to the ground. I spat on the cur and stepped over him, turning to Kai to share a triumphant grin. My face quickly dropped in anguish.

Kai was still looking down at the stricken Red Beard, his wide eyes and stitched-up face unmoving. The man he had punched with his shield had recovered, and in two quick steps was behind him, sword raised. 'No!' I had time to scream before the sword came crashing down, crunching into Kai's helmet. He slumped, wordless, to the mud.

With an enraged cry, I hacked at the man, cutting

through his shoulder, pulling free my sword and swiping at his neck, taking his head off in one outraged swing. The battle had descended into chaos around me, but I didn't notice. The shield walls were broken, and individual duels had broken out. I swept through the battle like a wraith, cutting at exposed limbs, screaming in my grief. I hacked and chopped and ducked and blocked, though I couldn't tell you how many I killed, or how many times I was hit in return. I was lost, senseless.

A blow on my left hip stunned me. As I turned to see where it had come from, there was an almighty blow to the top of my head. My helmet shook with the impact but just held itself together, and I sunk to one knee, seeing stars.

I don't know how long I stayed there, but when I eventually opened my eye, the din of battle seemed to have subsided. I dropped my sword and shield, and on all fours, vomited on the mud.

'There he is, lads!' a voice called out, dripping in mirth. 'The *great* Lord Alaric! Brought low at last.'

My head swam. I couldn't piece a thought together, let alone a word. There was a pulsating pain behind my one eye and I struggled to focus my vision on my hand. 'Alaric! Alaric, get up!' It was Hilde, shouting from somewhere. I managed to get one foot planted on the floor, but I could move no more. I vomited again, splattering my mail. I heard laughter and wondered briefly where my sword had gone.

'How does it feel? To be the loser, to be defeated.' Something hit my face. It was wet. 'But you've of course been here before. Your army defeated, you at the mercy of your enemy. Bringing back any memories?'

I thought of my mother. I remembered her being raped, the triumphant grins of the legionaries as they tied me and my father up, our faces planted in the grass. 'Just do as they say, Alaric,' my father had said. He wasn't a bad man, might have even been a good one. He'd just wanted to me to survive.

Trouble is, I'd never been much good at doing what I was told. From running away with my father's sword, to raising a warband and treating our land like a playground, I'd always strived to be different, to stand out from the rest.

With an effort, I got my other foot planted on the ground and slowly began to rise to my feet. I was battered, broken, bloody. I would not let them see me beaten.

I blinked, slowly clearing my vision, if not the pulsating pain in my head. The world seemed darker, dimmer, as if the sun had left and taken everything good with it. 'Any last words?' Sigimund said, striding up to me with all the arrogance of youth.

'Yes,' I said, my face gradually splitting into the wolf-like grin I had become so very fond of. 'Look behind you.'

Sigimund's face slipped, and a glance over his shoulder had him quaking in his boots. Metal glinted in the dying light; a banner hung in shadow in the sky. Boots trampled on dry mud, and out of the darkness marched an army.

Dagr had come.

30

It was a full three weeks later when I felt well enough to travel. I'd slept for two straight days after the battle and still woken with a pounding head. I had built a pyre for poor young Kai, and he had gone to the Heroes Hall in a blaze of glory. Sedric and I had stayed until the embers had died to ash, both of us lost to despair.

Dagr's men had made short work of cutting through Sigimund's hastily formed army, though the young lordling had been spared the slaughter. His father had arrived at dawn the following day, a hundred armed men at his back, as well the women and children of the Cimbri. He had been full of sorrow and regret, pleading his ignorance to his son's scheming and newfound riches. I hadn't believed him, neither had Dagr, but I reasoned Sigimund would live with rather less freedom from that day on.

The Cimbri would survive, and that gladdened my heart. They were a good people, a strong people, and with some help, they would rebuild their fortress and then their town and go on to prosper once more. Isvilt would lead them, with Hilde and Eadger at her shoulders. I wondered if a woman had ever served as a chief before. I hadn't heard of one, though if any woman were to make it possible, it was Isvilt. She'd already tied Haribert down to an agreement on trade of cattle and grain for amber, something the Cimbri were sure to never be short of, and there were plenty of hugs and tears as we said our final goodbyes on the shore of the beach.

My small Celox sailed well under the burden of the amber as we slipped down the east coast of Jylland. Our journey south was mercifully less eventful than the one north. I had eight men loaned from Dagr to help me man the ship, and Sedric and I spent our days in silent companionship, each of us not ready to speak of the thoughts that haunted us.

We were rowing down a river that cut through the lands of the Chauci, and I had my eye roaming the shore, desperate to see the spot I had left Saxa and our boys. 'Is it always like that?' Sedric said suddenly. He was folding the ship's sail with one of Dagr's warriors, each man holding a corner. I realised he must have been holding on to the question for weeks. I shared a look with Dagr's man and he gave me a nod and moved off, giving me and Sedric some privacy.

'Yes. Yes, it is always like that.'

He nodded, adjusting the cloth draped over his bald head. The wound above his eye was healing well, a scar forming where the stitches had been. He rubbed at it. 'I don't think it's the life for me,' he said after a time.

I smiled and reached over and hugged the young man tight. 'Reckon it's time for you to make your own way when we get home. No rush, mind, but you need to find yourself a girl, and a trade, settle down somewhere quiet.'

He nodded once more, unable to meet my eye. 'I could still serve you, Lord. You'll need a blacksmith or a carpenter, something like that...' He trailed off, emotion clogging his voice.

'No, lad. My business is war. I've too many enemies, too many old scores waiting to be settled. War will always follow me; it is my curse, but it doesn't have to be yours.'

'Surely even you don't want to fight again after that?'

I shook my head. 'No, but I will have to. There are men in the Suebi who would pay good coin for the location of my hall, not to mention Rome.' I thought of the cursed legions then, and my long-standing feud with the Fourteenth, and their senior centurion in particular, Silus. 'It's been a long time since I stuck my head above the sand and tasted the air, but no man can hide forever. Trust me, young Sedric, you're better off forging your own path. But you will be welcome at my fire whenever you wish.'

I hugged him tight, and he shook with tears in my arms. War is a cruel mistress, a savage and barbaric custom that seems as old as man. Some men spent their lives running from it, others flocked to battle like crows. I'd seen enough to know Sedric was better off being in the first.

A shout from one of Dagr's men broke up our embrace and I turned, scanning the horizon, to see three figures shouting and waving on the western bank. Saxa, Ludwig and Eric, my family, were there to greet me. We pulled the ship over to the bank, hauling her half onto the mud banks that lined the river. One of Dagr's men remarked that we'd never get the ship back off it, but I wasn't listening. I leaped from the ship and ran to my boys, scooping one up in each arm as I breathed in their heavenly scent. 'My boys,' I whispered, drinking in their pale faces.

'You took your time,' Saxa said, standing a pace from me, taking in the new scars on my face and arms.

'Trust me, my love,' I said, putting down our boys and pulling her close, 'you don't want to know the half of it.'

I held her close, our boys singing and dancing as they circled us. The sun was bright in the sky on a warm summer's day. I was home.

* * *

MORE FROM ADAM LOFTHOUSE

Another book from Adam Lofthouse, *Raven*, is available to order now here:

https://mybook.to/RavenBackAd

AUTHOR'S NOTE

This book is a complete work of fiction. The lives of the Germanic people throughout the reign of the Roman Empire are largely unknown. The sources we have from the time are of course all Roman and therefore do not paint a pretty picture of the tribes that caused them so much trouble.

We do of course know that Rome never sustained any ground east of the Rhine or north of the Danube. For a time, they held on to some land, building forts and roads. But it was too costly in men and coin, and with the ever-growing need for the legions in the invasion of Britain and on the eastern border, Rome eventually had to concede defeat and remove themselves from Germania entirely.

However, they never found themselves entirely at peace with their Germanic neighbours. *Frumentarii* agents, as mentioned in this novel, were indeed tasked with slipping through Germania, stirring trouble between neighbouring tribes, ensuring one never got as big as to cause a real threat to the *Pax Romana* – peace throughout the empire. That all came to a head in the second century though, when a tribal chief named Balomar, chief of the Marcomanni, managed to join a coalition of tribes together and invaded the empire through Pannonia. (If you've read my *Path of Nemesis* trilogy, starting with *The Centurion's Son*, you should already be familiar with this.)

It was in my debut novel mentioned above I first created the character of Alaric. A scoundrel to the core, his twisted mind scarred from a hard lived past. I loved writing him in both *The Centurion's Son* and *War in the Wilderness*. He was fun. I felt as though anything could happen when he was in a chapter, and once that trilogy had reached its conclusion, I found my mind thinking back to what his life could have been before the Marcomannic War, what could have driven him to that desperate need for revenge.

Hence I decided to write *Raven*. Like this novel, there was no real need to pore over textbooks and historical accounts; I could just let my imagination run riot. I loved what I'd written, and after finishing writing a book set in fourth century Roman Britain, and one very much focused on real historical events, I felt the need for a change of pace – a pallet cleanser, if you like.

And so I wrote this book. *Outlaw* picks up a few years after the events of *Raven,* and once again I found it an absolute joy to write. It's such a different challenge, writing without any real boundaries, not been guided by historical events or based around real figures from the past. If I can dream it, I can write it, and whilst that definitely presents its own challenges, it does provide a huge amount of satisfaction.

I do hope you have enjoyed this book. There will be one more Alaric adventure coming your way, working title is War Lord, so watch out for that. Should be published in the autumn of 2025. If you enjoyed this book, please do consider leaving a small review on Amazon or Goodreads. Each review helps a book's visibility so much and therefore puts it on the map for potential new readers. If you want to be among the first to know when my next novel is out, then be sure to sign up to my newsletter at adamlofthouse.com. Max four emails a year; no spam, ever – I don't have the time or energy for that! And as always, find me on Facebook, Instagram or X, where I'm very active and often share snippets of what's going on in my day-to-day life.

Thanks once more for taking the time to read this book.

ABOUT THE AUTHOR

Adam Lofthouse has for many years held a passion for the ancient world. As a teenager he picked up *Gates of Rome* by Conn Iggulden, and has been obsessed with all things Rome ever since. After ten years of immersing himself in stories of the Roman world, he decided to have a go at writing one for himself. He lives in Kent, UK.

Sign up to Adam Lofthouse's mailing list for news, competitions and updates on future books.

Follow Adam on social media here:

facebook.com/AdamPLofthouse

x.com/AdamPLofthouse

instagram.com/adamplofthouse

ALSO BY ADAM LOFTHOUSE

Enemy of the Empire

Raven

Outlaw: Nemesis of Rome

Eagle and the Flame

WARRIOR CHRONICLES

WELCOME TO THE CLAN ✕

THE HOME OF
BESTSELLING HISTORICAL
ADVENTURE FICTION!

WARNING:
MAY CONTAIN VIKINGS!

SIGN UP TO OUR
NEWSLETTER

BIT.LY/WARRIORCHRONICLES

Boldwood

Boldwood Books is an award-winning fiction publishing company seeking out the best stories from around the world.

Find out more at www.boldwoodbooks.com

Join our reader community for brilliant books, competitions and offers!

Follow us

@BoldwoodBooks

@TheBoldBookClub

Sign up to our weekly deals newsletter

https://bit.ly/BoldwoodBNewsletter

www.ingramcontent.com/pod-product-compliance
Lightning Source LLC
Chambersburg PA
CBHW010700100726
47900CB00010B/2737